THE BILL HAWLEY UNDERTAKINGS

Bill Hawley is a licensed undertaker running a reputable funeral parlor with his wife, Nat, and his brother, Jerry. But Hawley is also known as ™thesleuthing undertaker, an amateur private investigator with a knack for Ændingthe truth. Even when it's six feet under . . .

Final Viewing
Bill Hawley's debut! Lydia Scholtz's husband turns up dead in a motel room—minus $50,000 in cash. Hawley investigates to make sure the truth isn't buried with the body . . .

™EXEMPLARY . . COMPELLING . . . AN IMPRESSIVE DEBUT! – *The Armchair Detective*

Double Plot
Edward Kane thinks his father—a wealthy antique dealer—was murdered. The sleuthing undertaker takes over to Ændout if the death was an accident, a suicide, or something even more sinister . . .

And now . . .

Grave Matters
Bill Hawley's most harrowing undertaking yet!

MORE MYSTERIES FROM THE
BERKLEY PUBLISHING GROUP ...

DOG LOVERS' MYSTERIES STARRING HOLLY WINTER: With her Alaskan malamute Rowdy, Holly dogs the trails of dangerous criminals. "A gifted and original writer." —Carolyn G. Hart

by Susan Conant

A NEW LEASH ON DEATH	A BITE OF DEATH
DEAD AND DOGGONE	PAWS BEFORE DYING

DOG LOVERS' MYSTERIES STARRING JACKIE WALSH: She's starting a new life with her son and an ex–police dog named Jake ... teaching film classes and solving crimes!

by Melissa Cleary

A TAIL OF TWO MURDERS	SKULL AND DOG BONES
DOG COLLAR CRIME	FIRST PEDIGREE MURDER
HOUNDED TO DEATH	DEAD AND BURIED

CHARLOTTE GRAHAM MYSTERIES: She's an actress with a flair for dramatics—and an eye for detection. "You'll get hooked on Charlotte Graham!"
—*Rave Reviews*

by Stefanie Matteson

MURDER AT THE SPA	MURDER ON THE SILK ROAD
MURDER AT TEATIME	MURDER AT THE FALLS
MURDER ON THE CLIFF	MURDER ON HIGH

DEWEY JAMES MYSTERIES: America's favorite small-town sleuth! "Highly entertaining!" —*Booklist*

by Kate Morgan

DAYS OF CRIME AND ROSES	WANTED: DUDE OR ALIVE

BILL HAWLEY UNDERTAKINGS: Meet funeral director Bill Hawley—dead bodies are his business, and sleuthing is his passion ...

by Leo Axler

FINAL VIEWING	DOUBLE PLOT
GRAVE MATTERS	

PEACHES DANN MYSTERIES: Peaches has never had a very good memory. But she's learned to cope with it over the years ... Fortunately, though, when it comes to murder, this absentminded amateur sleuth doesn't forgive and forget!

by Elizabeth Daniels Squire

WHO KILLED WHAT'S-HER-NAME?	REMEMBER THE ALIBI

A BILL HAWLEY UNDERTAKING

GRAVE MATTERS

LEO AXLER

BERKLEY PRIME CRIME, NEW YORK

GRAVE MATTERS

A Berkley Prime Crime Book / published by arrangement with the author

PRINTING HISTORY
Berkley Prime Crime edition / February 1995

ISBN: 0-425-14581-6

Berkley Prime Crime Books are published by
The Berkley Publishing Group,
200 Madison Avenue, New York, NY 10016.
The name BERKLEY PRIME CRIME and the BERKLEY PRIME CRIME
design are trademarks belonging to Berkley Publishing
Corporation.

PRINTED IN THE UNITED STATES OF AMERICA

10 9 8 7 6 5 4 3 2 1

This story is respectfully dedicated to
Dr. W. Grayson Lappert...
It ain't Shakespeare, but I tried

ONE

■ ■ ■ ■ ■ ■ ■ ■

ELLIE LYTTLE WAS no older than twenty-two or twenty-three, and she had been married for less than a year. We were sitting in my office at eight o'clock in the morning on Monday, April 26, Mrs. Lyttle in the "family chair," and me behind my desk. Her husband had been mauled to death by some kind of dog, and found in a hole by a crew of contractors who were working on a housing development on the city's far west side. When she called to ask me to take care of his funeral, she had said that because of financial considerations there wouldn't be any viewing; just a direct burial in the least expensive casket I had. Therefore I had not had Frank Lyttle embalmed. He was now lying on my prep table in a bright yellow body bag, covered with what the coroner estimated were some one hundred and thirteen bite wounds, and chopped to ribbons by a pathologist's knife. Now, his wife wanted to see him, "one last time."

She was a tiny, petite little thing, so very short and trim that her pregnancy looked positively ominous. She was wearing blue jeans, a white maternity top that was a little tattered around its pink, flowered edges, and a pair of very improbable, red spike-heeled pumps that must have been uncomfortable for a woman in her condition. Her short brownish-blond hair was frizzed from too much teasing, and her green eyes, which were as large as the ones you see on those greeting cards featuring fuzzy baby animals and sayings like "Just for being YOU," were swollen and angry from crying.

I told her that I didn't think it was a good idea for her to see her husband right now, considering what his body had been through, and that she should try to remember him the way he was. . . .

Not that it made any difference.

Stubbornly she sat upright—a movement that emphasized her swollen belly, and brought to mind a private ambulance company I used to work for. If a pregnant woman went into labor in one of our vehicles, our standing orders were to: "Cross her legs, and go like hell." My problem at the moment was that if the shock of seeing her husband did induce Mrs. Ellie Lyttle into labor, I didn't have anywhere to go. Funeral homes don't come with sirens and accelerator pedals. And it had been a long time since I'd seen a baby born, let alone delivered one . . . which I had never done solo.

When Mrs. Lyttle spoke, I detected a trace of the East Coast in her accent, making me decide that she wasn't a native Midwesterner, but had recently been transplanted. Her features were clean and smooth . . . not really beautiful, since they seemed to hint at a hard, unforgiving life, but pretty, if only because of her youth. Thrusting out her chin, she said, "How do I even know you've got the right guy back there if you don't let me see him? How am I gon'na know it's Frank I'm prayin' over when I take his son to see his father's grave?" Her hand went to her belly and rested against it, fingers opening and closing slowly.

I frowned, sat silently for a moment, and then finally nodded, saying, "Okay. If that's what you really want. But remember, I warned you. And I'm warning you again.

It's my considered opinion . . . and I can't emphasize this enough: It's my *strong recommendation*, that you let this idea go. Your husband's body isn't a pretty sight, and we haven't done a thing to improve it, since you said you didn't want him embalmed. I think you're going to be sorry if you look at him now. And I'm not talking about just today. I think you're going to end up being sorry for the rest of your life, because every time you think of him you're going to remember what you see on that table. I just wanted to say that."

"Okay," she replied, rising clumsily to her feet. "You've said it. Now, let's go."

The prep room's located at the back of the funeral home, just off the garage. It's long, cold, and white: white linoleum on the floor, white tile on the walls, white acoustic tiles on the ceiling. The cabinets are covered with white Formica. And the slop and sanitary sinks are made of white porcelain. Practically the only color in the place is the silver of the stainless-steel embalming tables, and the blues and reds that depict the human body's vascular system on the four-foot anatomical chart that hangs on one wall. Flicking on the overhead lights, I left Mrs. Lyttle at the door and went over to the body bag, which was still stiff with the cold of the morgue's refrigerated holding area, unzipping it just enough to expose her husband's face. It was important that I be careful not to show her too much, since the top of his head had been sawed off during his autopsy. But even what I did reveal was enough to break any wife's heart.

Ellie Lyttle stepped up to the table and looked down at her husband. After one quick inhalation of breath, she made not so much as a single sound. No gasp. No cry. No whimper. The only sound in the room was the crinkle of the body bag's plastic, expanding as it warmed.

Frank Lyttle was forty-two years old when he died, with long, dark hair streaked with grey, brown eyes, a hooked, beaklike nose, and a hard, straight line of a mouth that made him look as if he'd been carved from wood. Now, his left eye was gone, as was most of his left cheek, ripped into a mess of torn flesh and muscle; his upper lip on his left side was also torn, and his forehead had three black puncture wounds dotted in a straight line running from directly between his eyes up into his hair. His mouth was slightly open, revealing two very white teeth. His remaining eye was closed. Blood had dried into dark brown speckles all over him.

The silence in the room was so interminable that when Mrs. Lyttle finally did speak, her words virtually boomed as they vibrated off all that tile and linoleum.

"He . . ." she began, her voice breaking so that she had to stop, swallow, and start again. "He said that he couldn't hide forever. That sooner or later this would happen. He said that it was just a matter of time. He said . . .

"Oh, Mr. Hawley."

This last she said as she turned and looked up at my face. I was a good five inches taller than she, even with her heels, so she had to lift her arms high to put them around me. Heavily, she leaned into me, holding me as hard as she dared as she first began to tremble, and then to cry. The tears started with a kind of bark that was her only sound of sorrow. Then, as I put my arms around her, trying to offer what comfort I could, she rested her head on my chest, with her belly pressing against me. The warmth of her tears soaked through my shirt as she simply stood there, shaking with the rhythm of her sobs, until after a while she stopped, and, without so much as lifting her head, said, "He was hiding, but they found him anyway. Oh God, they found him, and this is what they did. What am I gon'na do now, Mr. Hawley? Oh Jesus Christ, what am I gon'na do with him gone?" Then she was crying again, and she cried for a long, long time.

Later, after she'd gone home, I was left sitting behind my desk, feeling drained, with her story running through my head.

Her husband had stolen something, she'd told me, not because there was necessarily anything I could do about it, but because saying it, even to a virtual stranger, seemed to help. He'd been in jail once, she'd said, but he'd served his time, and paid his debt. He was a reformed man, a good husband who was looking forward to being a father. But a long time ago he'd stolen something he shouldn't have stolen, and someone was going to make him pay for it. So he was hiding. Lyttle wasn't even his real name. He never told her what his real name was, saying only that because of his past he couldn't ever go by his real name again. It was too dangerous. So, since he'd started over fresh, Lyttle was now as much his name as any other. So Mrs. Lyttle should think of herself as bearing an even better name than the one she would have had if she'd have met him before he had straightened himself out.

But he'd always have to hide, even if he lived to be a hundred years old, because someone was looking for him, and whoever it was, they'd never forgive, or forget.

The phone rang and I picked it up, saying, rather vaguely in my preoccupation, "Hawley Funeral Home. Bill Hawley speaking." The voice on the other end was familiar, though its tone was not. "Wild Bill," Rusty Simmons said, a little breathless, and very hushed. "Can you meet me, man? It's important."

Sure I could meet him, I said, asking what was wrong, and whether or not he was okay. Rusty was a friend, and in all the years I'd known him I'd never heard him sound the way he did now.

"I'm fine," he said. "It's you I'm worried 'bout. Where you wan'na meet?"

"How about the Coffee Grinder?"

"Fine. When?"

"An hour?"

"See ya there."

All the way downtown I thought about Mrs. Lyttle, but I never once linked her story with Rusty's obvious concern for my safety. If I had, I probably would have declined his invitation to meet. The last thing I needed at that point in my life was a complication. Particularly one involving a client. I was already in enough trouble with the Ohio Organization of Funeral Professionals without pushing my luck.

Because of all the publicity I'd gotten through the articles Aggie O'Toole had written about me in the *Cleveland Plain Dealer*, as well as a direct complaint lodged against me by the sheriff of a small, southern Ohio town, the events surrounding my last "case" had brought me to the attention of the O.O.F.P., a regulatory organization chartered by the governor to monitor the activities of funeral directors licensed in the state of Ohio. I'd been ordered to appear at an ethics hearing in Columbus, our state's capital, to answer charges that my "ancillary activities" represented a breach of my professional responsibilities. They'd been jerking me around pretty good for the past six months, making me drive down twice, only to find each time that the hearing had been postponed. It had been scheduled again for that coming Friday, and I have to admit, I was scared. With a flick of a pen, the board could suspend, or revoke, my license, and I had over a half a million dollars worth of debt and property on the line.

But even without associating her with Rusty's call, I had to admit that there was something about Mrs. Lyttle that troubled me. She had seemed sincere, but after almost twenty years in the funeral business, I've seen enough grief to know how it looks, and, more importantly, how it feels. Grief charges the atmosphere, radiating out like electricity from the person experiencing it. It's hard to let go of someone you love. And different people react to such a loss differently . . . some cry, some go passive, and some get angry. But emotional reactions, whatever form they might take, are simply the external symptoms of an underlying, spiritual condition. I've seen so many displays of emotion, so often in my life, that I can literally sense when they're genuine.

Mrs. Lyttle had had the symptoms, but I wasn't sure if she had the grief. There had been something else in the room with us . . . something that had gone unspoken. I had the feeling that she had intended to say more, but that something had made her hold back.

So why had she cried?

And, perhaps more to the point, why had she orchestrated her crying in such a way that I couldn't help but be there when she did it?

Rusty Simmons was waiting for me on the sidewalk outside the Coffee Grinder, which is located just three blocks from the county morgue, on the campus of the best medical college in Cleveland. It features about a hundred different types of coffee, so the kids who work the counter are always wired, making the service very fast. We found a booth near the back, but instead of getting right down to it, Rusty insisted on ordering breakfast, which we got almost immediately: decaf coffee and a bran muffin for me—my wife would be so proud—and the "Ranch Hand" for him, which included scrambled eggs, toast with butter, pancakes swimming in syrup, bacon, and sausage.

"Don't you worry about cholesterol?" I asked after the waitress left.

Rusty shrugged as he replied, "Nah, I get plenty. Now eat your muffin; you're gon'na need your strength."

Talking to Rusty is like talking to the morgue incarnate. After forty years behind the receiving desk he knows everyone, and sees everything. And he's smart. I've known him since I first started carrying bodies for North Coast Medical Services, way back in high school. He's black, six foot three, over two hundred and fifty pounds, has kinky grey hair cut very short, and he's gone bald on top. But he used to be a redhead, which explains his nickname.

As he started to eat he said, "This body you just got, Frank Lyttle, it's gon'na cause you some real trouble if you ain't careful."

"What's so special about Frank Lyttle?" I asked, breaking my muffin in half before smearing it with butter, because you can't let this health shit ruin your life.

"Oh, noth'n much," he returned, somehow managing to talk, shovel in the eggs, and look grim, all at the same time. "Except that we already had him once."

"Come again?" I said.

So he explained:

"'Bout two years ago a body was found in the basement of a warehouse over on East One Hundred Seventy-first Street by some homeless guy look'n for a spot to spend the night. He'd been burned with gasoline on the front, but the part touch'n the ground was okay. In his ass pocket they found a set'a parole papers issued from Lucasville three days before in the name'a Ronald Lancing Webster. They figured he'd been dead no more than a few hours . . . so it hadn't taken him long to get in trouble once he walked."

"Okay," I said. "But what's this got to do with Frank Lyttle?"

Rusty bobbed his fork as he said, "The Webster body was burned so bad that they had to use dental records to make the I.D. Okay?"

I nodded.

"Well, yesterday, when they stripped Frank Lyttle on the table, they found an old driver's license in his shoe. The one in his wallet was in his name. But the one in his shoe was in the name'a R.L. Webster. And the picture pretty much matched. After a little check'n, the boys in the office found that other than a social security number issued a couple'a years ago, there wasn't a single record of a Frank Lyttle, spelled with a Y, match'n that new social security number, anywhere. No credit cards, bank records, or medical history. So the Wolfman had 'em pull the dope on the Webster name, and that's when the shit really hit the fan."

The Wolfman was Dr. Gordon Wolf, who's been the county's head pathologist—the position directly beneath the coroner—for almost ten years. He'd been christened the Wolfman both because of his name, and because of the frightful shock of stark white hair that he brushes straight back off his looming forehead.

Having finished his breakfast, Rusty leaned back and pulled out a pack of Kools, offered me one, which I declined, lit up, and continued. "When the Wolfman compared the X-rays out'ta the Webster file to the ones he took of Frank Lyttle's body, what he got was a ten-point, no-shit, match. Which means that R.L. Webster and Frank Lyttle *are the same guy* . . . or at least one of 'em is.

"You with me so far?"

"More or less," I returned.

"Well, when I heard that we had two bodies match'n the same set'a D-Charts," Rusty went on, "the first thing I did was look up Webster in the Book. You know, just to see what had been goin' through my head at the time. . . ."

Rusty's "Book" is famous for being the most complete digest of Cleveland's homicidal history ever assembled. He's kept a copy of every police report and coroner's document filed on every murder case that's gone through the morgue since he first started working there back in 1953—solved, and unsolved. Most importantly, he's kept copies of the notes recorded about homicide victims when they first hit the morgue's big stainless steel scale. That's when everybody's blood is up, and their impressions are most acute. The "Book" numbers something like twenty volumes now, and it gets bigger every day.

"And what I found," he continued, "is that, even back then, I thought someth'n smelled funny. I got two different notes in there 'bout sloppy procedure, including one that says, 'So who the hell's try'n to keep this thing quiet anyway?' But what really brought it back clear in my mind was the bathtub, and the rent-a-cop."

"So that's what did it, huh?" I said.

Rusty's voice grew earnest as he explained.

"The warehouse where they found him," he said, "had a locker room in the basement where the guys could clean up at the end'a their shifts. There was a shower room with a bunch'a stalls and one bathtub. The dead guy was in the tub, burned black, with scorch marks runn'n up the wall. Directly over the shower room was the building's security office, where a rent-a-cop sat look'n at TV between his rounds. They had one'a those old-fashioned systems in the place, where the guy had to turn the key on a bunch'a different watch boxes all over the building every so many hours.

"Now the guy on duty that night said . . ."

"Wait a minute," I cut in. "You mean this place was occupied?"

"Yeah."

"But you just said that a homeless guy found him. What was a homeless man doing in the basement of an occupied warehouse where there was a security guard on duty?"

"Funny, ain't it?" Rusty agreed, adding, "But it ain't half as funny as what the rent-a-cop says he heard the night the guy died."

"Which was?"

"Nothin'."

"Is that a problem?"

"Damn straight it's a problem. The warehouse had a heating system, right? A bunch'a ducts, cold-air returns, and vents. There was even an exhaust fan in the shower room, and another one in the guard's office. They were on the same feed. If you listened, you could hear anything goin' on down in the shower room up in the guard's office through that vent. The cops tried it. But all that week, every night, all night long, when the building was totally empty and quiet, the guard swore that he never heard, or smelled, a thing. You get that? Alone, in an empty warehouse, he didn't hear or smell anything comin' from a tile shower room that was connected to his office by an exhaust fan vent one floor below."

"Bullshit!" I protested.

"That's what he say."

"Didn't anybody notice anything strange about that?"

"Apparently not."

I leaned back in my chair and crossed my arms over my chest, searching Rusty's big brown eyes for any sign of deception or humor. Finally I said, "But nobody said a word to me about Frank Lyttle being anybody but Frank Lyttle."

And Rusty replied, "Now it looks like Margaret Taylor's decided to make sure it stays that way."

"Who's Margaret Taylor?"

"She's some kind'a liaison lady from City Hall. A certified killer-bitch. As soon as the Wolfman realized somethin' screwy was goin' on, Ms. Taylor locked things up so tight ya couldn't hardly breathe in there. It was need-to-know all the way down the line. I don't think but maybe three or four people in the whole morgue have any idea what's been happen'n."

"So how'd you find out about it?" I asked.

Rusty cocked his head as if I'd just said something extremely stupid . . . which I had. But instead of retaliating, he lit another cigarette, and kept going.

"Ms. Taylor apparently thinks that it's worth takin' a chance that no one'll ever find out that the city identified R.L. Webster's body wrong the first time we had him on the table," he said. "I guess she figures that if it ever got out that the Wolfman fucked up, then anybody who's had a family member I.D.'d by the county while he was on the job has got a gripe comin'. The city could end up disinterin' God-knows how many bodies, just to check the Wolfman's work. And that would cost a bundle. Not to mention all the shit they'd have to eat."

"But if it did get out, hushing it up's the worst thing they could do," I protested.

To which Rusty replied, "Ms. Taylor must think that she can get away with it, 'cause she's already doctored the files."

"Meaning what?"

"Meaning that the dental charts the Wolfman used to make his original I.D. are gone. I looked. The way things stand now is that R.L. Webster was burned alive . . ."

"Alive?!" I cut in.

"Alive," he repeated. "Autopsy showed that before he died he was breathin' fire."

"Jeeze."

"And Frank Lyttle bled to death after bein' attacked by a dog, probably a rottweiler."

"But if the fix is already in," I said, "then what's it got to do with me?"

Apparently we had arrived at the crux of Rusty's concern, because his face grew positively rigid as he scootched forward in his seat, looked me dead in the eye, and said, with deliberate emphasis, "It wasn't Mrs. Lyttle who picked you to take care of her husband's funeral. She was told who to call by the Wolfman himself."

"What are you talking about?" I demanded.

He nodded as he said, "That's right, the nastiest piece'a female political work in town hand-picked you to take care of the funeral for a guy the city wants buried as quiet as can be. She also made the county's head pathologist and medical examiner do the dirty work by having him contact the widow personally. Now, you tell me: What the hell?"

I sank back in my seat, saying, "Since when does the coroner's office recommend a funeral home? That's unethical!"

"Since yesterday," Rusty responded. "Which is exactly one time that I know 'bout in the forty years I been behind the desk."

"And you're sure about all this? I mean, about them *telling* the widow who to call?"

"I heard the Wolfman on the phone myself."

I didn't know what to say in response to that, so I didn't say anything.

"So what I think," Rusty continued, "is that somebody's fix'n to sling some shit your way. And Bill, I'm sincerely afraid that if you ain't real careful, that shit's gon'na stick."

"But you just said that the files have already been fixed," I observed. "What could I possibly do to mess things up now?"

"That's just my point!" Rusty said in a suddenly loud voice. "As it stood before, everythin' was fine: All the bases were covered, with nobody's ass showin'. So why should Ms. Taylor go and tell the Wolfman to make sure that you, of all people, got Frank Lyttle's death call? Unless"— he tapped his finger on the table and looked around the restaurant as he lowered his voice—"they're diggin' you a hole.

"That lady's no good, Bill. I've seen her work before. If she wants you to do this, then she's got a reason . . . and whatever it is, I can promise that you ain't gon'na like it. So don't touch it . . . that's the best way to stay out'ta trouble. Just bury this sum'bitch, and go 'bout your business. As a friend, I'm tellin' ya, don't give that lady a chance to do ya."

It was good advice.

It's just too bad I didn't take it.

TWO

■ ■ ■ ■ ■ ■ ■ ■

AFTER BREAKFAST I sat in my dark blue Chrysler Grand Caravan, smoking a cigarette and watching college students walk past as I tried to organize a working scenario that matched the facts Rusty Simmons had just described. As I saw it, two years before, one of two things had happened:

Someone had committed murder, leaving a set of parole papers in the name of R.L. Webster on a body they had deliberately mutilated beyond all recognition in hopes of throwing the authorities off the track when they identified the victim.

Or, for whatever reason, a man named R.L. Webster had decided that it would be better if he were thought to be dead. So he killed and mutilated some anonymous, convenient victim, leaving a set of his own parole papers on the body so that it would be identified as him when the authorities made their official I.D. Dr. Wolf had used a set of dental X-rays he'd gotten from the Lucasville state prison to compare with the ones he took of the body in question, so if this second scenario were true, the implication was that whoever orchestrated this deception must have had access to the county morgue's records room . . .

since the security in what amounted to a business office would have to be easier to beat than the security in a prison infirmary.

Another possibility was that Dr. Wolf had said that the two sets of X-rays matched when they actually didn't—but that prospect opened a real can of worms, and I more or less sluffed it off.

The bottom line was that R.L. Webster had disappeared, leaving a body behind that the authorities had erroneously identified as his own. If I'd gotten it straight so far, he would have then told Ellie, the woman he was to eventually marry, that there was something in his past that was so dangerous it was sure to catch up with him, no matter how hard he tried to hide. And now, his prediction had evidently come true. . . .

Or at least it had if R.L. Webster and Frank Lyttle were in fact one and the same man.

Involuntarily I shuddered, thinking about the manner of Mr. Lyttle's death, lighting another Marlboro menthol off the first before throwing the butt out the window.

I hate dogs.

And I do mean hate.

It's like a phobia.

When I was eleven years old my folks took my brother and me on an all-day excursion to Loudenville, Ohio, where there's a place you can rent a canoe and take a trip down some river with a long, Indian-sounding name. On the way back we stopped at a gas station, and when I stepped around the corner of the building looking for a bathroom, a German shepherd guard dog the owner kept tied up there jumped me. Before I staggered back far enough for the animal's chain to check his attack, he did nearly sixty stitches worth of damage.

For years afterward I had nightmares about that event. I saw blazing eyes and flashing teeth and screamed in my sleep. I woke up in a cold sweat more times than I can count, and whenever I heard a dog bark, I literally jumped. I'm still sensitive when it comes to dogs, though I'm not as bad as I used to be. The idea that Frank Lyttle had died because a dog had been able to bite him over a hundred times made my skin crawl.

But it also did something else:

It made me wonder.

The dog that attacked me when I was a kid was an animal specifically trained to do what it did. Even so, it didn't maul me like the dog that had gotten hold of Frank Lyttle. It barked a lot, and bit me bad, but it also stood back and growled, putting up a fuss. It bit me, but it didn't *grab* me. The dog that killed Frank Lyttle had just grabbed hold and ripped the living shit out of him. A hundred bite wounds . . .

Jesus, I thought.

How long had that taken?

And hadn't anybody heard?

On to other separate, but apparently connected, concerns.

Aggie O'Toole's newspaper articles about me have always made me uncomfortable, because the more things people know about you, the more things they can use to complicate your life. That might sound like a paranoid point of view, but don't forget that my name is in the telephone book, as well as on the front of my funeral home, so if anyone wants to bug me, all they have to do is pick up a phone and call. Also, up until about four years ago, I was a drunk . . . or a substance abuser, if you want to get flowery with your terminology. I prefer the word "drunk" because it sounds more serious. Substance abusers wind up in private clinics, paying doctors to assure them that any rotten or stupid stunts they may have pulled in the past were actually somebody else's fault, and that, deep down, they are really good, well-meaning people, afflicted with an unfair disease. Drunks wind up in alleys where grease-ball punks beat them up for fun. I come from a working-class family, so I always knew that a clinic wasn't in my future. The only way I was going to keep my sorry ass out of an alley was to leave the bottle alone, which I have for the past three, going on four, years.

But between the ages of seventeen and thirty, I was a serious, though functional, drunk, working in my dad's funeral home by day, and making a thorough mess of my life by night. I don't even remember all the shit I did. Near the end, just before I quit, I was drinking myself into "blackouts"—blank passages of time during which I didn't have a clue as to where I'd been, or what I'd done. To this day I'm terrified that one morning a woman I've never met is going to show up at my door with a baby she claims is mine. It's a nightmare . . . and one of my fears has always been that Aggie O'Toole's articles are going to bring me to the attention of some unscrupulous person, leaving me open to shit that I don't need.

Now, according to Rusty's story, it looked like my fears had been justified in the person of one Margaret Taylor, "certified killer-bitch."

Angrily, I started the van and headed for Interstate 71 south, which would take me through some of Cleveland's more affluent suburbs.

God, I was frustrated.

The past few years had been going pretty good: Other than the two occasions when circumstances, and my own inquisitive—some might even say, self-destructive—nature had combined to put me in the center of situations I would probably have been better off leaving alone, I had built my own funeral home, walked away from the joy-juice, and contributed the best parts of myself to a marriage that was so good that sometimes it didn't even seem real. Business could have been better, but like my dad says, when you own a funeral home, you can't hold a sale; and it takes time for an undertaker to establish his reputation in a new city. I was even losing some weight, thanks to a diet program I'd bought in a health food store, which had me taking vitamins and eating like a rabbit—at five-eleven I weigh just over two hundred pounds, which is still probably twenty-five pounds too much.

So why did the prospect of getting my hands dirty with the riddles surrounding R.L. Webster/Frank Lyttle's life and death excite me so much? Why was it that, if I was really honest with myself, I couldn't avoid the inevitable conclusion that the absolute best moments of my life, the times when I had felt the most alive and energized, were exactly those times when I had stepped out of my daily routine and into the far more nebulous, and even unsavory role of private investigator? Was I addicted again? Had I traded the haze of alcohol for the adrenaline rush of discovery? Or had I touched on the truth about myself as a person without even realizing it?

I didn't know.

But one thing was certainly clear: The Ohio Organization of Funeral Professionals wasn't interested in giving me any more latitude as far as my public persona was concerned. They had a very specific image of how a funeral director was expected to behave, and I wasn't measuring up. If I gave them even the hint of trouble again, they'd pull my license. And even a year's worth of disciplinary suspension would bankrupt me for sure. I'd be ruined. And so would my brother, who worked for me, and my dad, who, when he co-signed my mortgage, had put his own funeral home on the line, a business in which he and his younger brother had invested twenty-five years of their lives.

Which is why, as I worked on my third cigarette of the day—I was down to three or four cigarettes, three or four days a week—the image of Margaret Taylor and Dr. Gordon Wolf, sitting together behind a locked door in a morgue office somewhere, and using my name in a secret conversation, made the hair on the back of my neck absolutely prickle.

Nobody in the coroner's office would ever advise a widow as to what funeral home she should call. The official rule is clear: There will be no bias exhibited by any county employee toward any particular place of business at any time. The reality, of course, is a little different. But to just pick up a phone and say, "Hello, Mrs. Lyttle? This is Dr. Gordon Wolf, respected member of the coroner's staff, and I think you ought to let the Hawley Funeral Home bury your husband." Nope. It just wouldn't happen. But since Rusty Simmons had insisted that he'd already heard it happen with his own ears, I was left with a couple of very disturbing questions. Such as:

Did I really believe Rusty?

Answer:

Yeah, I did. He's not a fanciful man. He doesn't look for trouble; he just notices it.

Did I really believe that Dr. Gordon Wolf was capable of covering up the fact that he had misidentified a body in the past?

Yup. No doubt about it. The Wolfman was a good pathologist, but he was also a vain, strutting peacock who covered his own ass in every circumstance.

And, did I really believe that the city administration would have a person like Margaret Taylor on its staff, whose sole function was to run around making sure that the mistakes perpetrated by its people never came to the attention of the voting public?

Sure I did. Don't you?

So what did she have to gain by involving me?

If Rusty had his way, my response to this whole thing would be to simply walk away. Which was certainly one option. But the problem with doing it was that it didn't explain anything. It left unanswered questions, like, Why was my name the topic of secret conversations, and who was to say that walking away would keep it from becoming the topic of such conversations again? Rusty's verdict seemed to be that Margaret Taylor expected me to do something specific after I took charge of Frank Lyttle's disposition, and that if I didn't do it, I'd keep myself out of trouble. But what if she actually didn't care what I did after I took Frank Lyttle's body back to my funeral home? What if she was going to cause me grief whether I did anything or not? Maybe by just signing the release form for Frank Lyttle's body, I had already given her what she wanted.

What then?

Was I supposed to just sit around and wait for the hammer to fall? And why did the "nastiest piece'a female political work in town" care about what I did or didn't do in the first place?

No. Walking away wouldn't do me any good. I had too much to lose, especially with my meeting with the O.O.F.P.

coming up in just a couple of days, to leave such ominous questions hanging over my head. I'd have to at least try and clarify my position, to which end I got off the freeway at the Southland exit, heading east down Maplecrest Road.

When I'd been told that Frank Lyttle's body had been found by some contractors in a ditch, I envisioned a hole like a trench. Not a basement. But that was, as it turned out, a more accurate description of the ditch where Frank Lyttle had died.

The housing development was immense, a section of wooded lots through which a street was being cut, with the foundations of at least ten homes already dug. There was a huge plywood sign positioned at the street's mouth bearing the name Hubbard Contracting. And there was an air about the place of furious activity as big yellow trucks and bulldozers hauled and pushed mounds of earth from one place to another.

The air was chilly-damp, making me pull up the collar on my black cashmere coat as I got out of the van, glanced around, and headed over to the one foundation hole in which no one was working. There were little orange flags on bouncy plastic sticks waving at its four corners, and, as I stood at the top of a plank that was apparently used to haul wheelbarrows full of concrete block down to where the cellar walls stood half-built, I decided that there was no point in my going down. We'd been getting a lot of rain that year, so the bottom of the cellar where Frank Lyttle had died was nothing but a churned-up, puddle-pocked pool of mud. There were no footprints, marks where his body had lain, or anything else I might have been able to use. Just mud, and two stacks of grey concrete block wrapped in tattered sheets of black plastic.

"Can I help you?" someone said.

I turned to find a man standing next to me. He was dressed in dirty jeans, big muddy boots, and a flannel lumberjack shirt over which he wore a sleeveless denim vest that was covered with patches: Disabled Vietnam Veterans; P.O.W., M.I.A.—You Are Not Forgotten; N.O.R.M.L.—

National Organization for the Reform of Marijuana Laws; Motorhead; etcetera. He looked to be roughly my own age, which is thirty-four, though his dark hair was considerably longer than mine, and his face was deeply marked with the lines of someone who spends a lot of time outdoors in the elements.

"Maybe you can," I said, trying to sound friendly as I pointed into the pit. "I'm looking for the guy who found Frank Lyttle's body Saturday morning. I understand he's the foreman on this job."

"Yeah?" the man replied, watching me. "What'ya want him for?"

"Is he around?" I asked.

"Who wants to know?"

"Bill Hawley," I said, removing my blue, apprentice private investigator's card from my wallet and handing it over. "The insurance company's giving Frank's wife a hard time, and she wants me to make sure they come across with the money. She's got a kid on the way, and nothing coming in, now that Frank's gone, so she can't afford any trouble, especially where money's concerned. Know what I mean?"

"Yeah," the man said, returning my card and then shaking my hand with a grip like a pipe wrench. "I'm the foreman. Name's Blukowski."

"Good hunky name." I grinned, trying to match his grip. "Mine was Hawlinski, once upon a time. It's Ukrainian."

"No shit? Mine too," the man replied.

Now we were friends.

"So what's the deal with Ellie?" he asked, getting right down to it. "The union ain't givin' her a rough time, is it? 'Cause if it is, I know some people who can straighten things out."

"It's not the union," I replied. "It's some private life insurance company Frank had. I guess if it's an accident, she gets so much. But if it's murder, or what they call an 'act of God,' like lightning striking or something, they calculate the payments different. So they're monkeying her around, analyzing the police report and requesting a stack of documents from the coroner. From the way they're talking, it could be two years before she sees a check. I think they're deliberately dragging their feet, and so does she."

"Jesus!" the man said, putting his hands on his hips. "You know, this whole thing's been screwed up from the get-go. Even the cops acted like they were walking around in a daze."

"How so?" I asked.

Mr. Blukowski then described how, on that previous Saturday morning, he had come onto the lot at about eleven o'clock to "kind'a look shit over when there wasn't nobody here. You know, just to get an idea of how things were goin'." He'd been walking around for about an hour, he said, when he approached this cellar hole, which was one of the ones they had been having trouble with because of the wet walls sliding, when he noticed a "bundle of rags" lying in the three or four inches of muddy water that had accumulated overnight.

"At first I didn't really pay much attention to it," he said, gazing down to where he had first spotted the remains of the man he had known as "Little Frank" because of his size. There was another guy named Frank who worked on the same crew and he outweighed Frank Lyttle by at least forty pounds. Rubbing a knuckle over his stubbly cheek and taking a deep breath, the foreman added, "But after a second I realized that the rags looked, you know, filled out. Like there was somebody in 'em. I didn't even go down there. I just called nine one one right off 'cause I could tell that somebody had been messed with bad.

"But the funny thing," he said, moving his eyes to mine, "was that it was like two different things happened that day. When the cops had me go over stuff for 'em on the spot while they was takin' Little Frank up on the stretcher, they seemed all hot and bothered . . . like something important was goin' on. But when I called the station later in the day, they said, like, 'Oh, that was no big deal. Just an accident. Don't call here anymore.' It was weird.

"Like, when I first told 'em about that Hell's Angel kind'a guy been hanging around the last couple'a weeks—first they wrote it all down and acted like, 'Okay, now we really got something.' But later, Christ . . ."

"What Hell's Angel?" I asked.

"Well, not really an Angel," the man replied. "But that kind'a guy. You know: long hair, beer gut, tattoos. And the *dog*."

"What kind of dog?"

"Christ, I don't know. Looked like a lion to me. About as big as a goddamn pony. Light brown . . . you know, like that saddle-tan color they make the upholstery out of in fancy sports cars? With a black snout, all baggy around the jowls, and a stubby little tail. But big . . . no shit. I mean, like this." He held his arms out as far as he could stretch them on either side, like a fisherman describing the one that got away. "Goddamn thing barely fit in the sidecar."

"Sidecar?"

"Yeah. The guy rode a Harley. Big black thing with a sidecar for the dog. Started comin' around a couple'a weeks ago, I guess. Made Little Frank real nervous . . . you could tell. But when I asked him one time who the hell this guy with the dog was, he just blew me off. Said it was just some guy he knew, and that he wouldn't be comin' round for long. Which was okay by me. We got a contractor who's just itching to give my guys shit about something. Makes him feel manly, I guess. So the last thing I needed was some goon on a black bike with straight pipes and a lunatic fringe hanging around. I mean, I get enough grief about the way *I* look. This guy could'a stepped right out of an old Peter Fonda movie, chains and all. Know what I'm sayin'?"

I nodded, adding, "I'll bet the cops were charged up when you told them about that."

Blukowski shrugged, saying, "Like I already said, they were at first. But then, later on, it was like, 'Nope, we got it all figured out: It was a stray that done it. That's all. Just a stray. Bad luck, but it happens sometimes. Well, thanks for your help. Don't call us, we'll call you.' Fucking cops . . . what a crock."

I asked a few more questions, like, "Why do you think Frank Lyttle was on the lot off hours in the first place?" And, "Did anyone ever hear him talking about somebody who might bear him a grudge?" But to each question, the foreman just shook his head.

"It was weird," he said, more than once. "But Little Frank's body was like, all deflated. When the cops turned him over and I saw his face, I hardly even recognized him. It was like, when he died, he got even smaller somehow. Really strange."

I told him that I'd noticed the same phenomenon in the dead bodies I'd seen over the years, and that's when he looked at me, cocked his head, and said, "Hawley? I know that name. You're that funeral director guy I read about in the paper! The one solves them crimes! Right?"

I admitted, less than enthusiastically, that I was, which seemed to prompt him to try harder, as if talking to "that" Bill Hawley somehow made a difference. As I was handing him my business card and telling him to call if he should remember anything else, he said, "There is one thing. I don't know if it means anything, and I wasn't gon'na even mention it. But, since you know about this kind of shit, maybe you can do something with it. But Frank was, well, he was kind'a funny in some ways. I don't mean that he was like a fag or nothing. But, he had, like, rules."

"Rules, meaning what?"

"Rules, like no overtime on Wednesdays. He'd work until midnight any other day of the week. Even Sundays if I'd'a asked. But not Wednesdays. They were out. And you couldn't just call him if you wanted him for something. You had to call someplace and he'd call you back."

"Maybe he didn't have a phone," I suggested.

"Yeah," the foreman agreed. "Or maybe he lived in his car, 'cause he didn't have an address either. Nobody knew where he lived. We had to give him his paycheck in his hand. Nothing mailed. And . . ."

He paused.

"And?" I prompted.

"And, well, he took off sometimes. That was the big one, his hard and fast rule of rules. Sometimes he'd get his wind up about something and disappear for two or three days. He never said why, and when he came back he never talked about what he'd been doing. But before he hired on he specifically said that he had other irons in the fire, and occasionally he'd have to take a day or two off so he could go and take care of this other business. The boss didn't like it, but Little Frank was so good at what he did that we kind of let it slide. You know what I'm sayin'?"

"What exactly did he do?" I asked.

To which the foreman replied, "Most of the time he labored like anybody else, but on the side he did what we call procurement. He could get shit for us when we needed it; that was his thing. Most of our materials come from building suppliers. Shit like wood and pipe and all that. But anywhere the company can cut a deal chops the cost on a job, and that makes the job more profitable. Get it?"

I told him that I thought I understood the concept.

"Well, Little Frank was connected," he continued. "I don't mean in a ... well ... how should I put it so that it sounds tactful? It wasn't that he was connected in a criminal sense, exactly. But he knew guys. Understand? He could get shit cheap."

"Are you talking about stolen merchandise?" I asked.

Blukowski frowned, looked around, and leaned his head toward me a little.

"All I'm sayin' is that, of all the guys who work on this crew, the one I was least surprised to find face-down in a ditch was Little Frank. Okay? Anything else you wan'na know, maybe you ought'a ask the guy with the dog. Seems to me, see'n how Little Frank got himself bit to death, that him and his dog might be a good place to start."

I agreed, shook the foreman's hand again, and returned to my van. But before I did I reminded him one last time that he could call me if he thought of anything else. "You never know what might help Frank's wife get her money," I said in parting, making him frown as he studied my card.

"I'll call if I think of something," he said. "But I don't think I will. I mean, what else is there to say about a guy you only knew for a couple'a summers? I just worked with him. I didn't really know who he was."

And that, I thought as I drove away, was probably the most telling thing he'd said about "Little Frank" throughout our conversation.

Mrs. Lyttle's car was sitting in the funeral home's parking lot when I got back, and my brother Jerry was irritated.

"What the hell's going on around here?" he asked from his wheelchair as I stepped from the attached garage into the service area off the hallway leading to the home's main foyer.

Younger than me by three years, Jerry had been a body builder before he broke his neck when his Camaro hit a telephone pole outside a bar where he'd found me, drunk and fighting, in the middle of the night. The accident had left him completely paralyzed from the neck down for over a year, and ended my alcoholic career.

For the past two years he's been steadily improving. Thanks to a lot of physical therapy, he's regained the use of his arms. But he's still almost completely dead from the waist down. He's gotten to the point where he can get around in his wheelchair like a real pro. And he's even started doing things like chin-ups, and some limited aerobics. I wouldn't be surprised if, in another couple of years, he doesn't end up like one of those guys you see on TV, competing in wheelchair basketball games. He's that kind of man: thirty-one years old, blond, handsome, clean-cut, and almost always searching for focus. When he was younger he had a hair-trigger temper, which has mellowed over the years into a quiet, almost smoldering stubbornness that seems to permanently keep him on low boil. Lately, he's been a little irritable, as if he's got something on his mind. But as of yet he hasn't let me in on what's been bothering him, and, with Jerry, I know it's best not to push.

When he's ready, he'll talk. Until then, let him simmer.

When I asked him how long Mrs. Lyttle had been at the funeral home, he replied, "All day. She showed up about half an hour after you left this morning. But that's not what I'm talking about."

What he was talking about was the stack of paper he was holding in his outstretched hand for me to take. Which I did. Running my eye over it, I said, "What is it?"

"That's what I want to know. It started coming in about an hour ago, and the fax ran for thirty straight minutes."

"Who sent it?"

"It doesn't say. There's no transmission identification code, and no call-back number."

"Did anybody call ahead to warn you that they were sending it?"

"Nope. The fax machine just started spitting it out at about one o'clock."

"Wow," I said under my breath as I went through the long chain of paper that Jerry had more or less folded into a stack. What I was looking at was nearly seventy pages of material, some hand-written, some typed, some dated, some not. As I spot-read random sections, the words "Classified" and "Departmental Consumption Only" caught my eye. As did the layout of some of the pages, which looked suspiciously like police department incident report forms.

What I was looking at, I finally concluded, were the original sheets filed by the cops on duty the day that R.L. Webster's burned body was discovered two years before. Next came the internal documentation outlining the investigation subsequently conducted by the Cleveland Police Department, as well as what looked like several items of private correspondence between someone in the department's Special Operations Division and some people in the mayor's office . . . including, if what I was seeing could be believed, the mayor himself.

But what was even more remarkable—or disturbing, depending on how you looked at it—was what I found on the final page. There, in the squishy blue dot-matrix letters of our fax machine's printer, was a name. No explanation, no description, no documentation of any kind. Just a name next to the words "Date of Death," which was listed as nearly three years ago.

"Bill," Jerry said as I lifted my eyes from the page. "What's happening?"

I shook my head. "Jer, I have no idea."

"Are you on another case?" he asked.

"No," I replied, as forcefully as I could without sounding angry, adding as I fluttered the roll of fax paper, "But I do seem to have an overzealous friend," thinking of Rusty Simmons, and wondering how he'd gotten his hands on confidential police reports. "Now, what's the deal with Mrs. Lyttle?"

The deal turned out to be that Ellie Lyttle was lonely. She'd left the funeral home that morning at nine after making the simple arrangements for her husband's disposition, gone to McDonalds for breakfast, rode around for a while thinking about the empty rooms that were waiting for her at home, and returned, looking for company. Which is exactly what she'd found in Jerry.

I know my brother very well, so it didn't take me long to figure out that he was quite taken with her . . . which, for an instant, left me a little flummoxed. After the accident that paralyzed him, Jerry pushed everyone who was close to him away, including the woman who was his girlfriend at the time, isolating himself in a kind of protective layer of bad temper and resentment. Since then, my dad and I, and my wife, Nat, have all gotten close to him again, but his girlfriend never came back. He made a few overtures, sending me into the bank where she worked to invite her to visit a couple of times. But his attempts to rekindle their romance were half-hearted at best.

"What woman would want half a man?" he'd say repeatedly whenever the topic of his relationship with women came up. Which wasn't often, since I'm a little embarrassed talking about it. It had been so long since he'd even acknowledged a woman that I wasn't really prepared when his tone of voice implied an interest in Ellie Lyttle. It took me a couple of seconds to reorient myself. And when I did, I realized that, yes, Ellie Lyttle was exactly the type of girl he would have found attractive before the accident: petite, fair, and heavy on the makeup—which he used to call "glamorous."

His interest disturbed me because it ran counter to the first, cardinal rule of working in the funeral profession, which is, never, ever, EVER allow yourself to become emotionally involved with a client, particularly when that client's loss is still fresh. Undertakers are already perceived by much of the general public as living off the misfortune of others, without the added slander of setting ourselves up to be accused of preying on the emotions of the bereaved.

But Jerry was my brother. And he was in a wheelchair, after all. And, though both he and my wife have made the argument that I'm being unreasonable, it's my deeply held conviction that his being in that chair is my fault. So I didn't mention my misgivings, hoping that I was reading too much into his tone, and that I was wrong about him and Ellie Lyttle.

Jerry stopped me just as I was about to enter my office, saying, "Bill? Hang on a second, okay?"

I turned to look at him, finding his face solemn, and his upturned eyes fixed on mine.

"Yeah?" I said.

"Do me a favor, all right?"

"Sure. What is it?"

He licked his lips nervously, and said, "Give her a break. She's having a rough time right now . . . going through a lot, you know? So, how about maybe cutting her a little slack?"

When I asked him what he was talking about, he said, "It's just that I've been listening to her for the last couple of hours, and she sounds like she's in a real mess. She doesn't have any family here in town, and what family she does have is all broke up and scattered around. Her old man used to beat her mom, and her brother's a junkie or something back in New York, and—"

"What are you saying?" I cut in.

Making him look embarrassed as he replied, "Nothing, I guess. Just go easy, okay?"

"Yeah," I said, reaching for the door.

"And Bill?"

"Yeah?"

"Just give her a chance. Okay?"

I nodded, lips tight with unspoken protest.

Ellie Lyttle looked quite a bit better than she had the last time I'd seen her. Apparently talking to Jerry had done her some good, because her eyes, instead of being red and swollen, were now a bright, sparkling shade of emerald green. She was standing in front of the window next to my desk, and when she turned as I entered the room, her face was so expectant that, for a brief instant, she appeared almost happy. But her expression faded when she saw that it was me, brightening again once Jerry followed me through the door.

I stood there for a moment, dropped the fax paper Jerry had given me on the desk, and said, "Okay. What's going on?" even though I knew full well what was happening. Still, it surprised me when Jerry, and not Ellie Lyttle, spoke up first.

"I told her you'd help," he said. "I probably shouldn't have. But I did."

"Uh-huh," I said skeptically.

"Don't be sore at him," Mrs. Lyttle offered. "He told me that you wouldn't be keen on the idea. But I pushed it."

"Did he mention how much I've got riding on this?" I asked, looking at Jerry. "Did he say how close I am to losing my license?"

"This is different," Jerry said.

"How?" I asked.

He narrowed his eyes, but didn't respond.

"Mrs. Lyttle," I said, still looking at my brother. "Did your husband know anyone who rode a motorcycle?"

"Yeah," she replied, obviously confused by the question. "He knew a lot of guys who rode bikes. He rode one, too. He was kind of in a gang. You know what I mean? I mean, he wasn't exactly in it, but he hung around with a lot'a guys who were. Some of them were in pretty deep."

"How about a dog? Any of these guys he hung out with have a dog?"

"Yeah, some'a the guys go in for dogs. Usually big, gnarly ones. Dobermans and stuff. Fits with the image, I guess. Why?"

I sat down behind my desk. I'm not exactly clear on the reason, but sometimes sitting behind my desk makes me feel safe. I would have given a lot to feel safe right that minute.

"Does the name Ronald Lancing Webster mean anything to you?" I asked.

The look on her face was enough in itself to answer my question.

"He's the man who wanted to kill my husband," she said, a spark of anger flashing in her eyes.

"Is that what he told you?"

She shook her head. "No, he never came right out and said as much, but one time one of his friends mentioned the name, and Frank really got pissed. Wigged out on the guy completely. Later, when I asked him what it had all been about, he said something like 'Noth'n. It's just that R.L. Webster's the guy who's keep'n me underground. He's the guy who ruined my life.' So I just assumed that he must be the guy who was out to get Frank killed."

"So at least one of his friends knew about R.L. Webster," I mused. "Can you remember which one it was?"

"Jeeze," she returned, one hand going protectively to her belly, the other running nervous fingers through her damaged hair. "I was really blitzed that night. And it was a while ago."

"How long?"

"A year. Maybe two."

"But no more than two, huh?"

"No. Not even that. Yeah, I'm sure. It was like nine months ago, because I wasn't pregnant yet. I stopped party'n when I got pregnant so I wouldn't hurt the kid. So it must'a been longer than nine months."

"Okay." I sighed, paging through the fax paper on the blotter before me. "Now I'm going to ask you a few questions, and I'd like some honest answers."

She glanced at Jerry, communicating silently with her eyes.

Oh boy, I thought. They've only known each other for a few hours and already they're finding their own wavelength. That wasn't good. Jerry and I were going to have to have a little talk after she was gone.

Jerry said, "So what are you doing, Bill? What's this all about?"

"I thought you said to give her a break," I shot back, maybe a little too strongly. "I thought you said she wanted me to help."

"Yeah," he agreed. "I did. But you never said yes or no. Where are we on that?"

"We'll see in a minute," I said, returning my attention to the paper. "There's a name I'm interested in: Bernard Hilton. Do you know it?"

Ellie Lyttle shook her head in the negative.

Then I asked my questions:

Where was she from?

The East Coast, around New York.

How long had she been in Cleveland?

Five years.

How had she met her husband?

At a party.

What kind of party?

A party with a lot of booze.

Where was her husband from?

As far as she knew, he was born in Kentucky. But he had moved around a lot, never settling in one place for very long. He didn't even have a Southern accent, which showed you how long he'd hung around home.

How long had they been married?

Not long. Frank was old-fashioned, and even though she had said it would be okay to just live together, once he found out that she was pregnant he insisted on getting married.

She answered my questions quickly, in a very sincere-sounding tone of voice, and with a lot of nonverbal coaching from my brother. When finally I ran out of things to ask, she fell silent, as if leaving the direction of the conversation to me.

I sighed once again. "So, what's your financial situation like?"

To which she replied, "Lousy. To be honest, I don't even know how I'm going to pay you for Frank's funeral."

"No insurance?"

"No."

"Anything from his union?"

"Not really. He wasn't much for paying dues."

"No savings?"

"No."

"What about health insurance for when your baby's born?"

"I wish."

"So what is it, exactly, that you think I can do for you?"

Moistening her lips, and glancing at Jerry, Ellie Lyttle reached her hand into her purse—a large, macramé affair with two frayed tassels—withdrawing something that she kept hidden in her fist. "I told you already that Frank stole something that he shouldn't have stole, and that he was hiding because of it. Well . . ."

Timidly, she placed the object she was holding in front of me. It was a General Motors car key.

"I think he had some money," she went on. "Or else something that was worth some money. He worked seasonally. During his off time, money got tight sometimes. When it got really bad, he'd take this key and go someplace. Sometimes he wouldn't come back for two or three days. But when he did, he always had enough cash to get us through whatever rough times we were having. I asked him once if he was stealing again, and he promised me that he wasn't. He was 'dipping into his stash,' he said. Which was something he only did in emergencies because he had big plans that he didn't want to piss away a nickel at a time."

"His 'stash'?" I asked. "Meaning what? Drugs?"

"I don't know," she replied. "It's possible, I guess, but I don't think so. Having been in jail once already, Frank was really shy about the heat. He always said that drugs were the easiest bust for the cops to make, even if you weren't holding. When they were slow, or needed to look good for some publicity thing, drugs were their ticket. The quickest way back into the joint for a guy like him, he always said, was to be anywhere near a drug deal, especially a big one."

I lifted the key from the blotter and dangled it between my fingers. It was sharp, jagged, and mysterious, attached to a ring by a thin stainless-steel chain, three links long. The key chain's fob was a single bullet of a make and caliber that I had never seen before.

"What did he do on Wednesday nights?" I asked, without taking my eyes off the bullet.

And for all the world, Ellie Lyttle sounded as if I had startled her.

"How did you know he did something on Wednesday nights?" she asked in return.

"You don't know what he did, do you?" I said.

Making her shake her head No.

"So, what'ya think, Bill?" Jerry cut in. "Can you help?"

"We'll see," I said, rising from my seat, and adding, "Which is all I can say for now."

THREE

■ ■ ■ ■ ■ ■ ■ ■ ■ ■

MY WIFE SPOKE to me through the intercom on the prep room's wall, her voice sounding small and plasticky. I had a surgeon's mask over my mouth and nose, and when I spoke back, my voice was so muffled I had to concentrate on forming the words just right. I was wearing the mask because Frank Lyttle had been dead since early Saturday morning, and it was now late Monday night. And Nat was talking to me from the living room of our upstairs apartment because she didn't want to be in the room while I did what I was doing . . . which was fine with me, because an unembalmed body, dead for almost three days, is ugly, stinks, and fills the air around it with all sorts of bacterial nasties.

"So why are you doing it?" she asked.

And I, loading a fresh film cartridge into my Polaroid camera, said, "Because I'm not going to let whoever's got it in for me downtown win without a fight."

"No, I don't mean about the case," she said. "Why are you taking pictures?"

"Oh," I replied, stepping back from the embalming table and looking through the viewfinder. "This guy's getting more awful every minute, and the sooner I get him locked in a casket, the better. But these bite marks are significant. I don't know what they mean yet, but I just know they're important. So I want a record of what they look like."

Rusty Simmons had not sent me the fax.

I think that one simple fact, more than anything else, had pushed me over the edge, committing me to the course of action I'd chosen. As soon as Ellie Lyttle had left the funeral home that afternoon, I'd called Rusty, waking him up—since he was working the graveyard shift that month, it was the middle of his night—and asking him point-blank where the hell he had gotten hold of confidential police reports. In return he asked me if I had started drinking again. Then he warned me, even more vehemently than he had in the Coffee Grinder, that all was not well in the world.

I agreed.

But if Rusty was not responsible for the fax, then who the hell was?

And why?

I took a whole roll of pictures of Frank Lyttle, checking each shot over as it developed before moving on to the next. Photographing the dead always makes me a little uncomfortable, even when I see it done in the morgue. When I was done, I had a set of Polaroids that were somewhat overexposed, washed-out, and a little grainy, but I shoved them in my pocket as soon as they were dry, having decided that they'd do for what I needed. "Okay," I said to Nat. "Finished." Then I sprinkled a little Hexaphene, a very strong drying and deodorizing powder, over the body, and zipped up the bag.

Nat kissed me as soon as I walked into my office.

Nat's my lifeline to rationality in this world, and I depend on her more than I like to admit. She's the same age as Jerry, and has long, deep mahogany-colored hair that is pencil-straight, as thick as a horse's tail, and reaches nearly to her waist. Her ancestry is predominantly German, but her great-grandmother on her father's side was a Sioux Indian. The Indian flavor in her lineage expresses itself most strongly in her olive-hued skin—which goes as dark as toffee in the summer sun—her hair, and her high cheekbones. Also, there's something about the way she holds herself, the grace of her upright carriage, and the proud way she lifts her chin, that calls up images in my mind of sleek, running animals . . . big cats, and horses. When I look at her I can't help but think that her great-grandmother must have been an amazingly lovely woman for her modest contribution to Nat's appearance to make such a profound impression.

Six months earlier she had been attacked in our funeral home by someone who was trying to discourage me from getting involved in an investigation. She ended up with a broken arm, a couple of cracked ribs, and a mild skull fracture. She has since healed, without a scar. But I haven't. The memory of her lying in a hospital bed is still so vivid in my mind that it can make my knees go weak just thinking about it. Never in my life have I been more motivated to bring a task to its conclusion than when I was looking for the man who had caused her pain.

Never.

I love my wife. I'm devoted to her. And I shall always so remain. God help anyone who ever touches her again.

"You want to see?" I asked, referring to the pictures I had just taken.

"No thank you," she replied dryly. "I'm sure they're very nice. So, what's the plan?"

"That's up to Mr. Fizner," I said, referring to the man sitting at my desk with a lighted cigarette in an ashtray at one elbow, and a highball glass at the other. The room was dark save for the desk lamp beneath which the fax I'd received earlier that day was lying, cut into sheets and arranged in a three-ring binder.

Larry Fizner is the "master investigator" under whom I was serving my private investigator's apprenticeship. He's about sixty-five years old, no more than five feet six inches tall, and very thin . . . wiry is the word that comes to mind, but it doesn't really do him justice. He looks if he's made of beef jerky, with arms that have those skinny, hard little muscles, covered with ropes of veins like you see in the hind legs of some short-haired dogs. His neck looks as if it's made of the same stuff. And his fists are like rocks. I've only intentionally touched him once, shoving him on the chest when we were arguing, and it felt like he had an oak plank under his shirt. He's got grey hair around the crown of his skull, and he's perfectly bald on top. He used to let the hair over his left ear grow long and then lace it over, but he stopped after Nat convinced him that it made him look ridiculous. He also used to wear thick glasses with black plastic frames, which he's traded for a pair of gold wire-rims that make him look oddly distinguished, also on Nat's advice.

The only thing she hasn't been able to alter in his appearance is the way he dresses, which is aggressively, almost outrageously, tasteless . . . tacky is more the word I would use. When I first met him I thought that his choice of clothes, which tends toward polyester pants, white belts and shoes, and loudly patterned shirts combined with completely mismatched bow ties, resulted from an all-powerful lack of style. Then I thought that he was just cheap, and bought his clothes from Good Will to save money. But after having known him for going on three years now, and after having seen the way his mind works when we're on a case, I realize that, like everything else he does, Larry Fizner has a reason for the way he presents himself to the world. I just haven't figured out what it is yet.

That evening his trousers were maroon, his shirt was yellow, and he was fidgeting, rocking in his seat as he tried to hide his impatience. He always gets like that when something's up. He's a bundle of nerves who smokes too much, drinks too much coffee and booze, and lives for the chase. He's been a private eye for all of his professional life, spending his service time with Army Intelligence, and then some thirty-odd years with the county's tax fraud division, reporting to a shadowy office in Washington, which he hardly ever speaks about. When he does mention it, it's only to say things like "Bill, you have no idea how much shit's goin' on behind the scenes every day. You just have no idea." It's that behind-the-scenes shit that fires up Larry Fizner's boiler. And despite the three Scotches-and-water he'd already had, he was cooking tonight.

"I think this is some pretty amazing stuff," he said, watching his language on account of Nat. "If it's legit, whoever sent it is really sticking their neck out."

"*If* it's legit," I agreed. "But how can we tell if it's real?"

"We can't," Larry replied, leaning back in my chair and picking his cigarette up out of the ashtray. Taking a drag, he continued speaking so that smoke punctuated his words. "But I recognize some of the names from when I worked for the county. It's been seven years I been gone, and the rungs on the ladder where these guys are sound about right given who they were, and what kind'a smarts they had when I knew 'em."

"So what's it all mean?" Nat asked.

She was wearing a blue terry cloth robe that she'd bought specifically to throw on over the frilly lace nightgowns she likes so much. It was going on eleven o'clock at night, at least two hours past her regular bedtime.

"It means," Larry said, crushing his cigarette and lifting himself out of my chair, "that somebody's gone renegade in City Hall. This stuff was copied from the mayor's private files. Whoever sent it is warning you that something's up. Either that, or he's trying to give you a fighting chance. According to what's described here, this R.L. Webster guy was in some pretty deep shit." He paused, and then asked:

"You about ready to go?"

I nodded, opening a cabinet door next to the wet bar and withdrawing a fringed leather coat that Nat had bought for me when we were in college because it reminded her of the one that David Crosby was wearing on the cover of the "Déjà Vu" album. I had on some old clothes I hadn't worn in years: a pair of very faded jeans, cowboy boots, and a red and black flannel shirt. My leather coat was so beat-up that it had taken on a color and shine like the bottom of a wet moccasin, which was all the better, because Larry Fizner had said that in the place we were going—chosen because

Mrs. Lyttle had said that the Hound's Tooth, reputed to be the hang-out of a group of men who ran, of all things, a floating dog fight, was her husband's favorite bar—a shirt and tie would have made me stand out more than if I'd have shown up dressed like Napoleon.

I kissed Nat good night, telling her as I did that she shouldn't wait up. Then I followed Larry out to his ratty old Dodge conversion van, which was mustard-yellow, and had a series of oddly placed geometric shapes done in peeling gold paint around a pair of smoked glass bubble windows, one on either side. It had a homemade moon roof over the driver's compartment, which leaked when it rained, a C.B. antenna affixed to its back bumper, and a set of chrome mag wheels that reminded me of the cars that had been popular with the guys I had known in high school. Inside, there was orange shag carpeting on the walls and ceiling, four plush captain's chairs lined up in two rows—the driver's seat sporting a headrest that looked like it belonged in an airplane's cockpit—and a fold-down hide-a-bed arranged against the rear doors, which had been permanently bolted shut. Larry had once said that when he was working a stake-out, he'd sometimes live in the van for weeks at a time. And, judging by the smell, he wasn't kidding.

"Isn't this fucking fantastic?" he exclaimed, slamming the van's door and putting both his hands on the steering wheel. "Goddamn!"

"Isn't what fantastic?" I asked, cracking my window and buckling up.

"This," he returned, starting the van and sweeping his free hand around in a wide arc. "A clear, cool night, two guys on the job, and all the fucking information we could possibly ask for bound up in a binder right out'ta the cops' own files. You know, it ain't often in this business that you get to see what the cops have on record about a case. We're already ahead of the game, and we haven't even started yet. Between the two of us, we're gon'na tear this muth'a up!"

"I'm glad you're so confident," I said grumpily. "Because when I read that fax, all I saw in my mind was a sea of boiling shit, stretching out to the horizon."

"That's appetizing," he replied as he rolled us onto the freeway. "What's your problem, anyway?"

"My problem is that my ass is in a sling on this one. To you, this shit's a hobby. To me, it's my fucking livelihood on the line. I got the funeral directors' board breathing down my neck, a pregnant woman making cow eyes at me to please help her find out what her murdered husband was doing before he died, a paralyzed brother who's rediscovering women, and people sending me classified documents about bullshit police investigations that happened two years ago. This has not been my idea of a good day."

"I told you already, somebody was warning you with that fax. You got a friend in the police department. That's a good and happy thing."

"Friends like that I don't need."

"That's the problem with you," Larry growled. "You're cynical."

"The problem with me," I returned, "is that it's the middle of the night, and instead of being in bed with my wife, I'm heading down to a bikers' bar where the patrons like to watch their pets rip each other's guts out, riding in the fucking Yellow Submarine, dressed like Daniel Boone."

"It's better than sittin' home, starin' at the tube," Larry said, concentrating on the road.

"Okay." I sighed. "So what's the poop?"

"How do you see it?"

"Well," I said, "to me it all looks so jumbled up that it's hard to pick a place to start. I think it's the fax that threw me. I followed the stuff about the investigation of R.L. Webster's body okay—but who's Bernard Hilton, and why was his name so prominently included in that fax? If we believe for a second that whoever sent me all that shit actually knows something, then the implication seems to be that whatever's going on involves not only one death, but Hilton's too, which happened at least three years ago."

"How do you figure that?"

"I don't know. It's just a feeling, I guess. Why, you don't like it?"

"No," Larry replied, shaking his head. "I don't like it. You're making too many assumptions from insufficient facts, and lumping separate events together as connected just because they happen to be written on the same piece of paper."

"Okay, then let's hear your take on it."

"Okay. One," he said, holding up a finger without taking his eyes from the road. "His widow told you that Frank Lyttle stole something and was hiding because of it. Would she lie? Who knows? But I think it's a good idea to keep holding her statements up to the light, looking for cracks.

"Two." He raised another finger, still without turning his head. "You've got the physical evidence of the driver's license found in the dead man's shoe, linking Frank Lyttle to a man who died two years ago named R.L. Webster. As a matter of fact, it looks like R.L. Webster and Frank Lyttle might even be the same man, given that the dental X-rays of the first matched the second. But, according to your inside source at the morgue, those X-rays, which were our only real proof that the two bodies were linked, have now disappeared, so again we should be skeptical.

"Three." Another finger went up. "Supposedly there's a woman from the 'mayor's office' looking to give you some shit by making sure that you're involved with Frank Lyttle's disposition. How you can get into trouble just by burying somebody hasn't been made clear. And why the hell the city administration should waste its time on you isn't clear either. But again, your inside source at the morgue insists that Dr. Wolf's telling Mrs. Lyttle to call you instead of another funeral director was a sinister act. I won't argue. It's unusual, so therefore it's suspect. Though truthfully, if it weren't for the fax, I don't think I'd have paid it too much mind.

"Which brings us to number four, the fax." He returned his hand to the steering wheel, and leaned back as he drove. "That's where things get interesting. As I see it, it's that fax that's really the problem. It's not the timing that's important, or what the fax said, or how it relates to what you've already been told by other sources. The rest of it's all hot air and locked doors. But that fax is tangible. It has substance. It exists. Somebody sent it, and whoever it was, they must have had a reason. It's the one solid piece of actual evidence we have that there's more to all this than a lot of people worrying about nothing.

"Now, how about you? What's the part that bothers you the most?"

"The dog," I said, without hesitation.

"Why the dog?" Larry asked.

I sighed, saying, "Because the dog exists too. It punched a whole lot of holes in Frank Lyttle's body, and the cops don't seem to care. The foreman on the construction site where Lyttle was found said that a guy who rode a motorcycle fitted with a sidecar for his dog had been coming around to see Lyttle off and on for the last couple of weeks. And yet nowhere in that fax did it say anything about the cops following up any leads like that. Who could shut down the cops? And why would they want to? And . . . well . . . there's something else. . . ."

"Yeah?" Larry prompted.

Making me turn in my seat to face him as I spoke.

"There's something about Mrs. Lyttle's story that's been bothering me."

"You think she lied to you?"

"Oh, I *know* she lied to me. I don't know what she lied about yet, but I've known she was lying about something from the first. But that's not what I'm talking about.

"What's been bothering me has to do with Frank Lyttle's behavior, as his wife described it. See, I'm an addictive personality type myself. I'm hooked on anything I've ever tried and liked. I understand the addictive cycle, and I know what it feels like to both want something, and not to want it, all at the same time."

Larry's eyes narrowed behind his glasses as he drove, but he didn't say a word.

"The way Mrs. Lyttle described her husband's behavior strikes a chord in me," I continued. "He stole something, right? Or at least he did, according to her. Whatever that something was, it turned out to be so dangerous that instead of trying to sell it, or give it back, or get rid of it, he had to hide it. Why? I think it's because he didn't want to part with it. He took the risk of stealing it, and once he had it in his hands, he didn't want to give it up."

"Okay." Larry nodded. "That's a possibility. You're stretching it again, but it fits, I guess."

"Just let me finish," I cut in, feeling a little irritated by his interruptions. "I told you it was just something I sensed. I never said that I thought it was the truth.

"Anyway, according to Mrs. Lyttle, her husband told her that whatever he stole was so hot that he could never come out of hiding. *Never!* You get that? Never's a long time. I've been turning it over in my brain since she said it. What the hell could he have stolen that somebody would spend forever looking for, or that somebody would think was worth killing somebody over no matter how long it took to find him? And who the hell would spend forever looking for anybody?

"It was making me nuts. And then it hit me. It couldn't be a salable commodity, like dope or something, because Lyttle would have sold it off a piece at a time, and then, once it was gone, there'd be nothing left to hide. It couldn't be a precious object, like a painting or something, because Lyttle would have known ahead of time how hard it would be to fence, so why would he go to the trouble of stealing it? No, it had to be something special that he could use whenever he wanted, and that would retain its value even if he waited years before taking advantage of it."

"Like what, for instance?" Larry asked.

I sighed. "I don't know. All I do know is that once he had it acted like an addict. He went to the trouble of getting what he wanted, got scared of it, and then couldn't leave it alone no matter how hard he tried, even though he knew he'd be a lot better off if he did. Addicts do that—they lie, cheat, and steal to get whatever they're hooked on; then, once they've been doing it for a while and they pay a few consequences, they get scared and try to quit. But sooner or later they all come back. That sounds like the Frank Lyttle his wife described to me. He stole something, and got burned because of it. But it was like he was an alcoholic who was trying to quit, all the while knowing that there was a bottle hidden under the kitchen sink. Even though he knew what would happen if he messed with it, he couldn't help himself, and, in the end, he paid his dues."

We had arrived at the Hound's Tooth, a notorious bikers' bar located in one of Cleveland's toughest neighborhoods. There were all sorts of things purported to go on at the Tooth, and the people who hung out there were constantly in trouble with the police. For a while the cops even had a squad car permanently stationed in the parking lot across the street. But after they lost a few windshields to bricks, and a few officers to brawls, they decided that they'd only respond when called, and otherwise pretty much leave the Hound's Tooth and its clientele alone.

The Tooth was a free-standing structure made of dirty red brick, perfectly square, and not overly large. It had two stories, with windows on the second floor only. Its parking lot surrounded it on all four sides, and there were a pair of spotlights mounted up high on the building's corners, aimed down to illuminate the area beneath. There must have been a hundred motorcycles parked in the lot that night. There were a few ratty cars, and pickup trucks too. But it was the bikes that caught my attention—all that chrome gleaming with reflected light in the dark, lined up in rows, leather and steel and rubber—but no sidecars. Absolutely none.

Larry parked across the street and the two of us sat and looked the place over for a minute or two before we got out.

He said, "You know, they run dog fights out'ta this joint."

I nodded, having heard about how the cops had tried to shut down the dog fights a couple of times, but that they just kept coming back. How could anyone possibly derive pleasure from such a spectacle, I wondered, trying to banish from my mind the images I had seen on the news of a circular pit the TV cameras had found in an abandoned building in which such fights had supposedly taken place. The pit had sawdust in it, and benches all around.

"Okay," Larry said, opening his door. "These guys are into everything from drug dealing to car stealing to pimping. Watch your mouth, don't look nobody in the eye. And listen. That's why we're here: to listen."

Right, I thought, smearing Vaseline in my hair and using a comb to slick it straight back on my head. Glancing into Larry's big wing mirror I decided that the effect was sufficiently sleazy. And when Larry saw me, he grunted his approval. Together, we crossed the street, and headed for the Tooth.

I've got to get this right. I've been in plenty of bars before, but this one I've got to be sure to get just right. You know how bars all seem to have their own atmosphere? Some are bouncy and light, with lots of music and hanging plants and people talking over glasses of wine. Some are dark and smoky, like the people in them, who just want to sit and drink in private. Some are cramped, others expensive. But the Hound's Tooth was . . . waiting.

That's the only word I can think of to describe what I felt as Larry and I stepped inside. There was this feeling of anticipation, a collective hush in the place, as if everybody was waiting for something to happen. It was eerie, and uncomfortable. And there were eyes following my every move from the moment I entered the front door. Tiny eyes, gleaming through the smoke in the dark.

"Grab a table," Larry ordered, nodding toward a corner. "I'll get us some beers."

Installing myself with my back to the wall, I looked over the bar, which was an island in the center of the room, oval-shaped, with a bartender on either side. Suspended overhead was a huge wooden latticework hung with glasses and mugs, through which multicolored lights shone dimly, picking up the facets of the glass and glinting with refracted, prismatic sparkle. Smoke hung in a boiling curl amid this looming clutter, fed by the cigarettes of the men hunched over their drinks, their shoulders rolled forward as their elbows propped their heads up, their asses half exposed as their jeans were pulled down by their spilling bellies.

If the Hound's Tooth had a motif, I guess you could say that it was dogs . . . or dog paraphernalia. There were huge leather collars dotted with spikes and studs hanging on the walls, as well as leather leashes, restrainers, muzzles, and chains. There were steel rings set into the floor around the bar, presumably for the convenience of the patrons, who could tie their animals' leashes to them while they drank. There were cartoon drawings of dogs, and T-shirts with dog sayings on them. And there were photographs. Lots and lots of photographs—mostly black-and-white, blown-up and framed—hung all over the walls. The one on the wall behind me was of ten bearded, beer-gutted, T-shirted, tattooed men, standing in a group, with their dogs positioned ominously before them. In ink someone had written "East 161st Street Kennel Club, May 8, 1990" across the bottom of the picture. And, examining it more closely, I noticed that most of the dogs in it were of the pit bull variety—large, square, and wide-jawed, with tiny, hateful eyes. The chains on the collars of these animals were considerably thicker than those sold in a pet store. And they were looped around the fists of the owners four or five times, presumably for the photographer's protection.

Larry returned with our beers, saying as he set them down, "Okay, we're in."

"In where?" I asked, lifting my glass and almost drinking before thinking better of it and replacing the mug on the table.

Larry was lighting a cigarette and waving his hands expressively as he spoke—loudly, because, as he always says, speak loud and no one hears; try to whisper, and the whole world wants to listen.

"This whole joint's jump'n about Frank Lyttle," he said. "I'm his uncle by the way, so that makes you his cousin."

"His cousin?"

"Yeah, it's the best I could come up with."

I shrugged, adding petulantly, "You know, you shouldn't smoke so much. It'll stunt your growth."

"No sense locking the barn door after the horse runs away," he answered. Then, "Anyway, when I told the bartender that I'd come in from out of town as soon as I heard about Frank's death, he gave me two beers on the house and started in about how everybody liked Frank, and what a swell guy he was . . ."

"What horse ran away?" I asked.

Larry blinked.

"Oh," he said. "I've got cancer."

I almost fell out of my chair.

"Since when?"

"Since I don't know," he replied. "I found out about it a little over six months ago. What can I say?"

I stared at my beer glass, my fingertips tingling. Finally I asked, "Didn't they have any soft drinks?"

To which Larry replied, "In here, beer *is* a soft drink. Anyway, when the bartender heard that I was Little Frank's uncle, he said that there was a guy I should talk to. Frank's best buddy, he says. He's sending him over."

I was finding it hard to look at Larry, and, even though I know I shouldn't have, I said, "Cancer? No kidding?"

He shrugged. "Listen, Bill. You're not the only person in the world who's got trouble. At least with your problem with the booze, you got an option. Know what I'm sayin'?

"Now straighten up, here comes our man."

Our man was a dilly . . . probably no more than five foot four, he was early middle-aged, had long, tangled brown hair that was heavily frosted with grey, round, wire-rimmed glasses, a moustache, nicotine-stained teeth, and on his arm a tattoo of a naked woman draped from the waist down in a Confederate flag. He shook Larry's hand, and then he shook mine, firing a blast of beer breath my way as he said, his voice thick with booze, and a lazy, Southern accent, "Little Frank's kin! I'll be goddamned. I'm sorry 'bout Frank, man, I truly am."

Then he stopped in mid-word, his eyes going round and his expression going blank. Staring at my beer glass, he lifted a finger and pointed. "Is that yours?" he asked.

I nodded, glancing at Larry.

"You drink from it yet?"

I shook my head.

"Oh man," the guy said. "Signs and portents. Signs and motherfucking portents." He placed one hand over his mouth thoughtfully.

"What are you talking about?" I asked.

And Larry said, "He'll read your fortune in the bubbles in your beer."

"Good deal," I said, without taking my eyes off Larry, looking for some sign as to what, if anything, I was supposed to be doing.

The man lifted the beer glass and drained it. Then, holding it up and staring at the ceiling through the glass, he said, "There's a guy named Jack. They call him Jackal. He ain't here right now, but you'll know him by the tattoo he's got. It's a swastika, prison-style, shoe polish and a straight pin so it's blue on his skin, and crooked. It's on his neck, just under his left ear. He went Aryan whatchamacallit while he was in the joint . . . a fucking American Nazi. Scum of the earth, but brainy. Reads books and all. Talk to him. He knows everything there is to know 'bout Little Frank. And he's pissed. Good and pissed. Bitchy might even be the word for what he is . . . if ya get my drift. The end of a perfect romance. He'll be a help, Jackal will . . . as I live and breathe.

"So, thanks for the beer, y'all."

He put the glass down on the table, directly atop a fifty-dollar bill that Larry must have placed there when I wasn't looking. With a rueful half-grin, the man shook his head and said, "Not this time, partner. This one's on the house. Little Frank was a good'un. T'aint right, what happened. Boo-koo fucked-up, if you please. Talk to Jackal. He'll be at the show, Wednesday night. He's always at the show on Wednesday night. Peace."

When the man had walked away, Larry slid the fifty out from under the beer glass and ran it between his index and middle fingers to squeegee the condensation off before he placed it back in his pocket. I looked at him and said, "What the hell was that?"

"That," he said, "was a drunk, transplanted-hillbilly biker-Vietnam-veteran helping a dead buddy's kin in their hour of need. Noble, don't you think?"

"Yeah, I'm all choked up. What's the show on Wednesday night?"

"The dog fights," Larry said, cocking a thumb over his shoulder at the photograph of the men and their dogs. "Nasty business. You know where they hold 'em, don't ya?"

"No," I said with a shake of my head.

"In an abandoned warehouse over on East One Hundred Seventy-first Street."

"East One Hundred Seventy-first? That's where R.L. We—"

"Shhh," Larry warned, looking at me over the top of his glass as he finished his beer.

"That's where they found the burned guy," I said more slowly.

"Uh-huh." He nodded. "Quit a coincidence, isn't it?"

"Yeah," I agreed. "But what was all that shit about the 'end of a perfect romance'?"

Larry shrugged. "I guess we'll just have to wait and see. But for now, I've got to tell you something that's even more important than that."

"What?"

"You're never going to get that Vaseline out of your hair. Now come on, let's blow."

On the way out of the bar, I was looking at the pictures hanging on the walls, and with a jolt, I realized that one near the men's room was important. Larry had gotten ahead of me, and I had to weave my way through a forest of hairy forearms and sweaty T-shirts to arrest his motion with a hand on his shoulder. Turning him around, I directed him back to the photograph, and pointed. He squinted, lifted his glasses, and then lowered them, looking around and finally settling on a particularly large man with a ponytail sitting on a stool and using a pinball machine as a table. There was a woman next to him, sleeping with her head on his shoulder.

Larry indicated the picture and asked, "Who's that?"

The man glanced up, and said, with exaggerated disinterest, "Captain Video."

"Really?" Larry asked.

The man shrugged.

"That's his name."

Doesn't anybody have a real name in this place? I thought, saying nothing.

The man in the photograph was huge, with a yawning gut, massive arms, and a neck like a fireplug. He was unshaven, though he didn't actually have a beard. And his eyes were covered by a pair of mirror sunglasses. The rest of his appearance was right in line with the uniforms we'd seen that night in the bar: leather, denim, and studs. But what was different was that he was standing in front of a Harley Davidson motorcycle, and that motorcycle was fitted with a sidecar. In his hand he held a chain, and that chain was connected to the largest, most dangerous-looking dog I had ever seen.

Larry said, "What kind of dog is that?"

To which the man at the pinball machine said, "That's Congo. He's a Tosa."

"What's a Tosa?" I asked.

Being questioned by the two of us at the same time seemed to disturb the man enough for him to say, "You guys into dogs?"

I nodded.

"You?" he asked Larry, who nodded as well.

"Japanese fighting dog," the man said. "There's only about two dozen of 'em in the whole country. Real special breed. Mean bastards too. In the pit there ain't noth'n can touch 'em."

"Tosa, huh?" Larry said, glancing back at the picture.

"Yeah, that's Congo," the man repeated. "Captain Video only fights him when he feels like it, or else he'd be champ for sure. Weighs in at one-eighty . . . and he's fast."

I felt a shudder run down my back as I looked at the picture of Congo on his leash, and saw, in my mind, the photographs of Frank Lyttle's body I had taken in my embalming room a few hours before.

"What color is it?" I asked. Since the photograph was in black-and-white, the Tosa came across as a kind of light grey.

"Saddle-tan," the man said, shifting in his seat. "You know, like sand."

"I'll bet Congo's an impressive sight," I said.

"Fucker walks like a lion," the man agreed. "I sure wouldn't want the video man aimin' that fucker my way . . . no shit."

"You think he'll be fighting this Wednesday?" Larry asked.

"I doubt it. He'll probably be there, since the Captain don't hardly ever miss a Wednesday night; but Congo don't fight much anymore. Only when there's a real challenge. Why? What's with you guys, anyway?"

"Noth'n," Larry said, indicating that I should walk ahead of him through the door. "Just making conversation. Take it easy."

And we left.

FOUR

■ ■ ■ ■ ■ ■ ■ ■ ■

" 'THE TOSA IS known as the Japanese fighting dog,' " Nat said into the phone, reading from a book on dogs she'd looked up as soon as she got to work. She's a reference librarian at the college where we met, which is located just a few blocks from my new funeral home. It was ten o'clock Tuesday morning, and she'd called to fill me in after I had asked her to do a little digging for me if she got a chance.

" 'The breed is fairly new to the West,' " she continued reading, " 'with fewer than a hundred specimens in the continental United States. It was bred in Japan over two hundred years ago in answer to the challenge of European fighting dogs such as the mastiff, which were far superior to anything the Japanese could offer up until that time. As a result of its careful breeding, the Tosa is a superior fighting animal, but its temperament makes it unsuited as a companion, pet, or guard. This is strictly a working dog, designed for one purpose, which is combat. Its speed is exceptional, particularly for an animal of its size, and its agility is quite startling. The Tosa is derived from mastiff, wolf, and rottweiler stocks, will fight to the death and beyond, its jaws often having to be pried open to release its victim even after the Tosa has expired, and it has been known to grow to some two hundred pounds, even in its leanest, pit-ready prime.'

"You want more?"

"I didn't want that," I said, leaning my elbow on my desk blotter. "It sounds like a monster."

"You should see its picture."

"I have."

"It's an amazing dog."

"It's a nightmare. God, I hate dogs."

All this talk of dogs was making my scars itch, so I changed the subject to googey talk, and hung up after telling Nat that I loved her about ten times, and that I wanted to take her out for dinner when she got off work.

Then I went back to the fax ... the new fax, that had just come in.

Whoever was doing this to me was serious, there was little doubt about that. The fax machine had started running at about nine that morning, and had gone on for twenty minutes. Again, I had about seventy pages of material in front of me, and it was of a sensitivity that I could hardly believe. This time, we were concentrating on the people who had died on the dates offered. There were three, with the last being R.L. Webster, and the first being Bernard Hilton, whose name had finally rung a bell. Reading the newspaper clippings included in the fax about him brought it all back.

Bernard Hilton was an entrepreneur who owned a great deal of real estate in Ohio, as well as a number of businesses ranging from a string of pizza parlors to a whole bunch of new and used-car lots. For a time he had been under investigation because of allegations that he employed "underworld characters" to steal cars for him to sell, as well as drugs, and enforcement muscle for local hustlers looking to intimidate mousy small-business owners into paying their protection money on time. But nothing ever came of the charges, at least not publicly, and they soon blew over. Still, Mr. Hilton was known to have all sorts of connections, particularly downtown. He had died two and a half, almost three, years before, and his death had been ruled from "natural causes" by the county coroner. Dr. Gordon Wolf himself had performed the autopsy, and it was said that no foul play had been involved.

Dr. Gordon Wolf.

Removing my glasses and rubbing my eyes, I leaned back and thought: Dr. Wolf?

Why did his name keep popping up?

Replacing my glasses, I looked down at a photograph of Bernard Hilton's wife, Elizabeth, emerging from the church on the day of her husband's funeral . . . a large affair, attended by many of the city's richest people. . . .

Elizabeth Hilton?

I paused.

Where had I heard that name before?

Why was it so familiar?

Then it hit me: Elizabeth Hilton and Dr. Gordon Wolf had been married just a little over a year ago. It had been in all the papers. "Socialite Matched with Man of Medicine," was the headline on one of the stories. I could literally see it in my mind. Aggie O'Toole, who was more or less the town's official gossip, had written the story from the angle of the couple's differing backgrounds. Dr. Wolf, whose first wife had died young, had remained unattached for years, concentrating his energies on his job and establishing a real name for himself as a frequent lecturer and author of articles in professional journals dealing with forensic pathology. Elizabeth Hilton, who was younger than he by about ten years, was known as a feisty, independent woman, who, even while her first husband had been alive, insisted on expressing herself in her own way. After Bernard Hilton's death, Elizabeth Hilton assumed control of her late husband's financial holdings, making no bones about the fact that she felt herself more than a match for any businessman to ever don a pair of wingtips.

And now she was married to Dr. Wolf.

Did that mean something?

And if so, what?

"Where is this shit coming from!" I demanded, slapping my hand down on the stack of paper before me, and gritting my teeth in anger.

If I only knew who was sending it, then maybe I'd know how seriously to take what it said. That morning, Larry Fizner was going to talk to somebody he knew who worked for the phone company. If he could obtain a computer record of the calls on my business line, we might be able to nail down the number from which the faxes had originated. The phone company keeps a record of all calls, coming and going, for all phones they service, and it's not unusual for the police to subpoena such records when they need them. A private eye's getting hold of them was another story. But if anybody could do it, I knew that it would be Larry Fizner.

So what to do?

I had already arranged one interview for the day: Ellie Lyttle had agreed to let me come to her home and look over her husband's possessions. I needed a sense of who Frank Lyttle was when he was at home, and having his wife there to answer questions would be a help. We were going to bury him tomorrow, which was Wednesday, in a private service at the cemetery. I'd be there, with Mrs. Lyttle, and Jerry, who insisted that he wanted to attend.

The other stop I had planned was going to take me to the one spot on earth that made me more uncomfortable than any place else. I didn't want to go there, and my palms got moist with nervous perspiration just thinking about it. But the photographs of Frank Lyttle's body I had taken needed to be analyzed by an expert, and I knew that the best person to do the job was surrounded by barking, prancing dogs. I would just have to swallow my discomfort and make the trip, heartened only by the knowledge that if worst came to worst, dog bites, statistically, are very rarely fatal.

Before Nat there had been Hildie. And the two were as different as pink and black. Where Nat was dark and mysterious, Hildie was fair and vivacious . . . a smiling, laughing, bright-eyed party girl who loved everybody, and never tired of being around people. I'd met her at a high-school mixer when I was just sixteen. The high school I had attended was all male, and once a month we had a dance with the all-girl school down the road. Hildie's last name was Schimmel, and she was blond, buxom, and beautiful. We dated for almost two years, our relationship falling apart only after I started college in town, while she went off to an out-of-state school specializing in veterinary medicine. Our parting was amicable, with no hard feelings, and to this day we are still friends. After she got her veterinary degree, she came home and set up practice at her father's kennels . . . which is the place I was referring to when I mentioned the most uncomfortable spot on earth. I remember it from when I used to pick Hildie up for dates . . . all those dogs running around, all that barking and snapping and noise. It would make my skin crawl, which she always thought was funny.

Hildie's father's name is Gunther, and at one time he was the head dog trainer for the Cleveland Police Department's K-9 unit. He's retired now, at least from working for the police. But at over seventy years of age he still runs The Schimmel Kennels, a private school where dog owners bring their animals to be transformed from stupid household pets to finely tuned companions.

This is a little off the subject, but when he was young, my dad was in the Army for like eight months. He hated it. I believe that it's from my dad that I got the stubborn, independent streak that is so much a part of my nature, and which is the same Ukrainian personality trait that my dad inherited from his father before him, a man who had been so hard-headed that even after the fifth doctor he'd seen told him to stop drinking or his ulcer would kill him, he kept right on putting it away, living for years on bourbon and baby food until—and I'm serious about this—his ulcer *disappeared*. I swear. For the last five years of his life my grandfather could eat and drink anything he wanted without pain. He stubborned the damned thing into finally giving up. Either that or his cancer was hurting so much that it made his ulcer pain irrelevant.

Anyway, my dad despised the Army, and when, after eight months a high-school football injury to the cartilage in his knee swelled up on a march, he took a medical discharge and got the hell out. But while he was in, there was one man in particular who made a real impression on him—his sergeant, whose name was Fritz Heimmelman, formerly of the German, as in Nazi, Army, this being around the time of the Korean war—who was known as Mr. Discipline. He used to make his men spit-shine the *bottoms* of their boots.

That description fits Gunther Schimmel to a tee. He's short, stout, and has an iron-grey crew cut. His eyes are steel-blue, and his posture ramrod-straight. When he barks an order at a dog, the dog listens so hard you'd swear it comprehends the words themselves. He can take any dog on the planet, no matter how surly, mean, or stupid, and make it understand what he expects from it, and when. And the reason he's so successful at teaching dogs to perform is because he loves them more than anything else in the world. People, Gunther Schimmel tolerates. Dogs, he loves.

I left my van on the gravel lot out front of the Schimmel Kennels, which were housed in a small, vanilla-colored brick building with a red tile roof and windows covered with venetian blinds. The silhouettes of two German shepherds, one standing, the other seated, formed the kennels' logo, which was painted on the door above the hours: Noon to Five, Monday through Saturday. Beneath that was pinned a three-by-five index card with the words "Other Times, Don't Call" written in red ink. There was also a more dignified, little brass plaque bolted to the wall next to the door that read "Hildegard Schimmel, D.V.M.," and, opening the door, I felt a little tingle of nerves. I still get like that when I see Hildie, even after all these years.

I don't think anybody ever completely gets over their first girlfriend, which is something I don't plan on ever mentioning to Nat.

Hildie greeted me with a kiss and a smile, asked a few questions, and then showed me through the office to the back yard, where her father was standing watch over three young men as they ran six leashed dogs of various breeds over an obstacle course of painted car tires, barrels, ladders, pretend window frames, and water puddles. The boys were dressed in jeans and white, medical-looking tunics. Gunther Schimmel was wearing a dark green jacket. When he saw me he smiled, blew a whistle, and told the boys to take a break. Then he stuck out his hand and said, "William Hawlinski? In my yard with dogs? What a surprise!"

I shook his hand and said that my fear of dogs wasn't nearly what it once was—which was true, though just barely. Then I complimented him on how fit he looked, and withdrew from my jacket pocket the series of Polaroids that I'd shot in my prep room, saying, "I've got a professional question for you, Mr. Schimmel. It concerns a bad dog, and I'm afraid these pictures aren't very nice."

Mr. Schimmel removed a pair of half-rim bifocals from his shirt pocket, and glanced through them at the pictures I'd handed him. Then, very glumly, he said, "No, they are not nice. Come with me," leading me into his private office, where he closed the door, and sat down behind a big metal desk. I sat down across from him as he opened a drawer, removed a magnifying glass, and turned on a green-shaded banker's lamp under which he held my pictures, one at a time. Finally, he grimaced, sighed, and dropped the photos on the blotter, leaning back and touching the magnifying glass to his chin as he asked, "So what exactly do you need to know?"

"Two things," I said. "What did that? And why?"

"The what," he said, "I can't tell from these pictures, because I can only get a rough idea as to the size of the wounds. I'd need measurements to determine a bite radius and tooth length before I could name a breed. But just going by what I see here, I'd say you've got a fairly big animal on your hands—mastiff-size, or thereabouts. We're talking anywhere from eighty to a hundred and forty pounds and up. A real man-stopper, that's for sure. But"—he paused, lifted one picture and held it under the magnifier as he squinted one eye shut—"there's something peculiar about this. It's a tenacious animal, no doubt there. But"—he paused once more, considered, seemed on the verge of saying something else, and then sighed, adding, "No," as he dropped the picture again and laid the glass aside. "I would need precise measurements to be sure.

"As to the why," he continued, "that's a little easier. This dog did this because it was trained to do it. That's the only explanation."

"Trained?" I said, lifting one of the pictures and frowning. I knew better than to say something stupid like, Are you sure? because Gunther Schimmel never said anything about dogs if he wasn't.

A movement caught my eye in the corner of the room as a huge brown head lifted itself from the pair of giant paws on which it had been resting, turning on me two sharp, amber-colored eyes. This was Ansel, a German shepherd I'd watched Gunther Schimmel raise from a pup. I'd always been terrified of this particular animal because of its size, and the ferocity with which I had seen it throw itself into its attack training. Seeing it lying curled in the shadows sent a quick shudder down my spine. Its name, Ansel, was derived from the old German, Anselm, which means "divine warrior." Ansel's black nose moved a little as he sniffed and started to rise. But Mr. Schimmel said, "Ansel, no," without even moving his eyes, as if he knew what the dog was doing without seeing it. Ansel lay back down, watching me serenely with his huge old head held at a high, stately angle.

Mr. Schimmel once told me that Ansel was the smartest dog he had ever trained, and that he preferred his company to just about any human being he could name, excluding his daughter.

"The bite pattern is the key," he said, lifting a pencil from the desk and arranging the four Polaroids so that they were facing me under the banker's lamp. Using the pencil to point, he continued, "See here, the attack is very general, spread out, unfocused. A dog has a real advantage going after a man. He's lower to the ground, covered with fur to protect him from assault, and equipped with his most effective weapons, which are his teeth and jaws, at the front. Men have a higher center of gravity, so it's hard to defend themselves from something coming up at such an angle. Plus, we're built for blocking blows."

He demonstrated with a quick forearm up, perpendicular to his face.

"Which, with a dog, only gives him something to slash and bite. Also, there's the human versus animal concept to deal with. Very ancient, and very pure. It's a clash of the species boiled down to its most basic level. When a human being draws blood, he generally stops his assault, satisfied with the result. But when a dog draws blood, it's the impetus he's looking for to motivate an escalation of his efforts."

As Mr. Schimmel spoke he was moving the pencil point over the pictures of Frank Lyttle's mauled body.

"Now there's two types of attack," he continued. "The snapping bite, like a Doberman pinscher employs, and the bite and shake, which is more in line with your pit bulls. This dog, which I'm almost positive is too big to be a Doberman, bit and held, as indicated by the bruising around some of these wounds; but he didn't shake. A mastiff, which is the breed I'm leaning toward, judging by the size of the jaw print—they shake when they bite. So I'm a little puzzled there.

"Also, and this is what really bothers me, the attack isn't concentrated. The animal didn't 'go for' any particular part of this man's body. It moved around. See here: hands, face, chest, arms. Straight snap-bites, but no concentrated mauling. So it wasn't going for a kill. It was just biting, over and over. Almost, and this is the part that's really bad, as if it specifically *didn't want its prey to die.*"

"But, how could a dog want or not want something like that?" I asked.

Gunther Schimmel put his pencil down, saying, "That's the point, William. Dogs don't work that way. A dog trained to do something like this is like a weapon in its master's hands."

I sure wouldn't want the Video man aimin' that fucker my way, I remembered the man in the bar saying.

"So it's your opinion that someone stood by and did, what?"

"Gave the bite and retreat commands, over and over again."

I shuddered, and glanced at Ansel, seeing that long muzzle full of gleaming white teeth beneath those deep, intelligent eyes.

"So you're saying that a person, a man, was present during the attack?" I said.

"Absolutely," Gunther Schimmel returned. "Because even if this dog was mad, by which I mean rabid, not just angry, it wouldn't bite so many times without going for the guts or the throat. Dogs bite to defend their pack-leaders, to defend themselves, or to kill. They don't generally do it for fun. They're not like cats, who play with their prey. They've got more heart than that."

An old argument:

A mother cat in the wild will deliberately wound and bring a creature back to her lair for her kittens to play with until it's dead. And while it might look like a cruel sport to the observer, it serves the function of teaching the kittens how to kill, which is, let's face it, what they're going to need to do in order to survive. Dogs, on the other hand, put wounded and sick animals out of their misery. That's almost their job in the wild. Wolves and jackals prey on the old and infirm beasts in a herd, and rarely kill anything healthy.

"So you think it was a well-trained mastiff then?" I asked, gathering up my pictures and putting them back in my pocket.

"I said that it's like a mastiff," Mr. Schimmel corrected. "Get me the bite measurements, and I can tell you better. But yes, it's well-trained. So well-trained," he added, taking off his bifocals and swinging them distractedly by one earpiece, "that its owner used it like a living instrument. Like an extension of his own hand."

"What do you mean?" I said, rising and looking down at him as he sat bathed in the green glow of his banker's lamp.

"I mean that he tortured that man to death with a dog," Gunther Schimmel replied, lifting his eyes to look up at me with a grim, almost angry expression. "Get me the measurements, William. What that man must have done to that dog to make it behave so much against its nature isn't right. A dog is a better creature than that. He misused it."

"Have you ever heard of a dog called a Tosa?" I asked.

Mr. Schimmel narrowed his eyes as he nodded. "They're rare in this part of the world, although in the East they're prized. I've only seen one once, at an obedience demonstration a few years back, and what I saw impressed me. It's a big dog, without a big dog's problems when it comes to mobility and stamina. A really strong beast. But crazy, or at least that's its reputation. Dangerous. Only the toughest trainers can handle them, I'm told, and even then it's usually a battle of wills."

"Meaning?"

"Meaning that it takes a strong-willed trainer to control a strong-willed dog. A tenacious dog will express its personality by testing its limitations, and trying to establish itself as the pack leader. It takes a powerful man to master a powerful dog."

"Could these wounds be the work of a Tosa?" I asked.

Mr. Schimmel shrugged. "I don't know enough about them to say for sure. But a Tosa would certainly be the right size . . . and have the necessary temperament. I'm not prepared to commit absolutely, but I will say that if you have some reason for suspecting that a Tosa did that, then you're probably on a pretty good track."

Glancing back down at Ansel, I asked one last question. It wasn't a question I necessarily wanted to ask, but it seemed important at the moment.

"How would you defend yourself against something like a Tosa? I mean, Ansel's what, about ninety pounds or so, right?"

"Give or take."

"So this Tosa thing would be like twice that size?"

"Give or take."

"And you say they're fast?"

Gunther Schimmel nodded, and removed a book from a shelf. Opening it, he pointed at a photograph of a Tosa, standing magnificently on a lawn with its rippling muscles distinct beneath its tight skin, its huge black jowls hanging beneath bright black eyes.

"That's a Tosa," he said. "And it's more than just a dog. That animal would eat Ansel alive. And Ansel is the best I've ever trained. It would eat him, Bill. Against that, a man without a gun has no defense. And even with a gun, there's no guarantee."

My hands didn't stop shaking until I had been on the freeway for nearly ten minutes. The photograph Mr. Schimmel had shown me was seared into my eyes. The thought of such a creature as the Tosa coming at me literally made me quiver, tweaking deep-seated terrors that I'd been carrying since childhood. I knew that I'd be having nightmares about dogs again soon. Maybe even tonight. It had been years since I'd had one, but it wouldn't be long now.

All this emotion, I knew, was serving to overshadow one simple fact. And that was that I had absolutely no proof that the animal I was looking for was a Tosa. All I had was one photograph in which a man with a sidecar coincidentally had a Tosa, which, coincidentally, was the type of dog that matched the description given to me by the foreman who had found Frank Lyttle's body. And that photograph, coincidentally, was hanging on the wall of Frank Lyttle's favorite bar.

Coincidentally.

Right.

My car phone rang, and when I answered it Larry Fizner came on the line with bad news. He'd chased down the phone records for the funeral home and had discovered that the two calls that matched the times and length of the faxes I'd gotten had been placed from two separate locations; one was a library that sold fax time by the minute, and the other was a Mail Boxes and More store that sold fax time at so many cents per page.

"So it's another dead end," I said.

"Not necessarily," Larry replied. "I'm gon'na head over to both places and see if anybody remembers anything about the person sending the fax. They were long transmissions, so chances are somebody noticed that whoever was sending 'em had a big stack of paper. We'll see. But I'll bet I come up with something today. It might not be much, but it'll be something. You just wait."

But Larry wasn't finished.

"I did find something useful, though," he added, and I could hear the smile in his voice.

This was the part he really enjoyed: the leg work. I was better at the mind games, at arranging and rearranging information until it made sense. Even Larry had said so, insisting that it was the matching of our two distinct talents that made us such an effective team. He was the man of action, and I the man of thought. Or so he said. He liked to run around looking under rocks because, intrinsically, he was the type of man who, if he was visiting your house for a dinner party, would be unable to resist peeking in your medicine cabinet when he used the bathroom. He just couldn't help it.

"I know who Captain Video, the guy with the Tosa, is," he said, triumphantly. "And, what's more, I know where he lives."

"How'd you do that?" I asked.

And Larry explained, "I went back to the Hound's Tooth last night after I put you to bed, and I asked around. Captain Video's real name is Mitch Krammer, and he's something of a local celebrity. You wan'na know why they call him Captain Video?"

"Tell me."

"'Cause he tapes everything he does. I guess he's a video nut. He's got every fight Congo's ever been in on tape, and every girl he's ever fucked, too."

"So?"

"I don't know. But I've got an idea."

"What's that?"

"You're gon'na have to go to the dog fights tomorrow night by yourself. I'm gon'na be busy."

"Doing what?"

"Breaking into Captain Video's house."

I almost swerved off the freeway. Holding the portable phone tight against my ear, I said, "Why? We don't even know that this guy's involved yet. He just happens to own the right kind of dog."

"Well, there's one way to find out," Larry said. "And besides, I want to leave a little calling card while I'm there. It might come in handy in the future."

"What kind of calling card?"

"You'll see."

Then Larry Fizner was gone.

I turned off the phone and returned it to its cradle, churning with misgivings about what he intended to do. Nat and I had discussed Larry's cancer earlier that morning. Thinking about it had kept me awake most of last night, and even Nat's level-headed reactions like "Well, he's pushing seventy, and he's been smoking most of his life," didn't do anything to make me feel better. Naturally, in my business, I've seen more than my share of cancer victims. Actually, you'd be surprised at just how many deaths are caused by cancer. Human beings seem to have a built-in mechanism where they self-destruct at a certain age, with cancer being one of that mechanism's most effective agents.

But Larry Fizner had always been such a formidable force in my mind. From the time I'd first met him there had been an air of toughness about the man that I found both comforting and disturbing. To think that he was in any way physically infirm shook something fundamental in my perception of the world. Suddenly, I found myself wanting to protect him . . . wanting to take his place and do the risky stuff myself so that he wouldn't have to. If I ever articulated those feelings, he'd probably slap me upside the head, but that's how I felt, and I couldn't help it. The idea of him breaking into the house of Mitch Krammer, Captain Video, Congo's owner and master, made me squirm. The only consolation was that the man in the Hound's Tooth had said that Captain Video rarely missed a Wednesday night dog fight, and always brought Congo with him so that he could show his prized dog off to an appreciative audience.

Still, I wished that it would be me doing the break-in—
one, because I wanted to protect Larry from further harm—
because I saw his illness as an injury he was carrying like
a scar—and two, because, truthfully, I didn't want to go to
the dog fights alone. I didn't want to go at all, if you really
want to get technical . . . and I think that I would have been
willing to do just about anything to get out of it.

Blinking, I came back to the world from the haze of my
distractions as I rolled the van into Ellie Lyttle's driveway.
I'd been flying on automatic pilot, and I honestly didn't
remember getting from the freeway exit to the house. I
turned off the motor, and looked the place over.

Frank Lyttle's foreman had said that he had never been
given Lyttle's address . . . that no one on the crew knew
where the man lived. With that in mind, I had been expecting something unusual, like a trailer park . . . not that a
trailer park is unusual in itself, but what I mean is that I
was not expecting a little blue house in the heart of
inner suburbia, with a lawn and a basketball hoop. With
everything else that had been going on, I didn't expect a
basketball hoop. But that's exactly what I found, on the
two-car garage behind the single-floor ranch-style house
with the tan shutters and the concrete porch with the red-
wood lawn furniture sitting under the picture window that
looked in on the living room.

There was a cyclone fence around the back yard, and,
before I opened the van's door, I looked around for "Beware
of the Dog" signs. I was a little surprised not to find any.

Ellie Lyttle opened the side door and smiled in greeting.
She was looking prettier and prettier every time I saw her.
Her clothes were a little newer, and her eyes a little bright-
er. They say that pregnant women glow, and Ellie Lyttle
seemed to prove it. I don't know much about pregnancy
and babies and all, but she looked like she was about
ready to be a mommy any minute. So I determined that
I'd go easy and not upset her. To that end I returned her
smile, and extended my hand. Instead of shaking hands, she
hugged me and asked me in. As soon as I stepped over the
threshold, the snoop in me took over.

"I did like you said," Mrs. Lyttle offered. And then, "That is to say, I didn't do anything. I didn't touch a thing I didn't have to. Everything's just like Frank left it. I remember, when my grandfather died, my grandma left all his stuff just like it was, and never moved it again. It was spooky, 'cause you'd go to the house and it looked like Grandpa was still there. The books and magazines and ashtrays and all. It was like he was just in the other room, and that every time you visited he'd hide. I ain't gon'na do that with Frank's stuff. When you're through I'm cleaning it all out."

She stopped and put a hand to her mouth, saying, "Oh, my. I'm babbling. I'm sorry, Mr. Hawley. I'm just a little nervous, I guess. It feels sort'a funny, letting you go through everything. It's . . . you know . . . kind'a weird."

I nodded, and told her that I understood her discomfort, while adding that her cooperation was the best thing she could do to insure the success of my investigation . . . like there was anything anybody could do to insure anything about what I was doing, since I wasn't even sure exactly what I was doing myself.

Asking me if I wanted anything to drink, "Coffee, or a soda? Maybe a beer?" Mrs. Lyttle bustled off to make coffee, leaving me gloriously alone for the first time since I'd entered the house. Then the phone rang, and when she answered it I could hear a change in the tone of her voice.

"It's your brother," she said, placing her hand over the mouthpiece.

"Does he want to talk to me?" I asked, reaching for the phone.

"Do you want to talk to him?" she said into the mouthpiece. Then she shook her head and said, "No. It's for me. You can just go ahead and do whatever it is you're doing."

I felt more than a little awkward, with my hand extended ready to take the phone . . . as if I'd reached out to shake hands with someone who had coldly rejected the gesture. I could feel my face burn, so I turned quickly away and stepped into the living room, thinking, *So, Jerry's calling her at home now*. And not liking it a bit.

Why was I so opposed to Ellie Lyttle and my brother getting together, I wondered. I mean, after all, what could they do? Jerry was paralyzed . . . and paralyzed people can't have sex. Can they?

I blinked, realizing that I didn't know the answer to that question . . . and what's more, that I'd never even thought about it before. I'd have to have Nat look into it for me. There had to be a book . . .

Asking Jerry never even crossed my mind.

The house was furnished in an "early Sears" style: lots of particle-board tables covered with sheets of imitation wood-grain paper, and vinyl chairs worn at the seat. The walls were painted neutral colors, the curtains nondescript, the carpets matted and frayed. But there was a wide-screen TV in the living room, two VCR's, and a stereo. Lots of CD's too, I noticed, no albums.

The pictures on the walls were innocuous, the type of thing sold in those "art" galleries in malls that frame posters of Marilyn Monroe. There was nothing of interest in the bathroom medicine cabinet or in the family room, which had been painted baby-blue, and outfitted with a crib over which hung a mobile of brightly colored plastic dinosaurs. A purple lizard bearing the improbable name Barney was painted on the foot of the crib, and there was an orange, stuffed alligator on the floor. Apparently, the youngest Lyttle would be introduced to a world dominated by reptiles. Lucky child.

It was in the Lyttles' bedroom that I started finding things. Frank Lyttle was apparently one of those men who kept everything that belonged to him in his dresser, the top drawer of which serving as his "junk box," which he had filled with odds and ends. Pulling the drawer from its frame, I set it down on the bed, going through it slowly and carefully. Then I searched the rest of the drawers, the closet, under the bed, and then, lastly, Ellie Lyttle's part of the room.

I examined the basement, the yard, and the garage. And then I stood on the sidewalk outside the house, staring at it. Ellie Lyttle's silhouette was just vaguely discernible through the front picture window. She was hanging back in the doorway to the kitchen, and her shape was dark and indistinct.

The things I had found were these:

In the junk drawer I discovered a stack of newspaper clippings, paper-clipped together, having to do with Bernard Hilton's death and the marriage of Mrs. Hilton and Dr. Gordon Wolf. Also there were roach clips for smoking marijuana, a tiny mirror and some razor blades, apparently for snorting coke, and a box of bullets. But I didn't find a gun. Since there had been no gun on Frank Lyttle's body, either, where was the gun for these bullets? Also in the junk drawer were a switch-blade knife, a set of Allen wrenches on a ring, and half a dozen tiny screwdrivers with their ends filed into various shapes. I knew automatically these had something to do with opening doors and windows that someone else didn't want opened.

In the basement I'd found a trunk full of dog-related items . . . dog-fighting-related items, I should say: studded collars, chains, and muzzles. When I asked Mrs. Lyttle about these she said that as far as she knew, her husband had never owned a dog. But she had never opened the trunk because she figured that if Frank wanted her to know what was in it, he'd have told her.

In the garage, I made my most important, though confusing, discovery . . . which was presently tucked safely under my arm.

Just who was Frank Lyttle? I wondered, lighting a cigarette and staring at the house. The question was beginning to burn inside me, curling in my gut like a parasite. It ate at me, and ruined my sleep. Who was he, and why did it feel as if this house, this yard, this wife, were all the trappings of his disguise, with little or no value in and of themselves? Could any man be so heartless as to marry a woman just because he needed to build the perception of a new life as a way of running from the old? Or was I extrapolating from insufficient evidence—as Larry Fizner had already said was my tendency—having formed a notion in my mind which I hadn't even articulated to myself yet, while searching unconsciously for evidence, not of the truth, but of the accuracy of my own preconceptions?

I found Mrs. Lyttle sitting at the kitchen table. The overhead lights were off, and the curtains over the sink drawn. The curtains on the window next to the table at which she sat were open slightly, throwing a harsh band of light that bisected her face, making one eye sparkle brightly as the other, dark with shadow, studied me.

The linoleum under my shoes was loud as I approached, stopped, and placed the object I'd found in the garage on the table. I let Mrs. Lyttle look at it for a moment before I asked my question.

"Who was he, Mrs. Lyttle?" I said. "Really, just who was your husband?"

"I already told you that I don't know," she said, lifting her coffee mug with both hands, which were trembling slightly.

"Not his name," I said, sitting down. "At least not yet. What I want to know now is, what kind of man was he? Was he good to you?"

"That depends on what you mean by good," she replied. "Compared to some'a the jerks I've known in my life, he was a fuckin' prince."

I opened the photo album I'd found in the garage, and paged through it for her benefit.

"Did he allow you to go in the garage?" I asked.

She shook her head. "Not really. He said that he had some paint and stuff in there that would be bad for the baby. 'Cause'a the fumes. Know what I mean?"

"But you went anyway, didn't you?"

She shrugged.

"You know a lot more about him than you're letting on. Even after asking me to help you, you're still acting like you can tell me only those things that you want me to know, and get me to jump through hoops with tricks instead of honesty. Who's this?"

She followed my finger to where it was pointing at a photograph of a man with a swastika tattooed beneath his left ear.

"Guy named Jackal," she said.

"And this?"

"Uh, Lemon, or Letton, or something. I'm not sure."

"And this?"

"That's Ron. R.L., they called him. R.L. Webster."

"So you've known who R.L. Webster was all along, haven't you?"

"More or less."

"Had you met Mr. Webster in the flesh?"

Mrs. Lyttle nodded, vaguely paging through the album as a look came into her eye that said that her thoughts were traveling. In the garage I had found a number of souvenirs from prison that her husband had kept, including this album, which was full of pictures.

Pictures from prison . . .

"Mrs. Lyttle," I said, drawing her attention back to me. "Who takes pictures in prison?"

"I think his name was Mitch . . . Hammer, or Flammer . . . I can't remember what Frank said his last name was . . ."

"Mitch Krammer?" I asked.

She nodded, her eyes narrowing as she studied me, obviously wondering how I knew a name that she hadn't been able to recall herself.

"Did they call him Captain Video?" I added.

She shook her head.

"Not then. They called him Shutterbug back then, I guess. They didn't start the Captain Video thing until later, when he got himself a Camcorder.

"Mr. Hawley," she added, reaching over and placing her hand atop mine in a gesture that I'm sure she meant to reassure me, to bond us somehow, but that succeeded only in making me feel uncomfortable. "You've got to understand, I don't really know these people. This was mostly before my time with Frank. He was older than me by quite a bit, and he had had a lot of life before I ever came along. I saw these pictures once, a long time ago. And that was it. He's hidden them ever since. This is the first time I've seen them in years, and these names are all hard for me to remember."

"The point is," I interrupted, removing my hand from beneath hers and rising to put a little distance between us, "that you did remember them; and you lied to me about it when I asked you. What else have you been lying about, Mrs. Lyttle? Even now, what else are you lying about, right this minute?"

Before she could answer, I removed a single photograph from my pocket and laid it on the table. It was of her and Frank Lyttle, standing together in front of the gates to a prison.

"Did you think I wouldn't find it?" I asked, continuing before she could answer, "Taken the day he got out, I'd assume. Did you know him before he went in, or was yours one of those prison romances where the lonely girl writes to a prisoner after seeing an article about him in the local newspaper, only to fall in love with him through the bars?"

"It wasn't like that," she responded, her cheeks coloring.

"Then you knew him before?"

She nodded.

"What was his name?"

"Joe Pace," she said, her shoulders sagging.

"Why didn't you tell me that before?"

"I didn't see how it made any difference. I want you to find his hiding place. What he did and who he was in New Jersey don't have anything to do with who he was in Ohio."

"Then he was in prison in New Jersey?"

Her eyes darkened as she nodded yes.

"And in Ohio?"

She shook her head, mumbling, "Only New Jersey."

I looked down at the photo album, at the picture she had identified as her husband, now named Joe Pace, dressed in prison-issue clothes, standing next to another prisoner, who she had named, R.L. Webster. So Webster and Lyttle/Pace were in fact two separate men. Right? Was that right? And if so, what was all that bullshit at the morgue about dental charts matching both bodies?

"Mrs. Lyttle," I said. "How old were you in this picture, fifteen? Sixteen?"

"Sixteen," she said.

"And you're how old now?"

"Twenty-two."

"Then you've known Frank Lyttle, or Joe Pace—call him what you will—for quite some time . . . at least, what, six years?"

"Right."

"And you're telling me that you don't know anything else about him other than what you've told me so far . . . and you're still expecting me to believe it?"

With a deep sigh, she nodded and said, "Okay. Okay. I was wrong to do it this way. I fucked up. But it's just that . . . Jesus . . . the way my life has gone, it's hard for me to open up to people. Understand? It's hard for me to lay it on the line, because every other time I've tried I've gotten nailed for it."

"Whew, let's see," she went on, rolling her eyes nervously and running one hand over her hair. "I don't even know where to start."

The story she related came in fits and starts, with a lot of asides, and a real problem with chronology. Once I'd waded through it and organized it in my mind, it went like this:

Apparently R.L. Webster and Joseph Pace—a.k.a. Frank Lyttle—had been friends for years. Neither of them was very successful at anything they ever tried, and they were both alcoholics and drug users. They screwed up everything they touched, drifting around the country together, getting high, pulling little robberies to tide them over when money got tight, and establishing connections with other criminal types. Finally, in New Jersey, they got busted when a stolen-car scam they had going fell apart. They'd been working for a dealer who had a couple of Cadillacs that he would sell to people who he knew couldn't make the payments. He'd offer a car at an amazingly low price, take a thousand dollars down on it, and arrange financing. The first time the buyer missed a payment, he'd have his "repossessors" steal it back; then he'd change the locks, and sell it again. Problem was, the cars had been stolen in the first place. All three men got popped, and R.L. Webster and Joe Pace ended up doing two years in a Jersey prison.

There they got tight with a couple of guys who said that they were on to a good thing in Ohio, and that as soon as they got out that's where they were heading. The men were named Mitch Krammer and Jackal—Mrs. Lyttle didn't know Jackal's real name, and doubted if even her husband had. Webster and Pace were invited up when they got out. And, when they did get out, they went, Pace taking his girlfriend, Ellie, with him when he moved.

"He went pretty straight when we got here," she explained, almost proudly.

Pretty straight, in her mind, apparently meant not carrying a gun when he went to work. But what he did for a living was essentially the same in Ohio as what he did in New Jersey. Small-time robbery, a few cars now and then, and whatever else came his way.

"But then something happened," she said, looking at me very seriously. "He came home one night and said that he was onto something. Something big. It involved Mitch Krammer, and the boss."

"What boss?" I asked.

She shrugged, and replied, "I don't know. Just 'the boss.' If it worked out, he said, we'd be set for life. No more bills, no more bullshit, 'cause this was the big one. The kind of thing that only came along once, and that was it. Like hitting the lottery. And him and R.L. were going to make sure that this chance didn't pass them by."

Whatever it was that they did, it involved stealing, and stealing was something at which the two partners were reasonably adept. They apparently pulled off their job, though Ellie Lyttle didn't know the details, and laid low for a while, waiting for the right time to take advantage of their prize.

"This was when?" I asked.

"'Bout three years ago."

"And then?"

"And then Ron got popped for a bullshit parole violation, and they sent him back to the joint. It was three months before he got out, and when he did, it was only like three days before he was killed . . . and Joe freaked."

"And is that when he changed his name from Pace to Lyttle?" I asked.

She nodded. "Yeah. That was when he did it. He laid low for the longest time . . . and then I got pregnant. And, hell, I don't know . . . I . . ."

She stopped, and wiped away a tear. Swallowing a mouthful of coffee, she sat, blinking.

"But you don't know what he stole?" I asked. "After all the rest, you really don't know?"

She shook her head.

"Mr. Hawley," she said softly, "why don't you like me?"

I was somewhat taken aback by her question, and it took me a second to order my thoughts. Buying time, I asked her to explain what she meant, to which she replied, "Your brother likes me. He talks to me. But he says you don't. He says you're hard to understand, and that you only see things your own way."

"My brother said that?" I asked. "To you?"

She nodded.

"Your brother's sweet," she said. "And he makes me laugh. It's been a long time since I laughed."

Wonderful, I thought.

"I like you fine, Mrs. Lyttle," I said, trying to keep my voice even, and professional. "And besides, me liking or not liking you isn't the point."

"But don't you see that what you think is important to your brother?"

I didn't answer.

"He looks up to you, you know," she went on. "He says that you've been blaming yourself for what happened to him for a long time, and that, in a way, he admires your ethics. But he also says that you're so hard on yourself that all you ever do is fall short of your own standards. That you're always angry at yourself for not being who you imagine yourself to be. So you do all sorts of risky things to make up for it. Like making allowances for everybody else's behavior, no matter how badly they treat you, and taking on these investigations, even though it could mean losing everything you own.

"So why do you do it, Mr. Hawley? What do you get out of it?"

"I thought you wanted me to find what your husband was hiding," I returned, wanting more than anything in the world to get the hell out of there. "I thought I was the one asking the questions."

"You are," she agreed. "But I asked you to help me before I knew anything about you. Your brother's told me a lot, and now I feel like I know you a little. I'd hate to see you get hurt . . . or to see Jerry get hurt . . . on account of me."

"I can take care of myself," I said, my voice tight with restrained emotion. "And I can take care of Jerry too. I don't need you looking out for me, and I don't need him to go around telling strangers my business. You can tell him that for me, too, since you'll probably be talking to him on the phone as soon as I go. But if, for some reason, you don't talk to him, you can bet that I will as soon as I get back to my funeral home!

"This is business, Mrs. Lyttle," I added, grabbing up the photo album. "Don't forget it. You asked me to do a job, and I'm doing it—for you, and for myself. My reasons are my business, but believe me when I say that they've got nothing to do with guilt or psychology. I don't need to be analyzed. And I don't need your sympathy. And you can tell Jerry that too!

"I do not need your sympathy!" I nearly shouted, turning, and slamming the kitchen door as I escaped the house and practically ran for my van, where I sat in the front seat, fuming for a long time before I finally started the engine.

How dare Jerry say those things to a stranger? How dare he talk like that about me, after all the things I'd done for him? If it wasn't for me, he'd never have left that first nursing home . . . he'd never have gotten the therapy that started him back to mobility . . . he'd never have gotten his own apartment, with his own money, and a job, and a life, and a whole new start, and—

If it wasn't for me, he wouldn't have gotten a broken neck.

It's during moments like these that I wish that I was still a drinking man.

FIVE

■ ■ ■ ■ ■ ■ ■ ■

JERRY AND I had a hell of an argument when I got back from Mrs. Lyttle's house, though nothing was resolved. We just yelled at each other a lot, dragging up old slights and resentments that had remained buried for years, as if we had been waiting for just such an opportunity to vent our frustrations and weren't going to let this chance go by without inflicting maximum damage. Nat missed the fight because she was still at work, but she noticed the tension in the air as soon as she got home. When she asked me if something was wrong, I lied and said that everything was just fine, so she dropped it. We went out for dinner that evening, made love that night, and afterwards I lay awake into the small hours, wondering what the hell was going on with my life, where I was heading, and how all this would end.

I buried Frank Lyttle the next morning, with Mrs. Lyttle and Jerry serving as the only mourners. I drove the hearse, with the casket in back and a priest from the local Roman Catholic church in front, babbling about the colors he was picking for his bathroom, which was being remodeled. Mrs. Lyttle followed us to the cemetery in an ancient baby-blue

Toyota Tercel, with Jerry in the passenger's seat, his wheelchair in the trunk. He and I weren't exactly on speaking
terms just then, and in the rearview mirror I could see
the thunderclouds cross his brow every time he glanced
forward at the hearse. The rest of the time he spent talking
to Mrs. Lyttle, and I couldn't help but think that I hadn't
seen him speak with such animation, or obvious pleasure,
in years. He certainly didn't talk to me that way . . . to
me, he hardly ever put more than two or three sentences
together in a row.

I spent a good part of Wednesday afternoon on the stair
machine I've got in the funeral home's basement, and then
I went up to my walk-in closet, where I keep an amplifier
hooked up to an effects pedal board and my electric guitar,
an old Gibson SG, which I played all through high school
and college. Jerry was our band's singer, and I played lead.
We were horrible . . . certifiably the worst garage band in
the history of garages. But we were loud, and drunk, and
on our way to the big time, right up until that inevitable
moment when it dawned on us that we weren't ever going
to be stars, and that it was time to grow up. That moment
came to each of the five of us at different times. But it came
to us all eventually. To this day, though, when I'm feeling
down I'll step into my closet, close the door, crank up that
old Marshall amp, and play a little heavy metal, clearing my
mind, and transporting me back to a time when the most
complicated things I had to worry about were the price of a
six-pack of Budweiser, and which girls were checking me
out . . . if any.

Today, however, no matter what I did, my mind didn't
clear, because there was one, solid, immovable, massive
obstruction to peace planted firmly in the center of my
brain. Like that black monolith at the beginning of *2001: A
Space Odyssey*, this obstruction was solid, dark, and heavy.
It had Frank Lyttle's name carved across it, and it was so
big that it blocked the light with the questions it raised . . .
such as:

If, as his wife maintained, Frank Lyttle was terrified of
having anything to do with drugs for fear of being sent back

to prison, then why did he have a roach clip and cocaine paraphernalia in his bedroom dresser drawer?

And if, as his wife maintained, Frank Lyttle was involved with a motorcycle gang, and rode a motorcycle himself, then where was it? It hadn't been in the garage. And I hadn't seen so much as a single object in that garage, such as a helmet, or a grease mark on the floor, to indicate that a motorcycle had ever been in there.

And if, as his wife maintained, Frank Lyttle was doing everything he could to distance himself from his old life, then why would he keep a photo album full of pictures of himself in prison? And who the hell takes pictures in a prison, anyway?

And if, as his wife maintained—and this was the big one—Frank Lyttle was such a "fuckin' prince" of a man, doing everything he could to be a good husband and father, why did I have the inexplicable, totally irrational, very disturbing feeling that he had never so much as stepped foot in the house where he and his wife had supposedly been living for at least the past two years?

Well, there it is. I know it sounds goofy, but that last one held the key to what was driving me nuts. I had come away from my interview with Mrs. Lyttle convinced that something was tragically amiss with both her and her story. I didn't have a single shred of physical evidence at which to point for confirmation of my hunch, but there was something about that house that seemed to hint that I was right . . . namely, that it didn't contain a single object that reflected the era of Frank Lyttle's youth.

For example:

As you'll recall, I said earlier that in the living room I had found a wide-screen TV, two VCR's, and a stereo with a bunch of CD's in a cabinet. Well, because I'm such a music fan, I try very hard to keep up with what's happening on the rock scene. I watch MTV when I can and buy a lot of new bands' stuff. When I was a kid my dad used to hang wallpaper on the days he wasn't at the fire station, and sometimes I'd go with him to help him paste. He played a lot of easy listening music on his portable radio, singing the lyrics to songs I'd never heard before. Anything new, he hated. He would only listen to stuff that he remembered from when he was a kid. I swore back then that I would never get like that. That I would never let myself get fixated at one point in time, ending my life in an old folks' home, perched in a wheelchair next to a jam box playing tapes of the same six Black Sabbath albums I had owned in high school, over and over while I complained that "kids today don't know what good music is."

Well, unless Frank Lyttle had made exactly that same vow, something was wrong with his record collection. It was, as I discovered when I glanced down at the titles, too new . . . too many new bands, and not enough old ones. Even I've got CD's of bands I remember from the old days that I pull out every once in a while. Frank Lyttle was forty-two years old, which means that in 1973 he would have been twenty-two . . . which means that in 1968 he would have been seventeen . . . which means that he should have had some old rock in his collection, if only for memory's sake—the Beatles, or Jimi Hendrix, or the Jefferson Airplane, or something.

Anything.

But he didn't have a one of them. The oldest thing in his collection was a little early Aerosmith. Everything else was completely up to date: Primus, Alice in Chains, Drivin' n' Cryin', the latest Ramones release. Apparently—at least as far as I was concerned—Frank Lyttle had very good taste in music. . . .

And that bothered me.

Like I said, I didn't have any physical evidence of Mrs. Lyttle's deception, but little inconsistencies like the newness of the record collection had made me suspicious. Something was wrong in that house, and in the end, I had come away with the feeling that Frank Lyttle was a much younger man than his forty-two years. Maybe it was all part of his disguise, all designed to keep his true identity hidden from those who would do him harm . . . but if that were the case, then he had taken great pains to erase some of the details of his old life, while overlooking other, more glaring proofs of exactly who he had been, such as that scrapbook full of souvenir pictures that I'd found in the garage.

So who the hell was Frank Lyttle/Joe Pace? And why was his wife still so jealous of his identity, even after his death?

Those questions rang in my head all Tuesday night, and through the day on Wednesday. By Wednesday evening, even though I was dreading the dog fights, I was almost glad that I had an obligation to attend, just as an excuse to get out of the house.

I left at ten o'clock, dressed like Daniel Boone again, sans Vaseline.

Larry Fizner had been right when he said that I wasn't going to be able to get the Vaseline out of my hair. I'd washed it half a dozen times already, and it was still greasy, which Nat thought was hysterical.

Speaking of Larry Fizner, he called just before I left and gave me my instructions. He was bound and determined to carry out his intended break-in at Mitch Krammer's house, and he wanted me to call him at a certain number if Captain Video and Congo failed to show up at the dog fight as scheduled.

So I was thinking about Larry, what he was doing, where he was, and the risk he was taking, all the way downtown. But once I left the freeway and drove onto the dark, inner-city streets of Cleveland, Larry's activities left my mind, and I concentrated on keeping my own ass safe.

Cleveland's changed a lot over the years. When I was a kid it was a fairly prosperous, industrial town. But during the seventies and eighties most of the steel mills and heavy industries scaled back, shut down, or moved away, leaving large sections of the city virtually abandoned. In some places, such as the warehouse district in the flats, which is the lower basin around the Cuyahoga river, enterprising people have converted what once was industrial space into nightclubs and bars, preserving a bit of the original, grungy ambiance of the past, while jazzing it up to party-people standards with fresh paint and hanging ferns. But in other places, such as the area toward which I was driving, the broken windows have simply been boarded over, and rusty chains and Yale locks are supposed to keep the vandals out.

I was leery of parking too close to the warehouse in which Larry Fizner had said the dog fights were taking place, for fear of having my van stolen. But I was just as leery of parking too far away and having to walk any distance, alone, in the dark. In the end I just tucked my van in among the motorcycles and cars I found lining an alley, and hoped it would be there when I came back out. Then, with the sounds of my own footsteps echoing over the sooty brick and cracked concrete, I started toward the warehouse.

The street was dead quiet, and still; dark, with every other street lamp either burned out or broken. Telephone wires hung low on crooked poles that should have been replaced years ago. And the warehouse, all black brick and jagged, broken glass, stretched on for blocks . . . three stories tall, boarded up, sprayed over with graffiti, obviously empty for quite some time. I looked around, seeing other buildings in the same condition and wondering if this indeed was the same warehouse in which R.L. Webster's body had been found two years before. I listened, hearing not a single sound. Judging by the number of motorcycles and cars parked outside, there were a lot of people gathered somewhere in the neighborhood, but they were either located well into the interior of the building, or keeping perfectly still.

Larry Fizner had explained the procedure:

"There's a door off an alley marked 'Violators will be fucked,' " he said. "That door'll be open. You just go right on in through there and follow the lights. Nobody's gon'na ask you who you are, and there ain't gon'na be no guard at the door or noth'n 'cause this is an invitation-only type of deal. If you know where to go, then they figure you must'a talked to somebody who sized you up as bein' okay, which is how you got there in the first place. But you're gon'na be expected to bet on the fights. This ain't a non-profit event, and spectators who keep their hands in their pockets aren't exactly welcome. Nobody's gon'na come up to you if you don't bet on the first couple of fights, but you'll be noticed if you wait too long . . . so take some money with you. You don't have to bet on every fight. But you better spread a little cash around or they'll boot your ass for sure."

I found the door he had described, and stepped through it.

I wasn't armed. At that time I didn't have a pistol permit, nor had I ever fired a weapon. No, I take that back. Once, when I was about thirteen, my dad, brother, and I went out to the country to collect wood for the fireplace in our den, and my dad produced a pistol that he allowed both Jerry and me to shoot. He set up an empty beer can on a tree stump and had us stand about five feet away. We each fired until the cylinder was empty, but neither of us could hit the can. It was my first experience with holding death in my hands like that, and I hated it. To this day I remember the feeling of the gun's kick when I squeezed the trigger, and the terrible concussion of the shot. It was an evil feeling. Guns are evil things.

As chilly as the night air was, the interior of the warehouse was downright cold—and my breath made steam. There was junk spread all over the floor, hidden in the shadows, and I had to watch my step. Overhead, on a single extension cord, was strung a series of what looked to be 25-watt bulbs—not bright enough to really illuminate anything; just there as a guide. I followed the lights— spaced about fifteen feet apart—around corners and down a flight of stairs, through the dark, and along what seemed like two miles' worth of corridors. There were lockers here, concrete-block walls there, broken office furniture in the smaller rooms I passed, and stalled, dusty equipment— broken-down forklifts and battered two-wheelers—in the larger areas where the splintered remains of broken pallets had been kicked into piles.

Finally, just as I was thinking that I should be emerging on the other side of the building soon, I stepped through a door that opened into what must have been the main storage area of the warehouse. The room was huge, high-ceilinged, and loud with people, laughing and shouting and talking in a circle about fifty yards from where I stood. There were Klieg lights positioned on tall stands aimed down into the center of the "pit," and what looked like the bleachers from a high-school athletic field arranged on the sides. There was sawdust and dirt on the concrete floor, and at least three stories worth of empty air overhead, surmounted by the shattered remains of skylights, hanging with broken frames and shards of cracked glass, through which the clear night sky shone with stars.

As Larry had promised, no one molested me as I approached the pit. No one even acknowledged my presence. What was happening here was absolutely illegal, I knew, and yet not a single person acted as if they were the least bit apprehensive about being arrested. There were no lookouts at the doors, nobody checking those who came and went, no signs of fear of the law at all. Somebody was protecting this "game," and, as I caught my first sight of the dogs, I wondered who it was, and how much it was costing them to keep the police away.

There seemed to be a pattern to the way the dogs were arranged, and, as I approached the pit, I passed through what was essentially a perimeter of stakes, set very far apart, that encircled the central area with another, larger circle about three times the size of the fighting area. This seemed to serve the dual function of keeping the animals far enough apart so that they wouldn't do each other dirt before they were supposed to, while allowing gamblers the opportunity of strolling around and getting a look at the combatants, who were all straining at their chains, growling low, vicious rumbles in their throats, and ignoring their owners, who were invariably posted nearby, beer can in one hand, stick in the other.

A haze of cigarette smoke hung in a perfect cloud over the center of the pit, rolling ominously in the harsh glow of the arc lights. A table had been set up off to one side, and next to it was a chalk board with the names of dogs that had been paired, and the odds given. Under the table was a metal strongbox, and on the table, before a man with a pencil behind his ear, were stacks of money, sorted according to denomination. Two powerful-looking bikers stood at the bookie's back, arms folded over their hairy chests, eyes following each person who approached with as much interest as the staked dogs had demonstrated as I had walked through their midst.

After my visit to the Hound's Tooth bar, I suppose that what I was expecting at the fights were the same people I had seen there. Which was what I got, though not in the way I had anticipated.

The Hound's Tooth crowd was present all right, but they were more or less running the show. They owned the dogs, and took the bets—one of the bartenders, I noticed, was acting as the bookie—but the crowd itself, and it was a crowd, probably a hundred and fifty strong, was anything but a biker bunch. I hadn't expected any women, but there were women there. I hadn't expected anything but denim and leather, but there were suits and neckties and polished loafers. I hadn't expected any jewelry, but there were sparklers on ladies' fingers, and a table off to one side serving mixed drinks.

I was a little shaken as the truth of the setup started sinking in. This was an entertainment run for people who had money. It wasn't just a bunch of drunken low-lifes getting together for the sick thrill of watching their dogs rip each other up. It was a business . . . an honest-to-God business, and the man at the money table was raking it in hand over fist. I, dressed in my denim jeans and fringed leather coat, didn't fit in with the spectators, who looked as if they were mostly middle-aged, well-to-do couples out for the evening: dinner, and a dog fight . . . how special. I looked like I belonged with the dog owners, dressed as I was, so I more or less hung back in the shadows in hopes of maintaining my anonymity.

Though no one seemed to be paying me any mind, I did have the strange feeling that I was being watched. I looked around, but didn't see anyone who looked as if they gave the slightest damn about me, so I put my feeling down to paranoia and hyped-up nerves. But it was a sensation that was hard to shake, and that only eased up when Captain Video and Congo made their entrance.

They arrived with all the pomp of a Roman emperor escorted by his champion gladiator. And seeing Congo, the Tosa, in the flesh for the first time, sent a chill through me that all but froze my blood.

I was standing off to one side, next to a light stand which was aimed toward the pit, so the area immediately around me was perfectly dark. From that vantage point I had a clear view of Congo's approach, and when I first caught sight of the animal striding forward on its chain, my hand gripped the metal struts of the light stand and I leaned heavily on it for support.

I don't know which of the two was more imposing, Congo, or his owner. Mitch Krammer must have been six foot five, tipping the scales at a good three hundred pounds. He was dressed in his hard-ass finery: black leather sleeveless vest, jeans, motorcycle boots, fingerless steel-stud-covered gloves, blue bandanna, long, flowing black hair, and tattoos . . . and I do mean tattoos, probably a hundred of them, covering his arms and chest with a bluish sheen and tangle of splashing color. He was unshaven, almost as hairy as his dog, shirtless, and proud. He swaggered like a king, and the people parted before him, or, more accurately, they parted before his dog.

Which was Congo.

I had seen his picture, but it was nothing when compared to the genuine, panting article. He was breathtaking. I have never in my life seen a creature so imposing that wasn't in a cage. He stood about three and a half feet tall at the shoulder, and was probably five feet long. Every square inch of his magnificent body was rippled with muscle, and his short, sandy fur was so smooth that it shone as he moved. His legs were long, and powerful, fluid in their steps. And his eyes gleamed like black ice, looking straight ahead, like a boxer approaching the ring.

But it was his jaws that held my gaze . . . those massive, muscular jaws. The Tosa has a lot of the mastiff in it; you can tell by its face. And the mastiff is known for its grip.

Congo's jaws were overhung with black, baggy jowls, but they didn't sway when he walked as you would expect them to do. They were firm and fixed, all muscle, folded and ready, backed up by the ropes of his powerful neck, and gleaming with teeth as the animal worked his tongue in and out in his obvious excitement. Congo was anticipating the pit, moving toward it with gusto, hoping for a chance. This dog craved confrontation, and you could tell by the way Mitch Krammer's body was cocked backward as he walked that it was only his considerable weight that was keeping Congo from bounding through the crowd.

It takes a strong-willed man to control a strong-willed dog, Gunther Schimmel had said, and here before me was his statement made flesh. I wondered at that moment how Larry Fizner was doing with his break-in, and if Mitch Krammer had any more at home like Congo . . . hoping, for Larry's sake, that he didn't, and suddenly glad for myself that it was Larry, and not me, who was doing the breaking and entering that night.

It was probably a full two minutes that I stood there, hearing nothing, seeing only Congo and his owner. Then, as I came back to myself, I realized that the noise in the warehouse had grown louder. In response to Congo's appearance, the dogs staked around the perimeter of the pit had started barking, creating a din over which the cheering of the crowd was barely audible. The dogs' barking seemed to excite the audience, and they clapped and stamped their feet until Mitch Krammer had seated himself in a chair at the head of the bleachers and Congo had taken his place next to him, looking like a reclining lion. Then a man stepped into the center of the pit with a bullhorn, and the evening's festivities began.

I'm not going to even try to pretend that I was unaffected by it all, because I wasn't . . . I was staggered. The sight of those men in their suits, holding highball glasses as they daintily took their seats on the dusty-planked bleachers, helping their wives and girlfriends step up without catching their heels on the hems of their skirts, while in the shadows two men smacked their dogs with sticks to get them as angry as possible, and a man at a table counted cash while two gorillas watched, all combined to turn my stomach and fill me with such a loathing that I nearly screamed. I didn't scream, of course . . . but neither did I have any intention of witnessing any more of this spectacle than I already had. I wasn't even sure what I was supposed to be finding out while I was there. For the moment at least, Mrs. Lyttle and her problem had exited my mind.

And that's when I finally caught sight of the man who was watching me. Jackal. It had to be. I recognized him from the picture I had seen in Frank Lyttle's garage, though he had aged considerably since that picture had been taken, paunch having replaced what had been hard, prison-yard muscle, and lines having formed tributary patterns over his cheeks and brow. His head was shaved, and he was wearing a sleeveless T-shirt and tattered denim jeans. He was probably my age, or older, obviously stoned, and standing, beer in hand, near the betting table, a length of chain wrapped around his waist, the butt of a pistol protruding from his hip pocket. He was looking right at me, and for a second I wondered what to do. Then I realized that he probably couldn't see me, standing amid the lights as he was, while I was in shadow.

The announcer in the pit pronounced the first combatants' names: Slag and Conan. The audience responded. The dogs appeared.

I stepped from the shadows directly into a pool of light, deliberately offering my face for Jackal's inspection. There was no doubt in my mind that he and I had achieved some weird intimacy . . . every other face in the building except his and mine was turned toward the pit, where a whistle was blowing and a horrendous din of snarling erupted as the fight began. But Jackal's eyes were locked on mine across the smoky distance. And I could see his jaw muscles working, making the swastika on his neck squirm. I wondered what the man who had drunk my beer the night before in the Hound's Tooth had told him about me. And I also wondered if Jackal was at all pleased that I had chosen to appear.

With hammering heart, I headed back toward the front of the warehouse, sure that Jackal, if he intended to speak to me, wouldn't want to do it where anyone else could see. In the doorway leading to that maze of corridors through which I had originally passed, I paused and turned back toward the lighted area around the pit, and found that Jackal was no longer standing at the betting table. He was nowhere to be seen, which I took to be a good sign—

Until I entered the corridor, and found that the string of ceiling lights that had guided me through the gloom had been extinguished, leaving the area before me pitch-black.

Removing a penlight from my back pocket, I snapped it on and consciously tried to control my breathing. I was scared shitless . . . sorry, but it's true. Condensed as it was into a single circle of monochromatic detail, the corridor slithered along before me as I carefully made my way forward, wondering how the hell I was going to retrace the twists and turns that had gotten me from the alleyway door to the warehouse's main floor, until it dawned on me that, even though they'd been turned off, the light bulbs were still strung along the ceiling. Aiming my flashlight up, I found the extension cord, breathed a quick sigh of relief, and started following it.

It wasn't until I had gone some little ways that the sound of the dog fight behind me faded, leaving me to appreciate just how quiet the rest of the building really was. I hadn't noticed it on my way in because I had been concentrating on a hundred and one other things. But now I had only one, single thought in my head: getting out.

It was because the building was so quiet that I heard the first sound of shuffling to my right. I froze, and swung my penlight beam down from the ceiling just in time to catch the tail end of something dark grey, or dirty brown, disappearing behind a pile of broken shelves.

Rats?

What would rats eat in here?

And then, thinking about what was going on in the pit, I decided that I'd rather not know.

As I stepped through a doorway that opened into the bottom of a shallow stairwell, an echoing voice said, "You really ought'a have your fucking head examined, cowboy," causing me to puff with surprise and swing my light up toward the speaker, located above, and to my right. At that same instant someone pushed me from behind, and I stumbled, my light racing wildly over the steel stairs as a great BOOM! resounded through the silence when the door through which I had just stepped slammed shut. Regaining my balance, I lunged at the door, and found it locked. Quickly I ran my light over the immediate area, realizing at once that my only choice was up, toward the owner of the voice.

"Jack?" I asked, trying hard to keep my tone even. "You're the man I wanted to talk to. They said at the Tooth that you'd want to talk to me too."

Nothing . . . not a thing.

I mounted the stairs, moving slowly, aiming my light up between the alternating flights and trying to catch a glimpse of the landings above. Sweat suddenly started running down the center of my back so profusely that I could smell my own fear. The bright circle cast by my penlight undulated, exaggerating the trembling of my hand.

"Jack?" I asked again, achieving the first landing and trying the door there, which was also locked. "Your name is Jack, isn't it? Jackal? Is that what they call you? Jackal?"

Two more landings in the dark, and two more locked doors. My nerves were about ready to pop. It wasn't until the fourth landing, and the end of the stairs, at the last door, that the knob turned, which was a mixed blessing, since I'd finally get out of the stairwell but I would also need to open that door outward to where I knew someone would be waiting.

I expected more darkness, but the doorway revealed moonlight that was bright when compared to the warehouse's interior. I was on the building's roof, and Jackal was standing about ten yards away, holding a knife. I think that I would have preferred it if he were holding a gun. Knives scare the shit out of me. I saw what they can do to a person when I worked the emergency room when I was in college. The gaping wounds, gushing blood as the victim, still conscious, howled with pain as he tried to hold himself closed with his hands, were enough to make me bring up my lunch . . . and I've got a strong stomach. This knife was short, with a wide, flat blade, and Jackal held it almost nonchalantly at his side, his elbow slightly cocked, as if he were nursing a vodka and tonic at a cocktail party.

"You got one chance," he said, his eyes gleaming in the same moonlight that was washing the pale skin on his bald head a milky, iridescent silver. "We'll see how you do. You really Little Frank's cousin, like you said you were?"

Without even considering any other reply, I said, "No. I'm not. That was a cover story my partner came up with on the spur of the moment."

"So far, so good," he said. "So if you're not a cousin, then who the hell are you?"

"I'm a private investigator that Frank's wife hired to look into his murder."

"Is that right?" Jackal asked, paused, repeated, and then, shaking his head and deftly turning the knife over in his hand so that it disappeared into a leather sheath strapped to his thigh, he turned his back on me and started laughing. "That's just about right," he said, running one hand over the top of his head in a curiously sensual motion. "That's just about absolutely, fuckingly perfect." Then he turned and pointed at me, saying, "You wear'n a wire?"

"No," I returned. "I mean, I'm not if you mean am I bugged or something."

"That's what I mean . . . are you bugged or something?"

"No," I repeated. "I'm on the level. I just wanted to talk to you . . . and I was honestly under the impression that you wanted to talk to me."

"Why would I want to talk to you?"

"If you didn't, why'd you bring me up here?"

"To see who you were."

"And to kill me?"

"Maybe. If I had to."

"Why would you have to?"

He motioned me toward him with a quick wave of his hand, his demeanor suddenly becoming lax, and nonthreatening. He was a remarkably fluid man, one of those individuals who express themselves with their movements, like an improvisational dancer. I stepped forward, and he put one hand on my shoulder, leaning his head toward me as if he intended to whisper in my ear. And then, with his free hand, he slapped me, opened-handed, across the side of the face, so hard that I saw stars. Instantly my cheek felt hot, and swollen, and my eyes teared as my ears rang. The hand on my shoulder suddenly had me by the hair, holding my head at a painful angle as Jackal's bright, crazy eyes came up close to mine as he hissed, "If I'd'a closed my fist, I'd'a taken some teeth, cowboy."

He let me go with a push, my knees buckling so that I almost fell. Righting myself, I looked at him, one hand on my burning cheek as I said, "Did Little Frank teach you to be tough when you were in the joint together, Jack? I'll bet he did. I'll bet he took you under his wing and protected you, him bein' older, and you so young. I'll bet they loved you in there, huh Jack? What did you have to do for Frank . . . or should I call him, Joe . . . Pace? What did you have to do for Joe Pace so that he'd keep you out of the other cons' way?"

Jackal's body stiffened, and for a moment I thought he was going to go for his knife again. Stepping back toward the door while keeping him in front of me, I went on, pushing him, turning the screws. "You're acting funny, Jack. And the stuff I've been told about you sounds a little funny too. Queer being the word that comes to mind. Funny, and queer. And with you knowing Joe Pace in prison, and then turning up here, all the way from New Jersey after you got out . . . and with you being so upset about him getting killed . . . killed the way he was . . . tortured to death. Did you know that he died that way, Jack? That he was bitten by some kind of dog over a hundred times? I've read the coroner's preliminary report . . . he lived a long time before he finally stopped breathing. Hours, probably. He lived for hours, lying in a muddy hole, bleeding to death, screaming for somebody to come along and save him as his body temperature dropped and he started convulsing with shock. Alone, screaming for help that never came. Maybe even screaming your name, Jack. Screaming for you to save him—that's how he died. Did you know that? *Could* you know that?"

Jackal's breathing was so harsh that I could hear each inhalation distinctly, its sound a good half-tone lower than the high pitch his nose produced when he breathed back out. His chest rose and fell. His fists were clenched . . . but still I saw no knife—

So I went for it.

"Homosexuals don't do too good in prison, do they, Jack? Which is a paradox because there's plenty of homosexual sex on the inside. It's just that, for some reason, the cons like you to fight it, at first. Makes it seem more like rape, I guess. And they like that. Don't they? If you fight it, it's okay. But if you enjoy it . . . if you *want* it, then you're a fag, and they see you as weak. You know what they do when they sense weakness. So you need protection. You need the Aryans and their swastikas, if they'll have you . . . because they don't really go for fags either, do they? They don't really like hardly anybody, but they especially hate fags. But you can get in if you're careful . . . and if you have a tough guy who's your friend. If you have a friend like that, you'll do anything for him, because he protects you, because you owe him your life. He can treat you any way he wants, because he owns you . . . and you both know it. Isn't that right, Jack? It can make for a very close relationship, even if that relationship is built on a foundation of fear."

"That's not the way it was," Jackal said in a voice so soft that I could barely catch the words. "There was more to it than just that . . . a hell of a lot more."

This was the second time in as many days that I had heard someone say that their relationship with Frank Lyttle/Joe Pace was something other than what it appeared to be on the surface. First his wife, and now his prison punk, had insisted that there was something about the man that made them feel special. Frank Lyttle . . . Little Frank . . . Joe Pace . . . must have been a very interesting person indeed. No wonder he needed so many names; he seemed to be a different man to everybody he knew.

"But when you got out of prison, it was over. Wasn't it?" I said, feeling a distinct change in the atmosphere as I did. The tension level, though still high, was shifting from an aura of potential physical aggression, to a tight, highly charged sensation of emotional expression. "When you got out of prison, things really changed between you and Joe, didn't they? I mean . . . they had to. It was a different thing entirely."

Jackal shrugged. "I knew it would happen that way," he said. "Joe was basically straight. That's just the way he was. It's different in the joint . . . things change for a while. While you're inside, they get sort'a rearranged. I'm not naive. I didn't expect it to last. I didn't even want it to."

"But there was still something special between the two of you, wasn't there? There couldn't help but be."

He nodded. And then, with the roof's gravel crunching beneath his boots, he turned and walked away from me. "Did you come here looking for revenge?" I asked. "Is that what it was? Were you hoping that I'd turn out to be the one who killed him so you could pay me back?"

Jackal grunted, shaking his head.

"You got a lot'a balls," he said. "But you don't know shit. You're guess'n."

"That's true," I agreed. "I'm guessing about a lot. But I know a lot too. And it's just a matter of time before I put the two together and my guesses start coming out right. That's the way it always happens with these things, Jack. And that's when you better hope I don't guess things about you . . . because I don't give up. I might be a little slow, but I don't ever give up."

"Are you for real?" Jackal asked, turning to face me from the very edge of the roof. His standing so close to the edge made me nervous, but I didn't express it.

"Yeah," I returned. "I'm for real."

"A private eye in a cowboy coat, armed with a penlight and an attitude? Don't you know what you're fucking with here? Don't you understand what can happen to you?"

"You mean, something like what happened to Joe?"

He nodded.

"That's my worry," I said. "I made a commitment to Joe's wife, and I mean to keep it."

Jackal was laughing again, and his hands were balled into fists where they rested on his hips.

"That's what I mean," he said, grinning sourly. "Right from the start you're twisted. Ellie's no more his wife than I am. She's his daughter."

I didn't know what to say, so I didn't say anything.

"Feelin' stupid?" Jackal asked. "Feelin' like maybe you ain't quite up to speed . . . like you're bettin' your ass on a bad horse?"

"Yeah," I said.

"Good. Then maybe you're not quite as dumb as you look. Now listen, and listen good. I'm only gon'na tell you this one time, for Joe, and because I kind'a like you. You're solid, somehow. You got something I kind'a like. So listen.

"The people who killed Joe are bad news. You've got no idea. You couldn't possibly have any idea. . . ."

"You know who did it?" I interrupted, astonished. "You know, and you're letting it go?"

"Sometimes things ain't simple," he explained, as if talking to a child. "Sometimes you can't just run around doin' as you please. There's other considerations. Financial. Health-wise. Professional. Sometimes, you got'ta let shit ride."

"Then why tell me at all?"

He looked at me, and finally said, "I don't know. That's a puzzler, all right. But it just feels right to do it, somehow.

"Ron and Joe was like this." He held up his right hand, with the index and middle fingers entwined. "Like twins or something. They had a thing together, like an E.S.P. sort'a deal goin'. A . . . oh, what's the word?"

"Synergy?"

"Sounds good. They had a big synergy, the two of 'em. And they used it. Come here."

He motioned me toward him as he walked away from the roof's edge and toward one of the many broken skylights. There he paused and pointed. I came up next to him, peering down through the smashed glass at the ring of people around the pit. The sound of the dog fight found us where we stood, faintly rising like a bad smell from the haze of light glowing so far below.

"That's the toilet," Jackal said. "See it? The toilet. It's the bottom of the barrel . . . I'm the bottom of the barrel; all the guys who hang out at the Hound's Tooth are; we're scum bags and retards and addicts. We can barely function, and most of us spend our lives bouncing from rehabs to jail to shooting galleries and street corners until we either O.D. or get snuffed by another low-life dirt-bag on a jag. That's how we live. That's who we are. That's reality, cowboy. Ain't it uplifting?"

I shifted my gaze to Jackal's face. He was looking down through the broken skylight as he spoke, musing distractedly, as if he were half-asleep. There was sadness in his eyes, and melancholy on his face. During that moment I was filled with the overpowering certainty that I would never look at people like him in the same way again. Self-understanding is a heavy load . . . and Jackal was carrying its full weight alone.

He looked up at me, his black eyes sparkling in the moonlight.

"You understand what I'm talkin' about, cowboy?" he asked. "It's up here," he said, pointing to his head, exposing for the first time the needle tracks on his arm. "Brains . . . it's what makes or breaks a guy out on the streets. Brains! The brains to know when you're running the show, and the brains to know when you're just a bum dancin' on somebody else's string. The brains to see the big picture, to understand the entire deal, and to see what your place in it really is. The brains to see the scheme of things, how you really fit into it, and what your ass is worth in nickels and dimes.

"Those guys down there don't got those kind'a brains, cowboy. They don't understand. I understand, but I don't have the brains to do anything about it. I can see it, but I can't change it in any way. I'm stuck . . . like a hamster in a cage. But, unlike all the other hamsters in there with me, all the other hamsters who think that our cage is the whole goddamn world, I can see the cage for what it is, and understand how I'm trapped. In the rodent world, that makes me a tragic figure, don't you think?"

I could feel myself blinking nervously, but I couldn't think of a single word with which to respond.

"You understand what I'm tellin' you, cowboy?" Jackal asked. "You following the story? You picking up on the lesson? It's a visual lesson, this time. Look at the way it's set up:

"They're down there, rolling around in the dirt with their dogs; we're up here, lookin' down on 'em from above; and the stars"—he waved his hands over his head demonstratively—"the stars are above it all, moving across the sky, unconcerned. That's the structure of the world, Mr. Detective. It's the way nature's designed.

"So, if you want to know what happened to Joe, you're gon'na have to lift your eyes up from the dirt and study the stars. Because it's the stars that dictate our lives, down here, in the hamster cage. Huh, cowboy? Understand? You ever read your horoscope? What's your sign?"

"Libra," I returned vaguely.

"Perfect for a snoop: the scales, symbol of justice; evidence weighed; you should be good at this."

Looking back down through the skylight at the combat pit, I said, "So what are you telling me, that Frank Lyttle was killed because . . . what? Because somebody higher up wanted him killed? That he was the victim of what . . . a contract killing? A hit, like in the movies?"

"What do you think they'd do down there if one of those dogs tried to bite its master?" Jackal asked.

"They'd shoot it," I said.

He smiled, nodded, walked toward the upright kiosk with the door leading to the stairs. "That's right," he said over his shoulder, stopping to cast me one final glance as the door opened and another man, presumably the one who had pushed me earlier, appeared. To my surprise, the man took Jackal's hand. "They'd shoot it," Jackal repeated with a shrug. "It's the way nature works, cowboy: One level presses down on the layers below it . . . and the stars control it all."

Then he turned, and before I could think of another question to ask, he walked, hand-in-hand with the second man, who was dressed in very much the same fashion as he, down the stairs, into the darkness, leaving me on the roof, alone, caught between the stars and the earth, hovering there, more confused than ever.

SIX

■ ■ ■ ■ ■ ■ ■

"IT DIDN'T HIT me, I mean really hit me, until I was back in the van," I told Nat when I got home. "Then it was like I ran full tilt into a wall. My whole body just went numb, my heart started pounding, and I started sweating all over. Jesus . . . I thought I was having a heart attack!"

Nat sat at our kitchen table, bleary-eyed. Larry Fizner sat next to her, virtually vibrating with excitement. It was two o'clock in the morning, and things felt as if they were finally starting to happen.

"I don't even think it was fear so much as shock," I said, taking a long pull of Diet Coke, and enjoying the way it felt cold all the way down my throat. "I was this close . . . I mean this close, to getting messed up bad. But I didn't! I got out of it; and not only that, I learned something to boot!"

Nat glowered at me, and I knew that she couldn't care less about what I had learned. The only part of my story that mattered to her was the part about my almost getting hurt. I had a black and blue handprint impressed onto the side of my face where Jackal had slapped me, perfectly formed and angry-looking, which she had seen as soon as

I stepped through the door. She had put her hands up to my face ever so gently and said, "Oh, Bill, what happened?" Ever since that moment, she had been watching my face. I knew what was going on in her head, and I couldn't blame her. If our roles had been reversed, if it were she who came home wearing the mark of someone else's hand, I would have flipped out on the spot. I'd have made such a scene that the roof would need to be nailed back down when I was through.

But she just didn't understand what it was like! She just didn't get it. . . .

I wasn't sure that I got it either, to tell you the truth. I knew that sooner or later I was going to have to try to explain it to her, what it had been like, how it had felt to risk something, to discover something, to do some-thing— That was the bottom line. It was all contained in that one concept: I had done something that night. I had gone out and made a difference . . . at least one small corner of the world would never be the same because of my actions . . . I mattered . . .

No.

It was more than that.

Actually, I didn't dare mention feeling like I mattered, because of the chances I had taken, because Nat would undoubtedly have responded by saying, as she had said so many times before, that I had always mattered to her, and wasn't that enough? To which I would have no reply.

In a split second, contained in her concerned eyes, I saw that it was hopeless for me to even try to verbalize what I was feeling . . . that this was something that Nat and I would never completely share. It saddened me. It made me feel untethered, somehow. It made me seriously wonder if I wasn't losing my mind.

But where Nat's expression radiated her disapproval, Larry Fizner's was like a powerful beacon, broadcasting his enthusiasm in waves.

"Jesus," he kept repeating, with obvious admiration. "You just don't know how good you did. It was too bad that you had to go in without backup like that, but I suppose it couldn't be helped. But at least ninety percent of all the cases a private dick solves is because of informants. You got'ta have stoolies or you're skunked. And you went out and you got yourself one. That's great, Bill. God! You're really comin' along."

I wanted to thank him. To sit down and pick his brain. To make him say it over and over again. *You did good; you're really comin' along*. The words just ran through me in ripples. But, as usual, I couldn't bear to be the center of attention too long, so, over my Coke bottle, I asked him how his evening had gone.

"Great," he said. "From here on out, the video man isn't gon'na take a shit without our knowing about it 'cause he's got three microphones in his house transmitting straight to a little receiver rigged to a voice-activated tape recorder in my van."

"You bugged his house?" I asked. "Isn't that illegal?"

Larry looked at me with amused astonishment. "After what you saw tonight, you're really worried about that kind'a shit?"

I had to admit that, no, I wasn't, adding, "So, where do we go from here?"

To which Larry responded, "We find out who's running the show. From what this Jackal guy told you, there's somebody pulling the strings. What we need is to figure out who that somebody is, and what Frank Lyttle could have stole that was important enough for this higher-up to have him killed."

"Is that what you think he did?" I asked. "Stole something from his boss?"

Larry shrugged.

"I don't know what else your stoolie could'a meant when he started talkin' about shoot'n dogs that bite their masters. Besides, we know for sure that Lyttle and his partner stole something . . . or at least they did according to Lyttle's wife, or daughter, or whatever the hell she is. Jesus, women drive me nuts sometimes. Anyway, both these guys were apparently tortured before they died, Webster with fire, Lyttle with a dog. So the way it looks to me is that somebody wanted something, and that the only way to get it was to squeeze the boys until they sang."

I nodded, placing my empty soda bottle down on the counter as I said, "Yeah. That listens. But how the hell are we going to pick up on this boss guy? If what Jackal said is true—and I don't see any reason to think that it is or isn't yet, since he didn't really say anything specific—then the implication is that whoever's running the show is keeping a really big distance between himself and the guys actually doing the dirty work. If that's the case, how are we going to come up with a name?"

"Why don't you ask me?" Nat said, making me look her way.

"I beg your pardon," I said.

She got up and excused herself, stepping into my office and returning with a stack of computer paper, which she laid on the kitchen table as she sat back down. Paging through the stack, she said, "While you were out, I couldn't sleep. I can never sleep when you're not home. You should know that. Anyway, what I did was hook up the modem on your computer to the reference memory over at the library so I could do a little research. I'm not saying that I've got anything conclusive, but since you said that you're looking for a place to start, I think you'll find some of this interesting. At least I know that I did.

"Now listen:

"The warehouse where R.L. Webster was found burned to death originally housed the Heartland Restaurant Supply Company, which filed Chapter Eleven nine months ago. Heartland Supply was a private company, so there's no way to know the names of all its directors, but it was common knowledge that a man named Bernard Hilton was C.E.O."

"Bernard Hilton?" I exclaimed. "You mean this Bernard Hilton?"

Removing the newspaper clippings I'd taken from Frank Lyttle's dresser drawer, I laid them on the table for Nat to see. She glanced at them perfunctorily, saying, "That's the one: local big shot. His name was in the faxed materials you had on your desk. He owned a lot of property . . .

and I do mean a *lot* of property, Bill. All over. They did a profile on him in *Cleveland Magazine* a couple of years back, not long before he died—rolled his car down the side of a ravine while he was drunk, by the way—and during that interview he went out of his way to show off. Word is that he was a real egotistical son of a bitch . . . a man about town, and a flirt."

"As in cheating on his wife?"

"As in not even trying to be discreet. Another article I dug up said that one of the businesses he owned was a limousine company, and that it wasn't unusual to see his private limo coming and going at every fancy restaurant and hotel in town at all hours of the day or night. There were even pictures of him 'entertaining' actresses and sing-ers and stuff. But never with his wife. She's not in a single shot. Not a one. He also had 'underworld ties,' or at least he did according to the newspaper."

"They say that about everybody who's got money," I grumbled.

Nat shrugged.

And Larry Fizner piped up, "They're usually right, too. If you got money, then you got the Outfit watch'n you. You can't get around it. When you reach a certain stage of influence, you're bound to get a visit. It can't be avoided. If you play ball, and you're smart, who knows? The sky's the limit with some'a these guys. No shit. The sky's the limit. There's just no telling where you might end up."

"Yeah," I grunted. "Like in a cemetery." Then, turn-ing back to Nat, I asked, "Who took over after Hilton died?"

To which she responded, "His wife. Lock, stock, and treasury bills. She's been running the show since her hus-band kicked off."

"Name's Elizabeth, right?" I said.

Nat nodded, adding, "Married a pathologist downtown named, ahh . . ."

"Wolf," I offered.

"Right. Gordon Wolf. Sharp guy, according to what I read."

"Yeah," I said. "Real sharp. According to our mystery faxer, he personally conducted the autopsy on Bernard Hilton when he died. He also did the posts on R.L. Webster and Frank Lyttle."

"Wolf did the autopsies on all three?" Larry Fizner asked.

I nodded.

"Isn't that quite a coincidence?" Nat put in.

I shrugged. "I don't know. He is the head pathologist, so he's at least peripherally involved in most of the posts that go on down there."

"But you said that he did these autopsies personally," Nat pointed out.

"Yeah, I did."

"Sounds to me like we should maybe take a closer look at the good doctor," Larry remarked, glancing at his wrist watch and rising as if to leave. "His is a name that interests me, the way it keeps popping up in this. That's something we need to keep in mind. Starting now, he warrants special attention. Agreed?"

Nat and I both nodded. Then, after a few more words of congratulations and encouragement, Larry Fizner went home.

Nat asked me if I was ready for bed, and I told her that I was too keyed-up to sleep, and that the prospect of lying awake, staring at the ceiling while my brain whirred away in my skull, didn't excite me. It was pushing three o'clock in the morning, so it looked as if I'd be up all night. "I think I'll just go soak in the bubbler for a while," I announced, unbuttoning my collar as I walked through the living room, heading for the patio.

We've got a four-person hot tub on the roof of the funeral home, on a patio enclosed by screens. Stripping off my clothes, I folded the cover on the tub back and lowered myself into the steaming water, feeling a shudder of pleasure as my muscles immediately started to relax. At the sound of the tub's cover rustling, Quincy, our cream-and-sand colored Persian, appeared, alive with curiosity, his gold eyes wide. This was a real change of routine for him, and he seemed to appreciate it. Batting at bubbles is one of his favorite pastimes, and he immediately took up his hunting position on the rim of the tub.

After five minutes of being submerged right up to my nose while I moved my finger around for Quincy to study and consider, Nat stepped through the patio door, a bottle of sparkling grape juice in one hand, two champagne glasses in the other, naked. Lithely, she slipped into the tub next to me, pouring out the drinks before fitting herself neatly in at my side. There we sat, looking out at the deep purple sky of darkest pre-dawn, silent and thoughtful. Finally, she said, "Tell me about this Dr. Wolf. What do you know about him, Bill?"

"Well," I began, setting my empty glass down on a little table near the tub and scootching Quincy away from it so that he wouldn't knock it over. "He collects Beatles junk, from what I hear . . . old records, figurines, shit like that. Ah, let's see . . . what else? He's about, I don't know, sixty, maybe a little younger. Tall, like six-two, real thin, has white-white hair, like that guy in *Mission Impossible*, or Leslie Nielsen. You know, silver-like. No facial hair. Serious. Professional. Competent. Typical pathologist type; likes jokes but never tells any himself. Self-absorbed, maybe a little unsteady socially. Or 'uneasy' might be closer to the mark. More at home in the laboratory than anywhere else, so he tends to overcompensate by being loud and obnoxious in a crowd."

"Do you think he's hiding something?"

"Whew," I sighed, putting my arm over Nat's shoulder to pull her in close. "That's a heavy proposition. The county coroner determines the cause of death on questionable cases all over this part of the state. She's the final word. If the coroner's head pathologist is diddling autopsy results, it means that somebody's getting a legal document that says that certain people died of natural causes, whether they did or not. That means that somebody's getting away with murder, legally. Short of disinterring the body and having an independent authority re-post it, the Wolfman's autopsy protocol is evidence most conclusive in any court. It's sacrosanct. It has to be."

"Why?"

"Because there's got to be a recognized authority who has the final word. Human nature is heavy on denial where death is concerned . . . people just automatically don't want to believe that something tragic could have happened to someone they loved. Given the chance, they'll argue forever. Not all of them, but enough. There's got to be a point where society says, 'That's it. No more questions. These are the answers regarding the death of so and so. There's nothing more to be said.' In order for that pronouncement to carry any weight, it has to come from a recognized court of last recourse, which is the county coroner. A document from the morgue is unimpeachable. It has to be."

"It sounds like Dr. Wolf's got a lot of responsibility," Nat observed.

I nodded.

"He's also got a lot of power. If he's abusing it, he's betraying a trust. He's saying that any document produced by the county coroner's office, any pronouncement, any diagnosis, is suspect. He's subverting the entire system, and making the very idea of a coroner useless . . . and even dangerous. The whole reason we've even got a coroner is to uncover the truth . . . that's the office's underlying function. Most people don't like the idea of their loved ones being chopped up after they're dead, and they especially resent the notion that, once the coroner becomes involved, they don't have anything to say about it. But in the end, the coroner is a control mechanism. It's a matter of collective self-defense. We need to know. In every case, we, as the citizens of a civilized society, need that. We can't give it up. It's important."

"Why?" Nat asked, looking at me curiously.

"Because," I said, "and excuse me if this gets a little philosophical, but death's the ultimate mystery; it's the last frontier, so to speak. Now I'm not saying that identifying a cause of death does anything to solve the deeper question of what death actually is, but at least it explains why it happened. That gives us all a certain sense of control. There's power in understanding. The enemy you don't know is always more dangerous than the one you do. So, understanding how a person died, since it's all we can ever hope to understand about death, is vital to our sense of order.

"At least I know that it's vital to my sense of order," I added, squirming a little mentally as I realized that what I was saying was not a spur of the moment pronouncement, but more the result of long hours of thought I hadn't even realized I had done over my years in the business. "If death were just a random event," I continued, "with no precipitators or explainable, definable causes, if it could just occur, without anyone ever having any idea of how or why—like, for example, if your heart could just stop, for absolutely no reason at all—then I think the whole arrangement, the whole prospect of death as an event, would drive me nuts. I don't think I'd be able to function, day to day . . . the anticipation would just overshadow every other aspect of my life. But knowing that there's at least the chance to determine how somebody died . . . to assign death a place in a series of events that make up a distinct, logical process, I don't know, but doing that just seems to take the edge off somehow.

"Then there's the totally unrelated fact that no human being has the right to decide when another person's life should end. We depend on the coroner to tell us when foul play's involved too. That's another, more practical function of the office. Given that the coroner's word is the last one on the subject, it's important that her word remain absolutely dependable. The slightest question ruins it completely."

"Do you think Dr. Wolf believes any of what you just said?" Nat asked.

I nodded. "I know he does. Anyone who holds a job like his has to, or they aren't qualified for their position. It goes with the territory."

"So if he's doctoring autopsy reports . . . I mean, that's what you think he might be doing, right?"

I nodded again.

"Then he's deliberately turning his back on everything he's supposed to stand for, right?"

"Absolutely."

"So he's not going to be easy to surprise."

"What do you mean?"

"If he knows he's doing something wrong, then he's going to be on the lookout for anybody who might be snooping around his door."

"So?"

"So, maybe our mystery faxer's somebody who believes in the role of the coroner as much as you seem to. Maybe he's somebody who knows for a fact that Dr. Wolf has been doing something wrong, but can't do anything about it himself. So he's giving you what you need to nail him instead."

I refilled Nat's glass, then my own. Then I leaned my head back on the waterproof pillow, sighing and sipping my juice.

"If that's true," I said, "and I'm not saying that it is—I'm just analyzing the proposition—then our faxer's certainly going about it the hard way."

"Maybe he has to."

"Meaning that maybe he's too scared to just go to the coroner, or the cops, with what he knows?"

"Maybe he can't go to either, safely. Or maybe he doesn't feel his evidence would hold up in court."

I sighed, musing somewhat vaguely, "So what are we really talking about here? A conspiracy in the coroner's office? A county morgue run by what . . . the Mob? Murder Incorporated with its own waste-treatment plant? Contract killings with a guaranteed 'natural causes' death certificate issued by the city itself—nice, neat, and legal down the line?"

Nat shrugged, her breast rising and falling against me as she said, "Maybe nothing that elaborate, but could Dr. Wolf do what you think he's been doing on his own? Wouldn't he need at least one other person to help him from the inside?"

"I don't know," I replied.

"What about Mrs. Lyttle?" Nat asked.

"What about her?"

"She isn't Mrs. Lyttle, right?"

"Right. But if you want to get technical, Mr. Lyttle wasn't Mr. Lyttle either. He was Joe Pace."

"It's confusing."

"No doubt."

"But what do you think it means?"

"I have no idea," I said, looking down at the wrinkle of concentration crossing Nat's brow. "What about you?"

"What about me?"

"Why do you think Mrs. Lyttle would lie to me like she did?"

Nat considered for a moment, then said, "I think she's scared."

"Scared?"

"Yeah, scared. She's pregnant, and people are being murdered around her. From what you said, even though she lied about the man she claimed was her husband—whether he was her father like that man on the warehouse roof told you, or whether he was actually someone else—it looks like this girl's been in contact with people who've been breaking the law since she was a teenager. Lies, crime, and prison must be her natural surroundings. She's reacting the only way she knows how: She's trying to manipulate her environment through deception. She thinks she's smart."

"If she was smart, she'd tell me the truth," I protested.

Nat shook her head. "I don't think she can. You're the 'Man,' Bill. You represent the establishment, in all its glory."

"Me? I can barely keep my own wheels on the road, and you know it. I'm this far from therapy. . . ."

"But Mrs. Lyttle doesn't know that. All she knows of you is your neckties and your business cards. She sees your picture in the newspaper, your name in the Yellow Pages, and she figures that you're a part of the world that she and the people she's known all her life have never been able to infiltrate. She's an outsider looking to you, an insider, for help."

"But if she's looking to me for help, why would she lie to me?"

"Because that's how you treat the straight world when you're bent. It's a matter of self-defense. How'd you behave when you were drinking? Remember all the lies you told? How many of your own lies did you eventually con yourself into believing?"

"Well, then, fuck her," I mumbled indignantly. "I've got my own self to defend too, you know."

"Oh, she'll talk," Nat said. "Eventually, she'll have to. I just don't think it'll be to you."

"Who then?"

"Probably Jerry."

"Jerry? Why Jerry?"

"Because he's an outsider too."

"Jerry's never broken the law in his life!"

"But he's a cripple. That makes him different. It puts him on the fringe."

I considered this for a long time without speaking. Then the phone rang, and I picked up the extension on the table next to the tub. It was a death call, and, immediately assuming my professional tone, I took the pertinent information about the person who had passed away, made an appointment for the family to come in later in the morning to make funeral arrangements, and sent an ambulance out to the house to remove the body. Hanging up the phone, I sighed and said, "That's all I need."

Nat didn't say anything.

Then I had an idea, which made me sit straight up. "You know, I never thought of Jerry as being an outsider before. But now that you put it that way, I think that you just might be right. So we're going to fix it right now."

"What are you going to do?" Nat asked as I got out of the tub and wrapped a towel around my waist.

"Listen," I said as I picked up the phone again and punched the intercom button to buzz Jerry's apartment downstairs. I had to buzz three times before he answered. When he did, his voice was thick with sleep.

"What'ya want?" he asked groggily.

"I want to know if you have a suit," I said.

"A suit? What time is it?"

"Don't worry about that. Just tell me if you have a suit that fits you or not."

"Yeah, I got a grey pinstripe around here someplace."

"Well, when you get up in the morning put it on, because you're making funeral arrangements at ten-thirty. The family's name is . . ."

Such and etcetera.

When I was finished giving him the information he'd need, despite his protests of "What's going on?" and "What the hell do you mean I'm making arrangements?" I hung up and looked at Nat, who appeared puzzled.

"I just invited him back in," I said.

She smiled. "I hope he decides to take you up on the offer."

"So do I."

Then the phone rang again. I was about to pick it up, when I noticed that it wasn't the business line that was ringing, but the independent, dedicated line for the fax machine. Still wrapped in my towel, I ran down the stairs to my office, snapping on the light and glancing at the digital clock on the shelf. It was almost three-thirty A.M., and the fax machine was running full tilt, a folded pile of paper already forming on the floor in front of it. As Nat appeared in the doorway, wearing her blue terry cloth robe, her long hair wetly tangled, I was sitting in my swivel chair, lifting the chain of paper as I read what was coming through.

"It's the autopsy protocol on Frank Lyttle," I announced. "Hot off the press. It's not even marked as filed with the city yet, so it can't have left the coroner's office. Whoever's doing this has got to have access to the offices down at the morgue. There's just no other way he could have gotten it so fast."

An autopsy protocol is the final version of the coroner's medical report. Unlike the death certificate, which just summarizes a person's cause of death, the autopsy protocol lists every detail . . . the weight in grams of each organ, its size, physical appearance, and condition. It also lists each procedure conducted, itemizes the results of toxicology exams and other serum analyses, and summarizes it all in didactic medical terms that are brutal, succinct, and unequivocal.

As soon as I saw the first page of Frank Lyttle's protocol, I knew that something was wrong.

Tearing off the page, which had a line drawing of a generic male figure—front view on the left side of the page, back view on the right—I laid it down on my desk, snapped on the desk lamp, and removed the Polaroids I had taken of Frank Lyttle's body that preceding Monday evening. The line drawings had been marked with each of the wounds Lyttle had suffered, cross-referenced with an explanation section which started at the bottom of the page, listing the size, shape, and depth of each trauma. As I'd suspected as soon as I saw the drawings, the wounds rendered on the protocol and the ones I had photographed on the body didn't match.

"What the hell?" I mumbled.

"Bill," Nat said, standing behind me.

I turned.

The fax machine had stopped. Nat had torn off the last of the transmission and was offering me the final page, saying, "Look."

I did.

Hand-written across the bottom of the autopsy protocol's summation page was this message:

"This is the last of the faxed material you will receive, Mr. Hawley. The rest of what you'll need I will hand-deliver tomorrow, at 6776 East 171st Street, at 9:00 A.M. Meet me there, alone. We have much to discuss."

"Curiouser and curiouser," I said, looking up at Nat from where I sat. "So, what do you think?"

She sighed, but didn't say a word.

Looking back down at my mystery faxer's note, I said, "Yeah, me too."

SEVEN

■ ■ ■ ■ ■ ■ ■ ■ ■ ■

IT STARTED RAINING at about five-thirty that morning, and the sun never really did come up. Dark, blue-black clouds streaked across the sky, pouring a steady stream of chilled drizzle onto wet, shiny pavement shimmering with the oily reflections of street lamps that kept right on glowing well after dawn. Driving downtown through the gloom, I felt absurdly like I had stepped into a Dashiell Hammett novel . . . all the clichés were there, except that I wasn't wearing a black fedora. I actually own a black fedora—I just never wear it because it makes my face look too round. Larry Fizner was shadowing me—"watching my back" as he called it. Though for the life of me I couldn't spot him. Nat was mad. She had wanted to come along, but I'd said no, which is not something we normally do in our family. We don't make pronouncements to one another. But this time I was adamant. I was going alone . . . no argument.

As I'd expected, I never did get to sleep, and morning found me so buzzed-up on coffee that I had developed a pretty fair case of the jitters. I had shaved, showered, dressed in a dark suit, and put on my black overcoat against the damp morning chill. When I entered the office at eight,

I found Jerry already behind the desk, coiffed to the nines, looking sharp. As soon as his eyes fixed on my face I knew that he was examining the slap-mark bruise left there by Jackal the night before. The mark was tender, though it wasn't glowing with pain as it had been for most of the night, having gone from dark blue to pale pink. After a moment's thought, Jerry's eyebrows twitched a little, and he asked, his face cast down to the desk drawer where he was apparently digging for a pen, "When's Uncle Joe coming to embalm?"

I said that Uncle Joe wouldn't be in until about noon because he had two bodies of his own to do first. Jerry nodded, and opened a new file folder.

"You sure you got it covered?" I asked. Meaning, was he sure he could make the arrangements unsupervised without messing it up.

He told me, curtly, that he had certainly seen it done often enough. There really wasn't all that much to it anyway. And besides, if he ran into trouble, he'd just call me down and I could fill in the gaps. That's when I told him that I wasn't going to be around that morning because of an appointment I'd made. Which pissed him off. Just where was I going to be, he wanted to know. And why wasn't I going to hang around to catch the phone? If there was one thing Dad had always drilled into us it was that you never have the guy who's making arrangements with the family interrupt himself to answer the telephone. It was rude.

Nat would be upstairs to get the phone, I said. She hadn't gotten much sleep last night, so she'd decided to take a sick day from the library. Besides, my appointment was important.

"It's got to do with your detective shit, doesn't it?" he asked.

I replied that it did . . . specifically, it had to do with the case he had personally gone out of his way to get me involved in, if he cared to recall.

"Well, as long as you take care of the important stuff," he grumbled, which hit a nerve.

"Excuse me," I said, my hand on the doorknob as I was heading out, "but if you'd care to take a look at a calendar, I think you'll find that tomorrow's Friday . . . which is D-Day with the O.O.F.P. My ass is on the line here. I need as much information as I can get."

"What you need is to decide what you're going to be when you grow up."

"What's that supposed to mean?"

"It means that if it wasn't for this detective shit, you wouldn't be having a meeting with the O.O.F.P. And I wouldn't be making arrangements alone. You know I don't have a license. If the state inspector walks in, we could end up getting fined for this too."

"Just shut up and do something useful for a change," I snapped, slamming the door behind me.

I felt remorseful as soon as the words were out of my mouth, but it was too late. Dammit! Why is it that Jerry, my own brother, can pull the nastiness out of me like nobody else on the planet? I'm usually such an easygoing guy . . . or at least I'm normally not the kind of guy who goes around randomly insulting the people I love. I like to believe that I'm more tactful than all that. But with him . . .

But Jerry's no better.

Some of the nonsense he says to me . . .

Sometimes . . . I swear, if it wasn't for that wheelchair . . .

I hadn't mentioned what I'd been told about Ellie Lyttle. I couldn't. One, because I was afraid of the effect it might have on him. And two, because I wasn't sure that he'd believe me. I wasn't sure I believed what Jackal had said about her myself. So before I started yet another fight, with Jerry taking up the position of defending his lady friend against the unfair barbs of a disapproving older brother, I decided to let it slide for a while. At least until I had something a little more definite.

The last time I'd seen the warehouse on East 171st Street it had been darkly forbidding. It was pretty much the same today, only now it was wet with rain. I parked in the alley, popped my umbrella, and glanced around, finding not another car in sight. I checked my watch: five to nine. Then I looked around, still unable to get a make on Larry. Either he wasn't watching out for me like he had promised he would, or he was better at staying unseen than I had imagined possible.

Remarkably, I wasn't nervous until I opened the warehouse door and saw the policeman.

He was waiting for me, a man of about fifty. Not a young beat officer, but an old-timer on the force, with sergeant's stripes and an insignia on his right shoulder that I couldn't peg as belonging to any branch of the police department with which I was familiar.

"You got some I.D.?" he asked, holding out his hand. When he moved, the handcuffs hanging from his belt jingled. He was in full kit: gun, bullets, cuffs, and walkie-talkie. His uniform was dark blue. He was wearing his hat with the patent-leather-looking brim.

Reaching for my wallet, I said, "I think I'd like a little I.D. from you too, Officer."

He leveled his eyes at me, producing his badge by unfolding a leather billfold.

John Harlevich, Sergeant, Special Operations.

I showed him my driver's license, and he led me into the warehouse, down the stairs, and into the shower room where I knew R.L. Webster's body had been found two years before. Waiting for us was a woman, standing at the bathtub with her back to us. The cop gestured with his arm, indicating that I should go on ahead, then left, closing the door behind him.

"Hello, Mr. Hawley," the woman said pleasantly as she turned to shake hands. "I'm Margaret Taylor. It's nice to finally meet you face to face."

As I shook her hand, finding the flesh warm and smooth, I was noticing all sorts of disjointed things. Behind her, I saw that the white tile wall over the bathtub was grimy with mildew, cracked in places, and missing large chunks of tile in others. In the tub there was a jumble of debris: shredded

paper and cloth, matted and chewed into what must have
been a rat's nest for the past few months. I also noticed the
exhaust fan vent set into the ceiling almost directly over my
head, just as Rusty Simmons had described it when he told
me about R.L. Webster and the mysterious circumstances
surrounding his murder. Then there was the woman herself,
younger than I had expected by a good twenty years, probably even younger than me. Thirty . . . perhaps even less.
Rusty had described her as a high-powered political force,
a liaison for the mayor, and someone who could shake up
an entire department by the simple virtue of her presence.

Looking into her eyes, I could see that his description
had been right on the money. It wasn't so much that she
was obviously a pro . . . though she was: dark-blue power
suit, crisp white blouse, blood-red ribbon tied into a kind of
bow at her throat. And it wasn't that she made any particular effort to be imposing, because she didn't. Nor was it her
physical size or appearance, since she was shorter than my
five foot ten by probably three inches, was slightly built,
with a moderate figure down-played by her costume, with
neatly cut, undistinguished brown hair, a thin nose, small
mouth unadorned by any lipstick, and a pale complexion
made all the more unremarkable by the dark circles of
fatigue that rimmed the underside of her light brown eyes.
It was more the sensation of self-assurance she exuded that
impressed me.

She met my look with a quiet confidence that implied that
she was perfectly at ease with this unusual situation . . .
a look that said without the need for words that she
was in control, and that, as inexplicable as I might
find our meeting, things were progressing in perfect
accord with some larger design that was exclusively of
her manufacture.

In her free hand she held an envelope, which she handed
to me without explanation, waiting for me to open it, which
I did. What the letter within said was this:

From the desk of Richard Comdeux, Executive Director, the Ohio Organization of Funeral Professionals, to

William Hawley, Ohio Funeral Director's License Number 5934–54

Re: Disciplinary Hearing.

Dear Mr. Hawley:

It has come to this body's attention that your activities of late (i.e. engaging in conduct unbecoming to a holder of an Ohio Funeral Director's License) has impacted negatively on the good reputation of our profession as a whole. Such behavior is unacceptable within the strict confines of the Ohio Revised Code, which clearly delineates the boundaries of legal, and ethical, business practice. Ordinarily, this body would have no recourse but to recommend that disciplinary action be taken against you, including the revocation of your license for a period deemed appropriate by the governing board.

However, certain mitigating circumstances have been brought to our attention, which speak in your favor. It is in light of this new information that, as of this date, we rescind all action contemplated against you for the present time. Please bear in mind that this is not a blanket endorsement of your activities, but a temporary amnesty made possible by the good graces of certain parties of impeccable reputation.

Therefore, as of this notification, all present disciplinary actions contemplated by this board are to be considered in abeyance.

Signed,
Richard Comdeux
E.D., O.O.F.P.

When I finished reading I looked up from the page, saying, "I don't get it," which caused Margaret Taylor to smile.

"It pays to have friends in high places," she said.

To which I replied, "I didn't realize I had any friends like that. Actually, on the way over here, I was wondering if I had any friends left at all."

There was something going on, and I desperately wanted to know what it was.

"Who's the 'impeccable' source of these 'mitigating circumstances'?" I asked, holding up the letter.

"That's not important," she replied.

"It is to me. I feel like I owe him a fruit basket or something."

"The bottom line, Mr. Hawley," she said, "is that, even though you probably didn't realize it, during these past few days you've been working for me, and, by extension, for the government. There are certain political administrators who, appreciating your efforts, have come to your defense regarding your license troubles with the bureaucratic machinery in Columbus. It's that simple. Consider it payment for services rendered, as well as services owed."

"So this isn't just a draft," I said, displaying the letter. "It's the state of affairs as they stand."

"Correct. Your state inspector put it together in my office a week ago, had the executive director sign it, and then trusted me to deliver it to you personally."

"Maybe I'm thick, but I don't remember rendering the city any services."

"Trust me, Mr. Hawley. Your activities have already had an impact."

"On whom?"

"We'll get to that."

Sliding the letter into the inside pocket of my suit jacket, I asked, "So why'd you do it, Ms. Taylor? What's the point?"

Margaret Taylor smiled, but didn't move from the spot where she was standing, just a few feet from the tub where R.L. Webster had died. It was then that I noticed her bad leg. As I've already said, she was wearing a dark-blue power suit, cut like a man's, including trousers. She was also wearing black flat-heeled shoes, and glancing down, I noticed that her right foot was turned slightly inward. I'd noticed it before, when she first turned around. But now, for some reason, the foot caught my attention. All her weight seemed to be resting on her left leg, making me realize at that moment that her right leg was shriveled.

"That question," she said, "the 'why' of it all, is exactly the thing that separates you from your less respectable colleagues in the private eye business, Mr. Hawley. Other men would have asked 'What': What's going on? What's it all about? What's in it for me? But you ask *why*. 'Why is this happening?' Your concern is motivational . . . you need reasons. That implies a certain judgmental bend to your very judgmental nature . . . which is, strictly speaking, the antithesis of the classic private eye."

"Yeah yeah yeah," I nodded dismissively. "I've heard all that crap before. All that hot air about how a private investigator's hired by a client to do a job, which, as long as it's legal, is all he needs to know. It's nonsense. I'm nobody's tool."

"No, you're autonomous," Margaret Taylor agreed. "Your independence is important to you. It makes you feel as if you're in control. It's exactly that vigilante streak that first drew me to you, Mr. Hawley. It's compelling, yet dangerous. No man is above the law."

"I never said that I was above any laws," I protested, trying to hide the fact that her observations had stung me.

"Oh, that reminds me," she said, reaching into her trouser pocket and handing me a pair of plastic cards, which I examined in silence before saying, "What are these?"

"What do they look like?"

"One's a private investigator's license valid for three years," I said, running my eye over my own name, embossed into the mauve-colored plastic. "The other's a pistol permit."

"Very good," Margaret Taylor said.

I looked her right in the eye.

"I don't deserve either of these. I haven't taken the test for my P.I.'s license, and I don't have the thirty-two hours gun training I need for the pistol permit."

"The pistol permit's just a formality. I doubt if you'll even use it," she returned. "As far as the test for the P.I.'s license, I think you've passed an equivalency on that one. Besides, the city's pretty sticky about that kind of thing. They've got rules about who they contract out with, and one of them is that, for investigative work, they employ only licensed professionals. From now on, consider yourself licensed."

"I don't know about this." I sighed, looking at the pair of cards again. "And you still haven't told me why."

"Because we've got a problem we need solved," Margaret Taylor said.

"What about the guy from Special Operations you've got guarding the door?" I asked, cocking a thumb over my shoulder. "If you need something investigated, he looks like a pretty good bet to me. Especially considering the resources the police department's got at its disposal. Why me? Why not them?"

"Let's try a little experiment," Margaret Taylor said, limping over to where a black leather briefcase lay in the basin of a beat-up sink. Removing a buff-colored folder, she stepped my way, favoring her weak right leg, and handing me a set of photographs she had taken from the file.

"These," she explained, "are crime-scene pictures taken by the investigating officer on the day Ronald Webster's body was found"—she pointed at the tub—"there. I know you've read the reports, since I faxed them to you myself. What I'd like you to do now is to compare these pictures to what you read, and tell me what you think."

"About what, specifically?"

"Just what you think."

I sighed, pushing my glasses up on my nose as I looked at the first photograph, then at the tub, as a point of reference.

"Well," I began, thinking aloud. "Let's see . . ."

The discrepancies were obvious immediately.

"You said that these pictures were taken by the investigating officers? That they were included in the official report?"

"They were taken by an investigating officer, yes," she replied. "But they were not included in the official report."

"But they don't match the details of the report at all," I protested.

"In what ways, specifically?"

"Well, for one thing, the body's positioned all wrong," I said. "In the report, Webster was described as having been found lying more or less on his left side, with his head turned up, facing the ceiling. But here he's flat on his back, head forward, with his chin tucked into his chest. And the arms are different. The report says that Webster had his left arm under him, and that his right arm was kind of folded over his stomach to form the fetal position most burn victims assume as a result of heat-related muscle contraction. But here he's got both arms up, over his head, elbows out, wrists together, as if his hands had been tied to the faucet handles."

Margaret Taylor nodded. "Very good. Anything else?"

"Well—" I said, glancing back and forth from the tub to the photographs. Then, "What the hell?"

"Yes?"

"The wall . . ."

"What about it?"

"It's . . . *clean*! There's no scorching!" I looked at her hard. "It specifically says in the report that there was scorching on the wall. Everything I've heard about this said that there was scorching running all the way up the goddamn wall! It's been the key to just about everything all along . . . the defining image: R.L. Webster was burned to death, while alive, *in this tub*. He died, in this tub. The autopsy proved it when it showed that he had smoke in his lungs. The physical evidence proved it by matching the circumstances with marks of fire. But . . ."

I looked at the body in the pictures more closely.

"But the burn marks shown on the body here aren't nearly as extensive as they're supposed to be. He's obviously been burned. But the scars aren't even close to the description given in the report."

"Now look at these," Margaret Taylor said, handing me a second set of pictures.

"But," I said, "these are different."

"Those are the official shots taken directly from Mr. Webster's file."

"But now he's burned worse. He's lying on his side; he's in the classic burn-victim posture, curled up, head tucked in close to his chest . . . and in these, the wall's scorched."

"Right."

"But that must mean that the body was altered at some point between the time when the cops first found it, and when this second set of pictures was taken. Who took the second set?"

But Margaret Taylor had apparently decided that it was time to answer a different question.

"These pictures aren't what started it, Mr. Hawley," she said, taking all the photographs back from me as she spoke. "They just happen to be the evidence that clinched things in my mind. What started it happened earlier . . . to another man entirely. A man named Bernard Hilton. Recognize it?"

"I should," I replied. "You sent me his autopsy results too."

"How did that report say he died?"

"Auto accident caused by operating under the influence. If I'm not mistaken, he ended up with a blood alcohol content of something like point three oh."

"Exactly point three oh, which is just a hairline under a stupor for a heavy drinker."

"Which he was, according to his reputation, and the lab report on the condition of his liver," I observed.

Ms. Taylor agreed. "I'm not arguing the point. What I'm questioning is the details of his death. He never drove his own car when he'd been drinking. That's a documented fact. When he was partying, he had himself chauffeured around in a limousine."

I nodded. "Yeah, I remember that."

"The limousine was a big part of his public persona," Margaret Taylor continued. "A part of his big-shot image. Yet on the night he died he drank himself to near unconsciousness, got in his car, and essentially killed himself. That behavior is very much out of character . . . which, in my mind at least, makes it suspect."

"So what are you saying?"

"I'm saying that you should keep the original photographs of Mr. Webster's body in mind, as compared to the official report filed by the county coroner. While you're doing that, imagine that a similar state of affairs exists in the case of Bernard Hilton's death."

"So it is Dr. Wolf that you're after," I said. "That's what this whole thing's been about from the beginning."

"Do you realize just how important the reputation of the coroner is to the city?" Margaret Taylor asked. Then she launched into a speech that encapsulated much of what Nat and I had discussed earlier in the morning, so I cut her off by holding up my hand and telling her to save the indoctrination for another day. I agreed with her, I explained. She didn't need to convince me of her virtue. But . . .

"I'm beginning to sense a bit of a problem with your methods."

Margaret Taylor's eyes gleamed as she pressed her thin lips tightly together.

"If I've got this straight," I said, "then the county coroner's head pathologist has gone rotten. You've even got evidence to prove it . . . hard evidence, nothing circumstantial. If you were to waltz into the coroner's office and slap down those original shots of R.L. Webster next to the ones that made it into the file, she'd have to take your charges seriously."

"But an altered crime scene doesn't point directly at any one person," Ms. Taylor cut in.

"Then what about Bernard Hilton? You said that his case bore similar discrepancies."

"Similar, but undocumented."

"And Frank Lyttle? I saw his body with my own eyes. I've got pictures of the bite patterns, as well as a copy of the autopsy protocol that you faxed me just a few hours ago. It's in black and white! The wounds don't match the drawings! Not only don't they match, they're not even close!"

"Who saw you take the pictures of the body?"

"Nobody. What difference does that make?"

"When and where did you take them?"

"After I had him picked up from the morgue, in my embalming room."

"In your embalming room . . . where you have surgical instruments that you could have used to alter the body yourself?"

"Why would I do that?"

"I didn't say you did. But Dr. Wolf's lawyer sure would. Do you know what else that lawyer would do? He'd sue you for saying what you just said. He'd sue you—and he'd win."

Stepping over to the bathtub, I removed a handkerchief from my breast pocket and dusted off the edge before sitting myself down. Looking up at Margaret Taylor, my mind clicking away, making patterns, I finally said, "Let me see if I've got this straight:

"What you're trying to make me see is that in both these cases the evidence of Dr. Wolf's misconduct is circumstantial . . . time passed between the discovery of the body and his actual contact with it. A judge, or for that matter, a jury, is going to take the pathologist's side every time, because they're going to hold the same preference for his point of view as the rest of society. They're going to want to believe him because the alternative is so unpleasant. Before you can do a thing to Dr. Wolf, you need evidence that's so damning it would hang a saint.

"That about sum it up?"

Margaret Taylor nodded glumly.

"You've been manipulating me into getting that evidence for you," I continued indignantly. "You've orchestrated it so that I'd be painted into a corner. If I don't play ball, the O.O.F.P. will just send me a second letter in a week or so that says, 'Oh, about that note you got that said that everything's okay . . . well, forget it. Your ass is still in a sling because the nice lady from City Hall changed her mind, and thinks we ought to boil you in oil now.' So I either play, or I pay. Right? All options exhausted. These license cards aren't rewards; they're threats."

A look that very much resembled pain crossed over Margaret Taylor's face as she said, the irritation clear in her voice, "That's grossly unfair, Mr. Hawley. Or should I call you Bill?"

"Mr. Hawley's fine," I said testily.

"Really? You struck me as the Bill type somehow. Anyway, I've already said that the letter you hold represents the state of affairs as they stand. It's a done deal, so to speak."

"And the license cards? The P.I. license, and the pistol permit? I suppose they're a done deal too?"

"Correct."

I looked at her carefully, saying finally, "I don't get it."

She stepped closer, glanced at the corner of the tub next to me, and sighed. Removing my handkerchief, I laid it over the tub's rim and she smiled, seating herself and hunching forward, with her elbows on her knees, in an exact duplication of my posture. There we sat, the two of us, dressed in suits, with shiny, expensive shoes, clean-lined haircuts, and worried eyes, talking like old pals amid the dust, dirt, and hanging decay of an abandoned warehouse's shower room. The empty air echoed her words off the concrete floors and ceiling. Sunlight knifed through the cobwebs from the glass-block windows high up on the walls, swirling with motes of dust and cutting milky white, geometric patterns on the floor at our feet. Apparently the rain had stopped and the sun had finally found its way out from behind the clouds.

"Mr. Hawley," Margaret Taylor began, "I squared things with the O.O.F.P. because I wanted your mind focused on a single problem—not clouded with professional worries. I swung things with the licensing board for your P.I.'s card and pistol permit because that's what I needed to do to satisfy the city. I didn't do either of those things to manipulate you. I don't twist the arms of people I respect. Arm-twisting is something you do when you can't reason with a person . . . when pain is all that person is likely to understand. All I did to manipulate you was send you some faxes. That's it. I just let you in on a secret. The rest you did yourself."

I sighed; shook my head; examined the fine layer of dust that had coated my shoes.

"So if I just walk away, if I just get up and walk out that door, that's it, right?" I asked. "The cop will let me go, the O.O.F.P. won't bother me anymore, and, if I want, I can carry a gun, legally, because this permit in my pocket is still going to be valid, even if I don't think about Frank Lyttle, or Dr. Wolf, for another second. Is that what I'm supposed to believe? Just like that? My troubles are over, the bills are paid . . . I can go about my business without a care in the world?"

"That's right," Margaret Taylor responded, looking at her own shoes, which, I noticed, were also covered with dust. "You can turn your back on the whole business, if that's what you want."

"What about Dr. Wolf?"

"What about him?"

"You know what I mean."

She shrugged. "He's my problem, not yours."

"How'd he get to be your problem, anyway?" I asked, turning my head in her direction. "What exactly are you?"

"What I am," she replied, "is a public relations specialist, five years out of college with a Master's in media . . . specifically, information-processing. Which is what they call lying, in the trade. I'm one of the people who reporters call a spin doctor. My main job is to keep my boss's butt firmly in the frying pan where it belongs, and out of the fire.

"How Dr. Wolf became my problem is a little more complicated."

"Does the mayor know about all this subterfuge?"

"The mayor? Is that who you think I'm working for? Hell no! He's got his own people: a staff of politicos who've never been more than a foot away from the buffet table in their lives. Small-time movers and shakers in sport coats and white socks who think Cleveland's the summit of the mountain . . . Olympus with a lake-front view. If the mayor or his staff ever got wind of this, they'd go blundering in like a bunch of drunken raiders and blow the whole thing sky-high. Like it or not, some of the things people say about Cleveland being essentially a hick town are true. Stereotypes don't just drop from the sky. They've got to start somewhere."

"Okay. So if not the mayor, then who?"

She bobbed her head back and forth a couple of times as if she were balancing two options in her mind that had actual, physical weight. Then she said, "Let's just say that I represent the interests of the medical community as a whole. How about that?"

"What, like the American Medical Association or something?"

"No, not the A.M.A., but that's a good guess. Let's put it this way: You know how people are always screaming about lobbyists in Congress?"

I nodded.

"Well, I guess you could say that I'm a lobbyist to local governments. Ohio's got a lot of potential in the medical field. There's a lot of money to be made by attracting research facilities and new hospital construction. Look at what the Cleveland Clinic's reputation does for the area. The Clinic's known world-wide. Or Metro's Burn Unit? Top drawer . . . one of the best in the country, if not one of the best in the world. Not only does the community benefit from simply having that kind of medical care available, the value of its prestige in dollars is incalculable. It's a real growth field for the state. We need it."

"So you're working out of the governor's office, then," I said. "No wonder you have so much pull with the O.O.F.P., and the licensing bureau, and everybody else down at the capital. I should have guessed."

"I think you just did."

I shrugged.

"The point, Mr. Hawley, is that with all the attention health care's been getting in this country lately, it's absolutely vital that the reputations of people and institutions of merit remain unstained. The story of a county pathologist going sour, not even considering what it would do to the coroner's office itself, would be a public relations nightmare. It's like a priest noodling little boys in the confessional. Fairly or not, it impacts on everyone who carries a stethoscope . . . from the Emergency Medical Technicians on city ambulances to the doctor in private practice."

"And the medical community can't stand that kind of heat right now," I observed.

Margaret Taylor nodded her head.

"Even under the best of conditions a scandal involving a medical man in such a position would be hard to weather, but considering public opinion right now, it's a potential disaster.

"Then there's the rest of it."

"The rest of what?"

"The rest of it meaning that your coroner turned over all responsibility in this matter to me. As soon as I approached her with my suspicions, she washed her hands of it completely, saying that it's out of her league."

"Out of her league?!" I said, my head snapping back as if I'd been slapped. "How can the coroner say that she's relinquishing control of her own office to you? She's the boss downtown. What she says goes. If she knows that Dr. Wolf's incompetent, or worse, she can boot him, no questions asked!"

"You're only half right, Mr. Hawley. The coroner can indeed 'boot him,' but as far as there not being any questions, that's naive."

"So then we're back to the beginning," I said, frustrated. "What is it specifically that you're trying to achieve?"

"A tactical victory, that looks like an accident."

"I'm going to need a lot more information, Ms. Taylor," I said. "A hell of a lot more information."

Margaret Taylor smiled. "Absolutely, Mr. Hawley. You're a licensed professional. And a professional can't be expected to function on anything less than the complete truth. That's only fair."

I was hearing the words as they came out of her mouth, but I was feeling something strange in the pit of my stomach as I listened. Margaret Taylor wasn't exactly a pretty woman. Actually, when you came right down to it, she was a little on the homely side; and with her bad foot, or whatever it was, she was awkward. Maybe it was her appearance that helped me study her comments so closely, because, I have to admit, one of my weaknesses is that I expect only the best from beautiful women. I'm often disappointed, and I've been rebuked for it any number of times. But I think it's a pretty common male failing that's not confined to males. I think women do it too. Why else would men and women constantly be able to hurt one another the way that they do? Somebody's believing a whole lot of rubbish, and they're doing it over and over again.

So maybe if Margaret Taylor had looked like Ann Margaret, she'd have hooked me through the brain. Instead, I went along more carefully. Even suspiciously. And the more she talked, the more nervous I got.

We parted company almost an hour later. I didn't see how she left the building, or what kind of car she'd used to get to our appointment. We just said our goodbyes at the shower room door, with the cop and Ms. Taylor going one way, and me going the other. As I stepped from the warehouse's side door, I found that the rain had indeed stopped, and that the sun was shining brightly. The air was warming up, hinting slightly at a clean, springlike breeze that never lasts long downtown. The smell of hot concrete, grime, and garbage would start rising as the sun heated up the ground. But, for now, the city felt refreshed.

My car phone was ringing as I opened the van's door. It was Larry Fizner, his voice taut with excitement.

"Bill!" he said. "Now don't freak out, but you got yourself a tail."

"A what?"

"A tail. Somebody who's following you."

"Where?"

"Don't look around. Look straight ahead. Take out a piece of paper and a pen and try to look natural. You want the guy to think you got business to do."

"Where are you?" I asked.

"Don't worry 'bout that. I'm someplace close where I can see both you and the guy on your ass."

"Where is he?"

"Down the street 'bout three blocks, crouched behind a parked car. He picked you up at the funeral home when you left this morning."

"The funeral home? Christ! Nat's there and . . ."

"Don't worry. It's you he's after, not Nat or Jerry. He obviously wants information. If he wanted to do you dirt, he'd have done it by now."

"Maybe he's got that planned for later."

"Maybe, but I doubt it."

"So what are we going to do?"

"We're gon'na turn it around on him," Larry responded through a laugh. "What I want you to do is take off. Go someplace, I don't care where. But someplace public, like a mall or something. Waste time. Fuck around. Make it obvious that you're not doing anything that's connected in any way with the case. What I figure is that he'll tail you for a while, and then give it up. When he does, I'm gon'na shadow him back to wherever he came from and see if I can't find out who sent him."

"But what if he spots you?" I asked.

"Stick it in your ass," Larry replied. "This guy's a dweeb. No craft at all. Just a punk. All you got'ta do is what I said, and that way your mind won't get all cluttered up with shit. Capish?"

"You shouldn't talk to me like that, Mr. Fizner," I said, starting the van's engine. "We're partners now. I'm not an apprentice anymore. It's strictly 'Hawley and Fizner, Inc.' from here on out. So you're going to have to start treating me with a modicum of respect."

"What are you talking about?" he asked.

"You'll see." I half-smiled, having to consciously keep myself from watching my rearview mirror for any sign of my uninvited guest as I pulled out of the alley and headed for the freeway.

Larry Fizner had been right, I realized almost immediately; the guy on my ass was a punk. I spotted him right away. I don't know how I'd missed him earlier, when I was heading downtown, but then I hadn't been looking. I'd have to start being more careful. He was in a dark green Chevy Nova, a 1979 model or thereabouts, with a fractured front grille that made the thing look like somebody had knocked a couple of its teeth out. Because of the sunlight on the car's windshield I only got a general impression of the person behind the wheel, and the feature that stuck out in my mind had to do with hair . . . frizzy, and tall—like I was being followed by Ronald McDonald. Maybe I was giddy from nerves, but I almost laughed, picturing the car pulling up behind me, like in an action movie, spilling out the bad guys who'd come to beat me up. They'd be dressed like clowns, right down to their big red shoes, and they'd just keep coming, about a hundred of them from the same clown car, like in the circus. . . .

Old funeral director joke:

First Funeral Director: We buried a clown from the Ringling Brothers Circus the other day. It was the shortest funeral procession I've ever seen.

Second Funeral Director: Oh yeah? Why was that?

First Funeral Director: Because everybody he knew rode in the same car.

Badoom-Boom!

The car phone rang. It was Larry Fizner again. "Will you cut the crap, Hawley!" he said. "You're acting like a kid. Quit fucking around!"

When I asked him what he was talking about, he said that I was grinning and watching my rearview mirror like I was nuts. "This is serious," he admonished. "Now behave."

"How the hell can you see me, anyway?" I asked. "Where are you?"

"One lane to your right and two cars up."

I looked, and recognized the back of his head in the driver's seat of a Lincoln Town Car.

"I didn't know you had a Lincoln," I said.

"There's a lot you don't know."

"Why aren't you behind the guy following me? I thought you were shadowing him."

"I am. He'll go wherever you go, and it's a lot harder to spot a tail when it's in front of you. Now quit fucking around, and drive."

"Okay," I said, feeling a little like I'd just been reprimanded by a nun. . . .

A nun who smoked Camels, drank Scotch, and liked loud sport coats. A nun who always needed a shave, and whose favorite word was "fuck."

I smiled again, but this time I kept it low-key.

I got off the freeway at the West 130th Street exit, headed south, crossed Pearl Road, and hung a left on Day Drive, which runs past Parmatown, the largest suburban shopping mall in the area. Parmatown started, years ago, as a May Company and Higbees, two big, free-standing department stores built close together. Over the years, private concerns built a series of enclosed corridors connecting the two magnet stores, filling them with smaller shops that wouldn't have been able to stay in business on their own. The concept caught on, and the mall grew until it covered almost five acres. M.B.A. marketing types use Parmatown as a gauge when studying buying trends because, with the people from the surrounding suburbs being predominantly of Eastern European extraction, the purchases made there are mostly cash transactions, and tend to anticipate the kind of business that stores in other areas will do in our part of the country.

I parked, tucked my cellular phone into my overcoat pocket, and headed inside. I didn't look around, fearing that I might tip off my tail, but my head was buzzing, trying to work out a plan for slipping away unseen, leaving Larry Fizner with the task of staying on my pursuer's ass. I wasn't inside more than two minutes before it hit me.

Parmatown is one of those places with a lot of linoleum floors, concrete fountains, and indoor trees planted in a line down the center of the mall. Babbling water and Muzak create an unobtrusive murmur wherever you go, and there are dozens of old people in tennis shoes, the "mall walkers," circling the place in groups, getting their exercise between stops for coffee and cigarettes with their friends. Women wander around carrying their purchases in big red bags, and high school kids hang out in the Picnic Place, eating French fries and congregating near the video arcade, preening for each other, and trying to look cool. I often wonder why the off-duty cops who work part-time as mall security don't ask them what they're doing out of school, but they only do that if the kids get rowdy. You can't go fifteen feet without somebody with a clipboard trying to ask you questions for some survey or another.

The movie complex is located down on the west end, and I headed straight for it, watching the windows of the shops I passed, trying to catch sight not so much of the clown following me, but of Larry Fizner, whose shape I knew so well. Try as I might, I didn't see either my tail or Larry, so I bought a ticket to see the noon showing of some movie or another, stepped into the lobby, and bought myself a bag of popcorn. Then I entered the darkened theater, and found a seat near the front, on the aisle.

The theater was almost empty, which disappointed me at first. But it was still early. I had twenty minutes before the movie was scheduled to start, and from where I was sitting I could see the light track across the screen every time someone entered through the theater's main door behind me. When the house lights finally went all the way down and the coming attractions started, I chanced a look around and found that the theater was almost half full. There was still no sign of a frizzy-haired clown, nor of Larry Fizner.

I waited until the feature started before dropping to the floor and crawling on my hands and knees toward the fire exit on the left side of the screen. It was one of those big steel doors with a bar across it, marked ALARM WILL SOUND in red letters that looked pink in the gloom. Still crouched low, I pushed the door hard, admitting a brief flood of outdoor light and immediately starting a bell ringing somewhere near the ceiling. People started murmuring, ushers came running, and it wasn't long before the lights came up. I watched it all from a seat near the wall down front, where I had planted myself as soon as the door had slammed shut. I'd taken off my overcoat and necktie, and was holding a paper napkin to my face, pretending to blow my nose, as a man with frizzy hair ran down the aisle and disappeared through the door I had just opened, and allowed to swing shut, followed by an usher in a red jacket. When he too had exited, I got up and made my way back up to the lobby.

I was counting seconds in my mind—one Mississippi, two Mississippi—imagining the man who was following me being hassled by the theater ushers in the parking lot. I figured it would take him about two minutes to explain that he hadn't been the one who originally set off the alarm, but had been following the person who did, to see who he was. The ushers would probably give him a hard time for a couple of minutes, and then back off. Then they'd all come back inside.

When I got to "fifty Mississippi," I ducked into a record store, stood by the "Bargain Barrel" for another two minutes, then ran for my van. As I skimmed between parked cars I was looking around wildly, seeing neither my tail nor Larry Fizner. The dark green Nova was parked about ten cars down from the van, with Larry's Lincoln positioned another five cars beyond that. I slid the side door of the van open and climbed in, lying flat on the floor behind the driver's seat, clutching my cellular phone.

I felt like an idiot, but I didn't make another move. The driver's window was open about an inch, and it wasn't five minutes before I heard the sound of running footsteps on the concrete nearby as someone hissed, "Shit!" I rolled myself up tightly in a ball, ducking my head down and holding my breath. Since the van is essentially a removal car, its side windows are tinted opaque to hide the cot I usually carry, and I was counting on my tail's being unable to see me where I crouched. The footsteps moved away. I stayed put. My phone rang about three minutes later.

"Okay," Larry Fizner said, breathing heavily when I answered. "Good going, Bill. He's moving again. I thought those ushers were gon'na call mall security on him for a second, but he talked his way out of it. He's on Ridge heading north. I think he's heading back to the freeway. I'm on his ass right now. I figure a couple of hours and we should be able to link up. Where you wan'na meet?"

"Give me your number," I whispered, poking my head up from behind the driver's seat and glancing around the parking lot to verify that I wasn't being watched. "I'll call you when I can."

"Why? What'ya doin'?"

"Just give me your number. I've got a stop to make on the way home."

Larry gave me the number of his car phone, and I hung up. Climbing behind the wheel, I straightened my suit, tossed my overcoat, which I had been clutching under my arm, on the passenger's seat, and dug out my keys.

Margaret Taylor's explanation of things was ringing in my head as I headed south out of the parking lot. Her explanation and one specific thing she had said just wouldn't stop running, like a loop tape replaying the same information over and over between my ears. There were two points that stood out: one, that Frank Lyttle had been employed by a company that was owned by the dead playboy, man-about-town, entrepreneur Bernard Hilton, and two, that one of the businesses Bernard Hilton owned was a junkyard/auto parts store down on Miles Ave. "A junkyard," I said aloud, both hands on the wheel. "A junkyard! That's absolutely perfect!"

Gunther Schimmel could hardly believe my request.

"Ansel?" he said, smiling through his perplexity. "You, Bill Hawley, who is so afraid of dogs, wants my Ansel to be your friend? This is certainly a surprise."

I assured Mr. Schimmel that there was no one in the world more surprised than I, but that I did indeed want to borrow the old German shepherd with the noble stature who was the "best" Gunther Schimmel had ever trained. "Will he be okay with me if I take him for a couple of hours, maybe even a day or two? I mean, will he accept me, or will he bite me on the ass the first chance he gets?"

Mr. Schimmel grinned. "Ansel wouldn't bite your ass. Unless of course he suspected that you were afraid of him. You can't be afraid of him, Bill. He's sensitive to fear. He's got a strong personality, so it's important that he believes that you respect him, or he won't respect you. Will you, Ansel?"

Gunther Schimmel looked down at the dog, who returned his gaze when he heard his name. We were standing behind the Schimmel Kennels' main building, where I had found Mr. Schimmel overseeing a training session in which ten or twelve dog owners were following his instructions as they tried to teach their pets how to heel. Ansel had been lying in the shade of a cherry tree when I stepped onto the grass. Other than lifting his head, he had hardly acknowledged my arrival. But as soon as Mr. Schimmel and I had started discussing my request, Ansel had come over, as if sensing that what I wanted had something to do with him, and had sniffed my trouser leg suspiciously, looking up at me with his expressive brown eyes, ears perked.

"So what do you think, Mr. Schimmel?" I concluded, having explained what I had in mind for the dog. "Can Ansel do it?"

"It rained this morning," Mr. Schimmel mused, running one hand over his clean-shaven jaw. "But you say that your subject visited this area often?"

"I think so. Or at least, if I'm on the right track, he should have."

"And all you need is for Ansel to locate one particular spot?"

"I think it's going to be a car," I said, producing the General Motors key that Ellie Lyttle had given me in my office . . . the key she said her "husband" had taken with him when he went off in search of money to tide them over during the dry spells. The key she had said he used when he went away for a day or two, only to return with a fist full of cash. "If I've got it right," I added, "then the car's been stationary for quite a while, and our man visited it any number of times."

Gunther Schimmel glanced back down at the dog, and said, "Up, Ansel," holding out his hands as if preparing to receive a baby. Ansel raised himself onto his back legs and placed his front paws into Mr. Schimmel's outstretched hands, looking his master straight in the face as if the two of them were discussing my offer. "So, Ansel," Mr. Schimmel said. "What do you think? Do you feel like working today? Does Ansel fancy a job? Huh, Ansel? Work? Huh, Ansel? Work?"

At the mention of the word "work," Ansel's tail started wagging and he barked twice, his tongue dangling as his mouth opened in that peculiar grin big dogs seem to have. His back feet were kind of jittering on the grass as he stood propped on his master, and he was breathing quickly.

"It's been a long time since Ansel had something important to do," Mr. Schimmel said, still holding his favorite dog's paws, but looking at me. "He's an old-timer, and he likes to show off. But you will be careful with him, Bill Hawley. He is my best friend in the world. You will be careful of my Ansel. You will take care of him, correct?"

"Absolutely," I agreed, watching Ansel drop back down to the grass and turn his head my way as if appraising his prospects.

"Good," said Mr. Schimmel. "Because if you take care of him, Ansel will take care of you. You will be friends. There is no better way to make Ansel love you than to give him a task. He is a working dog, who loves to work. This will be good for both of you, as long as you are careful. You may even get over your fear of dogs after you've spent some time with one like him. Isn't that right, Ansel? You will show Bill Hawley what a good friend a dog can be . . . won't you?"

Seeming to have understood every word his master said, Ansel glanced at Mr. Schimmel and then me, barking once as if in affirmation, and wagging his big, curled tail.

• • •

"My cat's name is Quincy," I said as I drove. Ansel was sitting on the passenger's seat to my right, watching me, ignoring the road outside. "We've had him for almost two years now; we got him just after our first cat died. Jesus, that was hard. I've buried human beings who I didn't care about as much as that cat. My wife, Nat, had him when I first met her in college. His name was Leo. He was an all-white male Persian with blue eyes. When they overbreed a Persian like that, they lose something, so every all-white male Persian with blue eyes is born deaf. Did you know that, Ansel? Do you know anything about cats, or are you pretty much exclusively interested in other dogs?"

Ansel cocked his head to one side when I said his name, but otherwise didn't respond.

"Don't look at me like that," I said. "I know I probably sound like a goof, but Mr. Schimmel said I was supposed to talk to you so that you can get used to the sound of my voice. I don't know what else to talk about. Okay? I've never talked to a dog before."

Ansel whined a little, and licked his chops.

"Wonderful." I sighed. "Listen, Ansel old buddy. I'm going to let you in on a little secret. You're really making me nervous. Okay? I don't like to admit it, but I can't help it. You're just like the dog that bit me when I was a kid. Okay? He looked just like you, except that, in my memory at least, he's about two hundred feet tall. You know what I mean? Like way up here, you know?"

I held one hand up to indicate the size of the remembered attack-dog from my youth. Ansel watched it rise and fall, moving his head appropriately before looking back at my face as if he expected some further explanation.

"Anyway," I said, "that's why I'm a little nervous, being alone with you like this. And that's why I probably smell like cat. Nat loved Leo like crazy. It was two solid years I knew her before she admitted she liked me better than him. What do you think of that, Ansel? How would you like to spend two years competing with a cat for a woman's affections?"

Ansel tilted his head the other way, licking his chops again.

"You'd probably get a kick out of Quincy," I said, pulling into the funeral home's parking lot. "I don't think he'd be all that thrilled with you. But you'd probably have a ball chasing him around. He doesn't have any claws. We had them all taken out when he was just a little guy, because he's all boy. He never goes outside, so he doesn't need claws anyway. If he had them, I swear, everything we own would be in tatters. He's a hellion. No kidding.

"Now, I'm going to go get some stuff for you to sniff, and I'm sure my wife is going to want to meet you. You're going to be nice to Nat. Right Ansel? You'll behave?"

Ansel didn't respond, but neither did he bark, which made me happy. When he had first climbed into the van, he'd apparently decided that barking was the right way to acknowledge anything I said. Every time he did it, I stiffened like an ironing board. I think he sensed that his barking was making me nervous, because it didn't take five minutes of being alone with me before he cut it out. For which I was grateful. I think it was that effort on his part to put me at ease—or at least the perception I had of his motivations—that first made me believe what Gunther Schimmel had said about the special understanding that can develop between a good dog and a man. I'd never been close enough to a dog for any period of time to experience such an understanding. And though I wasn't anywhere near relaxed in the company of the big German shepherd, I have to admit that the sensation of threat I'd initially felt radiating from him was diminishing.

"Okay," I said, throwing the van into Park. "I'll be right back."

When Nat saw Ansel watching us through the windshield with his big, sad eyes, she virtually melted on the spot.

"Oh, Bill," she exclaimed as she came out of the house and stepped into the parking lot. "He's beautiful!"

I tried to reiterate what I had already said upstairs about Ansel's being a trained guard dog and not a big, cuddly pet, but Nat ignored me, going straight to the van and opening the door. That was something I could never have done: go over to a strange dog and greet it with open arms. But Nat's an animal lover. She and animals have a kind of mental communion that's stronger than the bond she seems to feel to most other human beings. She simply opened the door and said, "Hello, Ansel. I'm Natalie!" Ansel spilled from the van, circled her twice, barked once—which made the hair on the nape of my neck prickle—and then stood on his hind legs and started licking her face.

"Oh, yes," Nat cooed. "You're a big nasty cuddle bear, aren't you, Ansel? You're a scary doggie. Big scary doggie, huh?"

Ansel was transported by joy, virtually wagging at both ends as I, standing there clutching the plastic garbage bag I had retrieved from the embalming room, shook my head and thought, Some fucking guard dog he is. While being, at that same moment, enchanted by his grace.

"Well, I guess there's no question of your coming along," I said, as Nat was dragged away at the end of Ansel's leash.

"That's right," she said. "Now go get a shovel."

A shovel?

Then I realized, Oh yeah. To Ansel, our front yard was one big litter box . . . which is something else I don't like about dogs.

EIGHT

■ ■ ■ ■ ■ ■ ■ ■ ■ ■

ON THE WAY to the junkyard I explained the situation to
Nat, who was sitting in the passenger seat, stroking the top
of Ansel's head. Ansel was lying on the floor with his head
and front paws resting between the seats. He had apparently
fixed on Nat as his own. I think he was in love.

I started by describing my meeting with Margaret Taylor
in the warehouse on East 171st Street, and when Nat interrupted to ask questions, I held up my hand to say that she
should just let me run through it the way I'd worked it out
in my mind, and save her questions for last in the event that
I didn't answer them as I went. She agreed. I ran through
the story, which went like this:

I hadn't been with Margaret Taylor for more than twenty
minutes before I realized that she was perfectly capable
of doing just about anything she set her mind to. Her
competence, and determination, impressed me, but also
made me a bit confused because, if she was so smart,
and had so many resources from the governor's office,
then what the hell could she need me, a lowly, all-but-
untried, part-time private investigator for? Then it dawned
on me: The problem for her was that she had exactly half

of the information she needed to complete a scenario. Her knowledge stemmed from her contacts in the morgue, and in City Hall. What she didn't know was the rest of it. The stuff she needed somebody like me to find out.

What had happened was that, two years ago, Bernard Hilton's death had coincided with an investigation initiated by the Cleveland Police Department's Organized Crime Task Force which was looking into allegations that Hilton's many business holdings had certain unsavory connections. Specifically, it seemed that a number of the people on Hilton's payroll were known as drug dealers and car thieves. They hung out at the Hound's Tooth bar, and were employed at either Hilton's junkyard, one of his car dealerships, or at his trucking depot. There wasn't anything concrete going on that the authorities could positively nail him for. But the coincidence of his dying just when the cops were getting interested was a little more than they could overlook.

Then came a tip-off in the form of a letter written to the Task Force's chief. It was from someone in the coroner's office—they never did find out who—who said that there was something funny about the way Bernard Hilton had been autopsied. That was it. Nothing specific. Just that Dr. Gordon Wolf, the Wolfman, of impeccable reputation, had been sloppy in his work. Coming as it did from an anonymous source, the letter was filed and forgotten. But then, not six months later, Bernard Hilton's widow, Elizabeth, married the Wolfman, which raised a few eyebrows.

Then came R.L. Webster, and the allegations of funny business in the morgue were more positively documented. A young officer took certain pictures, which I had already seen, showing that Webster's body looked one way, while, in the official report, it looked another. Upon investigation, it turned out that Dr. Wolf, in his role as head of the medical examination division, and another man from the morgue, had spent quite some time alone with Webster's body before it was removed.

"Aha!" Nat exclaimed. "I told you that Dr. Wolf would need an accomplice at the morgue. That proves it."

"What does?"

"That he examined the crime scene with another man."

"Maybe," I shrugged, returning to my story.

Then came Frank Lyttle, and the R.L. Webster driver's license that was found in his shoe.

That driver's license, by the way, was a point I raised particularly with Margaret Taylor. Since it was the first direct link between the bodies of R.L. Webster and Frank Lyttle, had it been examined carefully? In response she produced the license from the same file that had contained the crime scene photographs I had already seen, and handed it over. I looked at it, and decided that although it hadn't been tampered with in any way that I could see, the facial resemblance between the two men was too remarkable not to mean something.

"Could someone in the morgue have planted this license on Frank Lyttle's body specifically to cause a problem?" I asked.

Margaret Taylor, taking back the license and looking it over herself, admitted that the thought had already crossed her mind. After all, the person who had written the original letter about Dr. Wolf's sloppy autopsy habits had yet to be identified, so presumably he or she might still be hanging around. And it was strange that rather than being listed as a personal effect on the original property document, the license was not discovered until later, when the plastic bag holding the case's articles was examined a second time, by another investigator, to verify its contents. Clipped to the license when it was discovered in the bag was an I.D. tag that read "Shoe; Left Foot."

But beyond that, neither Margaret Taylor, nor I, could hazard more than a guess as to why Frank Lyttle would be carrying a dead man's driver's license . . . we could guess even less convincingly about why, if he had decided to keep that license on his person, he would choose to put it in his shoe.

Though none of these events directly pointed to any particular conclusion, Ms. Taylor had felt a tickle that all was not lily-white at the coroner's office. So, in her capacity as the governor's advisor on issues related to the medical profession in the state of Ohio, she had started pulling some strings, concluding that the only way that she was going to get any answers was to employ a disinterested outside party—namely, me—because she feared that using anyone connected to official investigative channels might tip off the bad guys.

Her exact words had been:

"Somebody's fiddling with autopsy reports for a reason. Whoever that somebody is, his ability to alter documents held in the coroner's own files indicates that he works within the city's investigative machinery itself. Though we might believe that we know what position this person holds, we can't be positive of his reach. So there's no telling what details he might notice: a memo, a note, a radio transcript, who knows? Anything done through official channels inevitably leaves an official paper trail. I can't afford to have a trail like that noticed. It's one of the oldest problems in the book: Who can police the police? That's why I've come to you, Mr. Hawley."

It was at this point that I asked her to start calling me Bill.

My job, if I decided to accept it—which, inadvertently, I'd already done, by taking the bait of the faxes she had sent me—was to first establish a positive link between the events she had described and then to find out why they had happened. Margaret Taylor knew what the Wolfman had been doing, but as far as her knowledge of Frank Lyttle or R.L. Webster or any of the other unsavories from the Hound's Tooth bar went, all she had were sketches, rumors, and her own, ill-defined suspicions.

She knew what she knew. Now I knew what she knew too. But I also knew more. Not much more, but enough so that when she mentioned that Frank Lyttle had worked for Bernard Hilton, and Bernard Hilton had owned a junkyard, my interest perked right up, and I ran off to borrow a dog who was trained to use his sniffer.

Most people don't realize that dogs trained to do police work get a lot of tracking experience. The German shepherd as a breed isn't as well known for its tracking ability as is, say, the bloodhound. But they're good nonetheless. The old adage goes that, when a fugitive is being chased by the cops, all he's got to do is run into a building, any building, and he's skunked. He might be able to hide well enough for the cops to miss him, but as soon as they bring in the dogs, which they will, no matter where he gets to, the dogs will find him. And that was good enough for me.

"So," I concluded, "what we're going to do is have you distract the guys in the junkyard's office, while Ansel and I give the grounds a quick going-over."

"What are you looking for?" Nat asked, still stroking Ansel's head.

"The lock that this key will fit," I said, holding up the General Motors car key Ellie Lyttle had given me. "If what Mr. Schimmel says is true, then it shouldn't take Ansel more than a few minutes to find it."

At least that was the plan. But as is usual with my plans, this one demonstrated an uncanny tendency to be easier said than done.

The junkyard was closed for the day, or at least that's what I though when Nat and I first pulled up. Then I realized that it wasn't just closed for the day, it was closed, period.

"This isn't what I expected," I said, the van's nose close to the big cyclone fence across which was bolted a pressed-tin sign that read "Uncle Junk's Precious Metals." "I figured on a couple of goons in greasy overalls in an office full of cigarette smoke."

"Maybe they're on break," Nat offered.

But I shook my head.

"Nope. This place is shut up tight. Look at the chain on the gate."

Atop the cyclone fence, which was a good nine feet high, was a spiral of razor wire that glinted in the early afternoon sun. I glanced around. Uncle Junk's was located in a pretty shabby part of town, with a big old brick building next to it that housed a carpet cleaning company, and an abandoned warehouse on its other side that had "Pepsi Cola" painted in faded letters across its bay doors.

"Wait here," I said, getting out of the van and taking a stroll along the perimeter of the fence.

Inside, the yard was a virtual jungle of dead cars stacked one atop the other into towers thirty and forty feet high. Some of the cars had been flattened by the weight of those on top of them. Others looked almost new, making me wonder how they had wound up in a junkyard in the first place. The ground was bare red clay, gleaming with leftover puddles from the night's rain. And there was a single structure, about thirty yards beyond the front gate, made of corrugated metal shingles painted a bleached and fading pink. What looked like brown butcher's paper covered the windows of this shack from the inside. And the front door was shut.

I tried the front gate, and found that I couldn't budge it. Then I went back to the van to retrieve the shovel I'd brought along for Ansel's convenience.

"What are you going to do?" Nat asked as I pulled the shovel out and said, "Come on, Ansel. This'll only take a second."

To her I said, "You keep an eye out for anybody watching."

"How am I supposed to tell?" she returned.

I shrugged. "In this neighborhood, nobody's going to give a shit anyway, so you got the easy job. Just keep your doors locked, and your head down."

About twenty yards down the fence there was a line of ragged bushes. I stepped behind them and planted the shovel in the soft, muddy earth. It took me about ten minutes to scoop out enough dirt for Ansel to squeeze under, and another three minutes for me to clear enough space for myself. Glancing down at my suit, I thought, Oh well, looks like the governor's office is going to be getting a dry-cleaning bill. Then I knelt down in the mud, and crawled under the fence. Getting to my feet with my necktie sopping wet I looked around for Ansel, didn't see him, and whistled once. He came on the run, tongue lolling, eyes bright. I was really warming up to the big guy. Opening up the plastic trash bag I'd brought along, I said, "Okay, Ansel. It's show time. Take a sniff."

Ansel nosed around the trash bag as I withdrew the shirt that had come with Frank Lyttle when I'd picked him up from the morgue. Ansel sniffed it, blinked, and took a step back. Then he sniffed it again, and looked up at me as if I were crazy.

"What's the problem, boy?" I asked. "You're supposed to be some kind of hot-shot sniffer. So, sniff."

Ansel sniffed again, and I swear I could see him thinking something over. His eyes grew intense, and he pressed his nose deep into Frank Lyttle's shirt, emitting a soft, rumbling growl that seemed to come up from his chest as if of its own accord. That growl made me stiffen a little, but I didn't say a word or try to draw my hand away. Gunther Schimmel had told me not to show any fear of Ansel. It was time I started doing as I had been told. After a time Ansel stopped growling and looked up at me as if to say, "Okay. I got it. Now what?" When he did, I said, "Okay . . . go!"

With a yap he turned and ran, leaving me flummoxed for an instant during which I stood there like an oaf before I said, "No. Not so fast!" lifting my hand and running after him on the slick mud, splashing through puddles with my spit-shined wingtips, Frank Lyttle's shirt flapping in my hand like a flag. Barreling along, I was cursing the stupid mutt under my breath as I turned the first corner of stacked, wrecked cars, flapping black birds chattering angrily overhead from where they had been spooked from their places, when I found Ansel, twenty yards ahead, body facing away, head turned back to where I was coming from, waiting.

"Son of a bitch!" I whispered admiringly. Mr. Schimmel had been right. Ansel was a good one.

When Ansel was apparently satisfied that I had the idea, and that I indeed intended to follow him at my own, painfully slow pace, he took off again, silently trotting with his head down, nose close to the ground. I settled into a trot of my own, confident that even if I couldn't see him, Ansel would be waiting within sight so that I wouldn't lose him.

We were working together as a team . . . or, if not exactly
working, then at least trying to learn.

The third time I made a blind turn amid the cars I found
Ansel standing stiff, his legs planted, his spine rigid, the fur
on his muscular body standing upright like the quills of a
porcupine. At first I thought that this posture was the one
he had been trained to assume when the object of his hunt
came into view. But as I trotted to a halt alongside him, I
realized that I was sorely mistaken. It wasn't excitement at
a job completed that had ruffled the big guy's composure.
It was pure, anticipatory fear, penetrating the dog's very
bones.

"What is it?" I asked, trying to see what he was looking
at. The tension he felt was seeping into my own bones,
making me cautious. "What do you see?"

Ansel didn't respond, but continued standing, the growling in his throat like a tiny outboard motor purring in
shallow water.

Then I saw it too, and my heart skipped a beat.

"Oh, shit!" I heard myself mumble. But the words sounded
strangely far away.

Ansel had led us around to the back of the pink shack I
had seen through the junkyard's front gate. Standing near
the van, I'd assumed that because the yard and the shack
looked so abandoned, they actually were. But I saw now
that I was wrong: On the ground near the back door was a
trio of bright yellow dog dishes, and a whole lot of dog shit
deposited in piles as if marking the limits of the animal's
personal property. Sitting off to one side was the hulk of a
wrecked station wagon, lying on its belly, minus its wheels
and doors. And through the gap where the driver's door
should have been I could see that the front seat was locked
in a reclining position, which instantly made me realize
that this car wasn't just a car, but the doghouse for the
junkyard's resident canine.

That was bad enough, but then I glanced at Ansel, who
was still standing rigidly in place at my side, growling, low
and mean, and then at Frank Lyttle's bloody shirt, which I
was still holding in my hand.

Frank Lyttle's bloody shirt, which smelled of the dead man . . .

And the dog that had killed him.

Ansel hadn't known which of the two scents I'd been asking him to follow, so he had led me to the strongest one he could find in the yard. He'd led me to the dog . . . who wasn't in his station wagon, nor on the end of his chain. For there was a chain lying at the end of what looked like a tent post that had been driven into the ground at the center of the yard behind the shack. The chain was probably thirty feet long, and had a ring at its end that was obviously meant to hook onto a dog's collar. That ring glistened where it lay in the mud, loudly broadcasting by its emptiness the fact that the dog whose collar it had been attached to was no longer chained up.

"Good boy," I murmured, trying hard to keep the tension out of my voice, for my own sake as much as for Ansel's. "That's a good boy. So you found where he lives, huh? The dog that did it. You found Congo's house. Now find the other one, Ansel. The man, Ansel. Find the man."

Ansel looked up at me as if to say, "Don't you get it? That monster lives here! He's loose someplace around here, you know? This is his back yard."

But I simply repeated my command. "The man, Ansel. Find the man," hoping like hell that Congo and his master, Captain Video, weren't home. I didn't see the video man's motorcycle, so I was hoping for the best. I was sweating, even though the air was cool. I just couldn't allow myself to imagine that I was wandering around a junkyard, with the animal I'd seen at the dog fights the night before, loose, somewhere in the crazy-quilt maze of wrecked cars around me. I just wouldn't let myself believe that. And after the first couple of seconds during which the image formed itself firmly in my mind, I banished it, sorry it had ever come.

Of course Congo wasn't here. If he was, he'd have shown himself by now. Wouldn't he? Did dogs stalk their prey like cats do? I'd seen Quincy stalk catnip-stuffed mice across our living room floor, and I'd found the image cute, though vaguely chilling because I realized that, if he had claws, and were outside, the mouse would be stuffed with warm juice, and not catnip. The calculation that went into the game from the cat's point of view was obvious . . . blotting out every other consideration from his little mind. The building could fall down around him, and Quincy would not break off the hunt until he had made that final, climactic pounce.

Did dogs do that?

Was Congo, that two-hundred-pound, saddle-brown, just-this-side-of-a-grizzly-bear-beast doing it right now?—moving through the rows, keeping himself up-wind from Ansel's sensitive nose, working himself in closer and closer as we moved ever deeper into the yard, ever further away from the little ditch I'd dug which was our only retreat, since the cyclone fence and its razor-wire top encircled us everywhere else. Was Congo here, or away?

I looked at Ansel, and he cocked his head and looked back at me, as if to say, "Hey, this was your idea, man. Three hours ago I didn't even know who you were. So what's the deal? We going or staying or what?"

"We're staying," I said. "We came this far, and I'm sure Congo's not here. Him and his owner are sitting in a bar somewhere, or else they're smoking dope in somebody's crash pad, or they're doing something else that's illegal. But they're not here. I simply will not allow myself to believe that the son of a bitch is anywhere within ten miles of this place. So go on, Ansel. Do your thing. We got a car to find . . ."

I reached into my pocket and withdrew the GM car key, held it in my fist, and returned Frank Lyttle's shirt to where Ansel could get another sniff of it, saying, "Go ahead, Ansel. This time, find the man. Go ahead, find him."

Ansel whined softly, sniffed, glanced around, and started, more carefully—and with what I can only describe as a deliberate calculation—to track a man who had been killed by a dog that may or may not have been watching us through the rusting steel and iron of the dead-car graveyard stretching out on our every side.

• • •

The car that Ansel led me to was a two-door Oldsmobile Cutlass Supreme—a 1980 model, or earlier—with a shattered windshield, ripped-up seats, and no engine. The hood was gone, leaving a huge, blackened hole that looked as if it had been made by a mortar shell. It was resting at the top of a stack, five cars deep, next to another stack that was twice as tall. The junkyard's fence was right next to the second stack, separated from the sidewalk and the street by an overgrowth of weeds and a smattering of broken beer bottles. From where I was standing I could see a hotel, and something else . . .

"Wait here, Ansel," I said, patting the dog's head where he was standing at the foot of the stack, gazing up at the Cutlass and whining.

I knew that the Cutlass was the object of our search, because of the five cars in the stack Ansel had chosen after leading me unerringly to it, it was the only GM vehicle I could see. The rest were Toyotas, one Chrysler, and a Honda.

Stepping over to the fence, I examined a piece of wire that was looped around the post and through the cyclone mesh. It was attached like a twist tie on a garbage bag, and there was another, identical loop about three feet down, closer to the ground. I turned, and looked from the spot on the fence where the wire loops were located, to the stack of junked cars surmounted by the Oldsmobile, and then back across the street at the hotel. An idea was forming in my mind, and, just to test it out, I touched the first wire loop and found that it came undone with just a little effort. When I'd gotten both loops off, the cyclone fence peeled back in a flap big enough for a man to squeeze through.

"So this is where he came in," I said aloud. "Instead of working his way all the way through the yard from the front gate, he snuck in here. But what about Congo? Could he get in and out for sure without running into the dog?"

I turned back, approached the stack of wrecked cars, and sighed, saying to Ansel, "Well, this suit's going to be for shit by the time this day's out."

The dog's only response was to stand where he was and watch as I settled myself, grabbed the bumper of a car at about face level, and started heaving myself up the stack, with the car key dangling from its fob in my mouth. Almost instantly I noticed how easy the climb actually was. I had expected it to be more of a problem, but the cars were situated in such a way as to afford easy access, and I even noticed a couple of spots that looked as if they had been dented from the pressure of a man's shoe. My first thought was of the trunk, but it only took me a minute to realize that the angle was so awkward it was unlikely that Frank Lyttle would choose to place himself in such a position, especially if he was in a hurry. So, pulling myself up to the driver's door, I tried it, and found it locked.

"Okay," I mumbled. "Drum roll please."

I inserted the key into the door's lock, found that it fit, turned it, and pulled on the door, which opened with a rusty creak.

"Bingo!"

Pulling myself into the driver's seat, and feeling the stack of cars beneath me sway ever so slightly, I searched around the floor, under the seats, and in the map pockets on the doors, finding nothing. Then I tried the glove compartment, and found it locked. I tried the key but it was no soap. I looked at it, wondering why Frank Lyttle would have the door key, but not the one to the locked glove compartment. Then I climbed back down the stack of cars, searched around until I spotted a pile of ripped-up junk, and selected what I imagine had once been part of the reinforcement structure inside a car door. It was a chunk of rusty steel about two feet long, shaped gratifyingly like a crowbar, and, once I had climbed back up into the Cutlass, it took me like five seconds to use it to break the glove compartment open.

Inside I found a single VHS video cassette. Unmarked. Holding it up, I though instantly of Congo's owner: Captain Video, and of the things Larry Fizner had said about him:

"They call him Captain Video because he videotapes everything he does. He's goofy about that. Compulsive, even."

So what did he tape? I wondered. What was on the cassette that was worth so much trouble, and—I had to assume—worth the lives of both R.L. Webster and Frank Lyttle?

The two sounds came almost simultaneously, although in my mind they were horribly distinct. The first was a car horn. And the second was the ominous rumble of an approaching motorcycle's engine.

My head snapped up, and from where I was sitting I could see the pink shack in the center of the junkyard over the tops of some of the other stacks of cars. It was then, in that split second, that the sense of what Frank Lyttle had been doing flooded over at me. It was simple, and it was brilliant:

The first hint I had that the man called Captain Video, or Mitch Krammer, as I later learned, was involved with Frank Lyttle had come, you'll remember, from Blukowski, the foreman on the construction job where Little Frank had died. Blukowski had said that a big "Hell's Angel-looking guy" on a black Harley Davidson fitted with a sidecar for his big brown dog, which looked like a lion, had been coming around for a couple of weeks, bothering Little Frank. Then I saw the video man's photograph on the wall of the Hound's Tooth bar the night Larry Fizner and I first visited it; and then came Mrs. Lyttle's admission that the pictures in the photo album I had found in her garage were taken by that same Mitch Krammer, Captain Video, Congo-owning biker.

Okay.

That was point one.

Point two:

I knew also that Frank Lyttle had recently started going someplace on Wednesday nights. Not every Wednesday night, but often enough for it to be a reasonably regular thing. Captain Video, coincidentally, attended the dog fights held in the warehouse on East 171st Street on Wednesday nights. And he took his dog, Congo, with him. If Frank Lyttle needed to come to this junkyard and retrieve the tape I was now holding in my hand, what better time to do it than on a Wednesday evening when he knew that neither the man nor the dog would be home? And from the place in which the tape was hidden, he could see the shack that the video man and Congo used as their digs.

It made perfect sense.

The pieces were fitting together.

But . . .

Where was the glove compartment key?

And what did Frank Lyttle do with the tape that could make him a quick profit, while keeping the tape safely hidden in the one place that Captain Video would not think to look in a million years: namely, his own back yard?

That's when I thought of the hotel . . .

But the car horn was still blowing, and I could hear a motorcycle's approach. I knew that Nat was trying to warn me that Captain Video had returned.

Scrambling out of the Cutlass, I worked my way down two cars, and jumped, landing on the slick, muddy clay and feeling my feet slide out from under me so that I ended up dropping onto my ass with a WHUMP! that knocked the wind out of me and almost popped the fillings out of my teeth. I must have looked like an idiot, staggering around, cheeks puffed as I tried to draw breath, going "Hoooo! Hoooo!" and waving one arm around as I bent at the waist while Ansel yapped, and the motorcycle roared, and Nat blew the van's horn.

"Come on," I finally wheezed, signaling for Ansel and bumbling toward the flap in the fence. I snagged my jacket on the wire, tore it, cursed, and more or less put the mesh back in place before running to the street, my breath finally easing my burning lungs, though my butt was soaking wet. I ran as well as I could, and as I turned the corner I saw the Harley with the sidecar parked next to my van, with the hulking shape of Mitch Krammer standing at the driver's window, waving his hands at Nat as she continued to pump the horn. Congo was sitting in the sidecar, silently watching this bizarre show, apparently indifferent, until he caught sight of me heading up the sidewalk . . . or, more specifically, until he caught sight of Ansel at my side. When he saw Ansel, Congo started barking, and I think he'd have plunged right out of that sidecar if it weren't for the restraining chain his owner had hooked around his collar and anchored to the bike's frame.

Ansel, to my surprise, didn't return Congo's fuss in kind. The bigger dog's challenge elicited a more subtly chilling reaction from the old German shepherd. Ansel simply stiffened, his eyes narrowing and his ears pointing straight ahead. Then he started breathing in long drawn-out hisses, as if he were trying his best to control himself as he studied, plotted, and planned his moves. There was an intelligence in the shepherd's eyes the like of which I had never seen in a dog before. A calculation that seemed to imply that, if he needed to, he could confront the larger—and from what I had been told, faster and stronger—Tosa, with a cold, strangely calm mental attitude that was as unlike Congo's brute rage as it could be.

"Easy, Ansel," I soothed, stooping to pat the big guy's flank as I slipped the video cassette into my muddy shirt. Ansel growled low, without taking his eyes off Congo. I straightened up, shouting, "Hey! What goes on here?"

Mitch Krammer turned his big woolly head my way, but Nat went right on blowing the horn.

"What's with this broad?" he said, his face growing interested when he saw how filthy I was. "And who the fuck are you?"

I had the absurd impulse to offer him my hand. I'd been studying him and his activities so intensely the past few days that I almost forgot that we had never actually met. He didn't know me, but I knew him. An advantage that I used.

"That's my wife," I said, stepping around the van and pounding on the sliding door. Nat glanced my way and hit the automatic door lock button so that I could put Ansel inside. As soon as the door was closed she hit the lock button again, watching Captain Video and me through the closed window.

"What?" I said, trying to sound pissed off. "You get a kick out of intimidating women? You think it's funny?"

"Intimidating?" the big man said, puffing up his chest. "This is my place. I pulled up and she freaked out!"

"And you didn't do anything to scare her, huh? Nothing? That's what I'm supposed to believe?"

"Listen, asshole . . ."

"No, you listen . . ."

Then we had at it. Me in my muddy suit, which Mitch Krammer never did have a chance to comment on, and him in his leather and denim, with his dog barking like crazy in the sidecar. When I threatened to call the cops, he told me to go ahead. We were trespassing. Couldn't we read the sign that said that the yard was closed?

Since when was leaving your van in a driveway while you walked around looking for somebody to talk to trespassing? I wanted to know.

The driveway was private property!

Oh yeah?

Yeah!

Well, all right then!

I climbed into the van and slammed the door.

And another thing . . .

Yuppie asshole!

Dirt-bag punk!

Shouts through a closed window.

Oh yeah?

Yeah!

I spun my wheels getting out of there, my forehead dripping with sweat, my heart racing. We were three blocks away before Nat, staring straight ahead with her hands bunched into fists in her lap, asked, "So, was it worth it?"

I shrugged, not trusting my voice.

I looked at her, she looked at me; and then, at absolutely the same second, we both burst out in a loud, relieved gale of laughter, which Ansel joined by barking between the seats.

NINE

■ ■ ■ ■ ■ ■ ■ ■

"WHY THE HELL didn't you tell me that he lived in that junkyard?" I asked Larry Fizner angrily.

Larry replied, just as angrily, "Why the hell didn't you ask?"

We were standing in my living room, Larry dressed like Larry dresses, me in a pair of black boxer shorts and an "Archie McFee" T-shirt. My suit was ruined. It looked like the governor's office would be getting a claim for a whole new outfit rather than a dry-cleaning bill.

"How was I supposed to know that's where you were going?" Larry added, his face red, his eyes bright with indignation. "You just drove off and left me in the dark!"

"You were busy following the guy who'd been tailing me," I returned. "I figured you had enough on your mind."

"You got'ta talk to me, Bill. You don't talk, and I don't know what's goin' down. We got'ta communicate."

I nodded, glowering.

"When they gon'na be here?" he asked.

"An hour or so," I said. "We got more than enough time to look at this thing again."

Popping the video cassette I'd found into the VCR atop our 54-inch wide-screen TV, I took the remote control and returned to the breakfast bar that separates the living room from the kitchen. Nat was sitting on a stool at the bar, and before I hit PLAY I asked her if she was sure she wanted to sit through this thing a second time. We'd already played it once; now I was going for the details.

She nodded but said nothing. I hit PLAY, and the TV screen went fuzzy with electronic snow.

When Nat and I got back to the funeral home from the junkyard, we'd found Larry Fizner waiting for us in the parking lot. He'd followed the man who had been tailing me that morning back to Ellie Lyttle's house, and had watched as he went inside. "Mrs. Lyttle's house!" both Nat and I exclaimed. And suddenly all those awful things I'd been suspecting, and fearing, about Mrs. Lyttle came home to roost. How the hell could she have known to send somebody to tail me? Who was the person she had sent? Who was she really? And just how was she actually related to Frank Lyttle/Joe Pace?

Blasting through the office door, covered with mud and grime, sweat running down my face, my glasses streaked and sliding down my nose, I'd found Jerry behind the desk busy with phone calls related to the funeral arrangements he'd been making when I'd left him earlier that morning. As he looked up from the folder on the blotter before him, his expression was one of utter amazement at the condition of my clothes.

"I've got to talk to you," I said.

He held up his hand. "Lem'me make one more call for the vault order, and then I'll be done."

"Now!" I said sharply.

He hung up, his expression settling into that hard, poker-face mask he wears when he's feeling his temper rise.

"What did you tell Ellie Lyttle about what I was doing today?" I demanded.

His mouth dropped open, chewing air wordlessly for an instant as he contemplated a reply.

"Don't think about it," I barked. "Just tell me what you told her."

"Nothing," he protested. "She called early, and I just said that you were working hard on the case, following some kind of lead. I didn't say anything specific, because I didn't know anything specific. You don't usually tell me anything about what you're doing. It's always a big, goddamn secret. But I had to tell her something. She was worried sick. So I told her you had a lead and you were going to be chasing around, looking for clues."

"When did you tell her that?" I demanded. "When did she call?"

"Early this morning, just before you came down."

It was then that I remembered the phone's ringing while I was in the shower.

"I didn't tell you I was leaving until just before I left. How did you know I wasn't going to be here?"

"Why else would you have me make arrangements?" Jerry asked back. "The only time I'm good for anything around here is when there's nobody else home."

I stopped, and stared at him.

"What do you mean by that?" I asked.

"You know damn well what I mean," he shot back, two spots of color dappling his cheeks high up, just under his eyes. "Don't play dumb. All I do is answer the phone, and look out the window while you go running around God knows where. Other than the two hours it took to bury Frank Lyttle, I haven't been out of this fucking building in two weeks. Two weeks! Do you realize that? Do you know what it's like to stay locked up in a funeral home for weeks at a time? No. You wouldn't. I can see it in your face. You didn't even realize I haven't been outside in that long. You just don't give a shit."

"I do too," I argued. "That's a lousy thing to say—"

"After all you've done for me. Yeah, I know. I've heard that speech before. I guess I'm just an ungrateful son of a bitch. Huh?"

"Maybe you are."

"And maybe you should just go fuck yourself, because

I've had it. I'm out'ta here."

"Meaning what?"

"Meaning you can take this place and jam it."

"Meaning that you're going to leave?"

"Yeah. I'm going to leave."

"And go where?"

"What do you care?"

"If you think Ellie Lyttle's your way out, you're dreaming," I said cruelly. "Because she's been messing with you, man. I wasn't going to say anything until I was sure, but I think all that stuff she said about Frank Lyttle being her husband was bullshit. I think Frank Lyttle was actually her dad."

Jerry's eyes smoldered as he looked at me across the desk, his hands opening and closing slowly.

"That's a shitty thing to say," he murmured, low and mean. "That's really low."

"Call her," I said, showing him the video cassette I had found in the junkyard, and explaining briefly how I had come by it. "Call her, and tell her to come over here. Then come upstairs and we'll look at this tape together. After we see what's on it, we'll know what Frank Lyttle was doing. Then, when Mrs. Lyttle gets here, we can have it out."

"I'm not calling her," he returned. "I'm not accusing her of lying just because you don't like the fact that she and I get along."

Throwing my hands up in the air, I said, "I don't care what you do! Goddamn it! That's not what this is all about . . ."

"Bullshit," he cried. "That's exactly what it's about. That's what it's been about from the first.

"You're doing penance for what happened to me in the parking lot of that bar, and you're making me a part of it too. I'm not a human being any more. I'm not your brother. I'm nothing but a symbol of your guilt. I'm a switch you use to beat yourself with every day. Day after day after day, it's the same thing. Over and over. How long is it going to go on, Bill? How long are you going to keep using me to punish yourself? And how the hell long are you going to keep punishing me too?"

"Just what the hell are you talking about?"

"This!" he screamed, waving his hands to encompass everything around him. "This funeral home, with its apartment for me, and its elevator for me, and its wheelchair ramps and the goddamn automatic doors for me . . . it's not a business. It's never been a goddamn business. It's a fucking monument to your mistake. And I'm the resident albatross. You've built this humongus chain, Bill. You designed it, and built it, and wrapped it around your neck. Then you hung me at the end of it, and that's where I've been dangling in my wheelchair for almost two years now. Every move I make, you're there to watch me. Everything I touch, you're there to take it away and do it for me. Everybody I talk to, you're there to chaperone. You're guarding, and protecting, and strangling me to death. I'm thirty years old, and you're acting like I'm your personal responsibility. I can't do anything for myself . . . because YOU WON'T LET ME!"

His hands were fists now, hard and white.

"Well," he finished, looking down at them, "if that's the punishment you've devised for yourself, I don't want to have any part of it. I'm not your child. I'll be damned if I'm going to hang around here and be treated like an invalid for another second."

He looked up.

"Fuck you!" he hissed. "Fuck you and everything about you, because you're the cripple around here, Bill, not me. You're the one without the legs. You paralyzed yourself, and you've been dragging me down with you. Well, I won't let it happen. I've got the rest of my life ahead of me, and I'll be damned if I'm going to spend it locked in this mausoleum, staring at the phone, with you looking over my shoulder. I'm out'ta here. That's it."

He had thrown down the pen he was holding, and with his final word he swept his arm across the desk, flinging the file and all the papers in it away from him to go sailing over the room, fluttering to the floor in a heap. He was breathing hard, and his eyes were rimmed with pale white flesh, as if all the blood in him had drained away.

Blinking, my eyes flickered to the papers on the carpet. My dirty fingers fidgeted on the video cassette I was still holding in my hand. Softly, I said, "Call her, Jer. Please. I'm not telling, I'm asking. But call her, and then come upstairs. Whatever you want to do . . . it's your business. But—" I lifted the cassette languidly, as if it had become suddenly heavy—"after everything . . . we should both see what this has all been about."

Then I went to clean myself up, and to change my clothes. When I got out of the shower and stepped back into the living room, Jerry was sitting in his wheelchair in front of the TV, with Nat sitting next to him, looking at me. Larry Fizner was on the couch, looking uncomfortable. Jerry didn't even turn his head when he said, "So, let's see it."

Wordlessly, I put the cassette into the VCR and hit PLAY.

That had been earlier.

Now Jerry was downstairs, waiting in the office for Ellie Lyttle to arrive, and Nat, Larry, and I were upstairs watching the tape again.

The first time through I don't think the images really connected. I saw them, and understood them for what they were, but I didn't comprehend them where it counts . . . deep down, inside. The second time, I stood in the center of the living room, arms folded over my chest, feeling something tight and hot untangling itself inside me. It was like . . . I don't know . . . a sigh, but deeper. It was like my eyes were opening for the first time on a world I had suspected but never wanted to believe existed. It was lousy. That's the only thing I can say.

As the electronic snow sputtered and coagulated into crisp, vertical bands before resolving into an image, I was thinking, This time it'll be different. The first time it was a dream. This time we'll see what's really on the tape, and it'll be totally different. It won't hurt, this time.

But, of course, it wasn't different. Neither was it the same. The second time, it was worse.

The tape had about twenty minutes worth of coherent material. It started in a room—where, there was no way to tell. It was a nice room, looking very much like a business office, with a huge, carved wood desk, a green leather couch against one wall, olive-colored carpeting, and wood-paneled walls hung with oil paintings and the kind of civic awards a business man is awarded from the community for donating to church groups and charities. The video camera used to record these images was apparently mounted on a tripod, because, though the view changed when the lens panned one way or another, the frame never jiggled, remaining always perfectly stable. Someone was working the camera, because the focus always remained on the man standing. The man standing occasionally gave the person behind the camera a word or two of instruction. There was a man seated, and he was, as the standing man pointed out, the star of the show.

The seated man was Bernard Hilton. I recognized him from the photographs Nat had dug up from *Cleveland Magazine*. His arms were crossed over his chest, and he had been wrapped first in a bed sheet, and then with duct tape, until the area over his chest looked like a body cast. The first time I had seen this arrangement I had briefly wondered why it had been done this way. Then I understood: He had been bound in this manner so as not to leave any marks. Ropes leave burns and abrasions on the skin. With the sheet and tape, the arms were bound securely without a telltale trace. Hilton's eyes were wide with fear. His mouth was hanging open as if he couldn't breathe through his nose. He was a handsome man . . . or at least he had been in those magazine pictures I'd seen . . . with grey-tinged black hair, and clean, even features. But here, his complexion was ashen, and his lips quivered, with drool running incontinently from the corner of his mouth. His only utterance was "No. Please." No elucidation. No details. Just "No. Please." Apparently he had been briefed on his fate before the taping had begun, and was too frightened to think; too tired, or too resigned, to beg. His words had the hollow, empty ring of reflex ... of sounds made for their own sake, more than for any meaning they might impart. There was a defeated, utterly desperate air about him. The attitude of one who knows that he's already dead.

The man standing was Mitch Krammer, Captain Video, Congo's master. He was dressed in a voluminous flannel shirt, open at the collar, and he was wearing a pair of leather gloves. Looking directly at the camera—which produces the effect that he was looking directly into the eye of the viewer—he said simply, "Scene Two: proof positive, as promised," as he motioned with one finger, inviting the viewer to approach.

Scene Two, I thought. *Where is Scene One?*

In response to his instruction, whoever was operating the camera zoomed in on the face of Bernard Hilton and held the shot for about twenty seconds before Mitch Krammer's hand appeared on the top of Hilton's head, turning it to one side so that the camera recorded the bound man's profile.

The camera panned back to a full shot, and Mitch Krammer lifted a bottle from the desk next to him, saying, "Grain alcohol. Two hundred proof." Then he lifted a huge syringe, like the ones I had seen the X-ray techs use to inject barium into patients for the dye-series they would sometimes shoot when I worked as an orderly in the hospital emergency room. Popping the needle off the syringe, Mitch Krammer inserted it into the alcohol bottle, tipped it, and drew fifty cc's of the alcohol. Then he replaced the needle, crouched, and, as the camera zoomed in again, injected it into an artery he had raised near Hilton's knee by means of a rubber tourniquet around his thigh.

As he did so, Hilton whimpered and tried to squirm. That's when the second man, the one operating the camera, made his one, and only, appearance on screen. Quickly, a blurred shape stepped into view, and the Camcorder's automatic focus struggled for a second to accommodate the abrupt change in perspective. Then the man came into crystal-clear focus, kneeling on the floor, back to the camera, holding Hilton's legs still as Mitch Krammer depressed the plunger on the syringe, pumping straight grain alcohol into his blood stream. The second man's face was never exposed, but I recognized his bald head, and the swastika tattoo on his neck, just under his left ear. It was the man called Jackal . . . the same man who had told me, on the roof of the warehouse on East 171st Street, that the dog fights were the toilet, and that if I wanted to know what had really happened to Frank Lyttle, I should "look to the stars."

I had thought then that he had meant that I should look to the literal stars . . . the ones overhead. But now I knew that he had been speaking metaphorically. The stars to which he referred were the stars of Captain Video's tapes . . . because if there was one tape, I had to assume that there were more.

As the Captain had said himself, Bernard Hilton was "the star of our show."

Look to the stars.

And:

What do you think they'd do down there if one of those dogs should try to bite his master?

Standing in my living room . . . my safe, secure, well-appointed, tastefully decorated, thoroughly comfortable living room . . . with my arms clasped protectively over my chest, I wondered, Who is the master here? And who was trying to do the biting?

When Mitch Krammer had emptied the syringe, Jackal again disappeared behind the camera, being careful not to let his face ever be caught on-screen. Then Captain Video stood back up, saying, in a bogus, Humphrey Bogart imitation, "And now we's gon'na take him for a little ride."

Quick cut.

Scene three:

Outside, on the side of the road. Mitch Krammer standing next to a car. Driver's door open. Bernard Hilton sitting in the driver's seat, head lolled forward. Sheet and duct tape gone from around his torso. Car running.

"Okay," Krammer says, "so our contractual obligation is fulfilled."

And with that, he reaches into the car, past the now unconscious form of Bernard Hilton—fifty cc's of grain alcohol straight to his brain, I thought; no wonder he's unconscious—and slides the gear shift into Drive. Pulling himself back out as the car starts to roll, he stands on the gravel of the road's shoulder, waving goodbye as the car wobbles out onto the pavement, picks up speed . . .

They must have propped Hilton's foot on the accelerator, I had thought the first time I saw it, as I did again the second time. Or else they wedged something against the pedal that would pop loose in the wreck, and not arouse suspicion by its presence, like a rolled-up road map, or, given his condition, an empty whiskey bottle or beer can. There was a whiskey bottle and a half-dozen beer cans on the car's floor, according to the police report Margaret Taylor had faxed me. So, who knew?

The spot they had chosen was a two-lane road, running along a sheer rock wall on a precipice overlooking the city skyline. The first time through I hadn't recognized the area. But the second time I did. It was in a suburb called Valley View, thus named because its eastern border was demarcated by a sheer drop-off hundreds of feet down into the great Cuyahoga River Valley basin. The road, which was called Skyline Drive, descended that rock wall.

The door on Hilton's Cadillac bumped shut as the car picked up speed rolling down the hill. Mitch Krammer was still waving as the Camcorder's viewfinder zoomed past him, keeping firmly on the taillights of the Cadillac— it was either dusk or early dawn; twilit either way—as it bounced across the center line, going faster and faster as the incline steepened. The red glow of the taillights blurred into a smear as the car veered, bounced over the shoulder, glanced off the rock wall, righted itself, crossed the center line again, and headed, like a huge silver pin ball, back to the left, rolling faster and faster, and finally hitting the guardrail, which for a hopeful moment seemed as if it were going to halt its momentum. But, in the end, as I had already seen, the rail gave way, allowing the car to dip, and then disappear, over the side.

The man operating the video camera was running now; the image bounced with his steps. He arrived at the edge in time to catch the Cadillac rolling, over and over on its side, spinning crazily, too fast to be real, lights still on, down the cliff wall, into the darkness below. There was no fire, no substantial sound. Just the inconsequential bumping of steel, and the tinkle of little pieces of junk peeling off the hulk and skittering over the rocks.

Another quick cut.

Mitch Krammer's face again.

Big grin.

"Highway Patrolman Bob says, 'Don't drink and drive.' "

Fuzz.

"I'll be downstairs," I said, hitting REWIND before handing Nat the remote control. "Let me know when Mrs. Lyttle shows up. Okay?"

Larry Fizner was rooting around in the kitchen cabinet, looking for something. Nat looked at me, asking, "Are you all right?"

I shrugged, smiled wanly, and said, "Yeah. I'm fine. I just have to think about a couple of things."

Then I kissed her on the forehead and went down to the prep room, closed the door, and left the lights out so that the room remained perfectly dark as I lay down on an embalming table and closed my eyes.

Please don't think that I'm nuts. I chose the embalming table for a very specific reason: namely, I needed it for perspective. I simply had to reestablish myself, and my place in relation to the rest of the world. My equilibrium had gone soft, and I was stumbling around inside my skull like a drunken sailor in a gale.

Sound extreme?

Think about it.

I had just seen a man killed. I hadn't seen a man die. I hadn't been standing in the Intensive Care Unit of some hospital as an elderly relative drew his last breath after a long, full life, and an illness so debilitating that it made death a blessing. I had seen a man murdered, in living color, in my living room. And, what's more, someone had ordered that murder, and, for all I knew, paid for it.

That was the big one:

Somebody had paid the bill.

There had been a "contractual obligation" involved, and Mitch Krammer, the video man, had used his Camcorder to make a record of the event . . . probably as proof that it had been carried out exactly to the specifications of whoever had hired him to do it. Then, once the deed was done, Dr. Gordon Wolf had come along and . . .

What?

Margaret Taylor had said that an anonymous letter was sent to the coroner by someone who claimed that they worked in the morgue, someone who believed that Dr. Wolf's autopsy of Bernard Hilton had been "sloppy." So what? What the hell did that prove?

It's quiet in an embalming room. So quiet that you wouldn't believe it. The embalming table is usually the last place where a person experiences any real physical contact on this planet. Oh, sure, sometimes a wife might plant a kiss on a dead man's forehead. But people don't do that much kissing of dead bodies anymore. It's not really safe, and most people know it. So the embalmer is the last person who touches the deceased. Short of the person who does the actual dressing, I suppose. It's the last time a person requires care. Embalming is the last service.

I was lying in the dark, at the very spot where those who are brought into my funeral home are transformed from human beings into objects to be displayed. I had literally, in a very physical sense, placed myself at the dividing line between two completely different states of being: life, and death . . . existence, and oblivion. And I had done it for a reason. . . .

It was just too bad that I didn't know what that reason was. I had been walking in a daze. It was physical, not mental, action that had taken me down to the prep room to that borderland between one world and another.

One world . . .

And another.

"There's us, down here, and the stars above, controlling our fate," the man called Jackal had said on the warehouse roof.

Up here, and down there . . . two separate places.

Two worlds.

The concept fit, and I mulled it over. Contained in Jackal's description were many layers of meaning. The stars overhead could be the stars of Captain Video's movies—the people Mitch Krammer killed. Or they could have been the higher-ups, the controlling powers who called the shots, who paid the bills, who hired men like Mitch Krammer to do the things they wanted done, but didn't feel they wanted to dirty their hands doing themselves.

And that was the heart of it, I knew. The sensation I'd been experiencing from the very first moment I stepped into the Hound's Tooth bar. The people there, the low-life scum bags, as Jackal had described them, including himself in the mix, strutted and preened and posed. They decked themselves out in their finest costumes, primped and postured, and thought of themselves as knowing all the angles. They were the tough guys, just ask them. They were the men who, if you sat down and drank with them, would tell you, sooner or later, that they were the ones who really knew what was going on in the world . . . who saw life from the perspective of the streets, and were therefore closer to "reality" than anybody else. Business people, the suits and ties, the ones they saw commuting back and forth every day on the buses and trains and freeways, they were sheep who didn't have a clue. They just didn't know. But those guys in the bar knew, they would be quick to tell you. Oh yeah, they were with it . . . in on the ground floor. Smart guys. Tough guys. Real men.

But Jackal had them pegged when he said that they were living in a hamster cage. What people like them, the small-time dealers, the muscle men, the hoods, don't realize, is that they're expendable . . . they're labor . . . they're nothing but the hands that do the dirty jobs. Where they thought they had the game all figured out, they were really doomed never to understand it because, from their perspective down on the playing field, they could never hope to view the big picture, never hope to understand the greater strategy. They compensated for their lack of influence by pumping themselves full of alcohol, and whatever else they could lay their hands on, until they got high enough to think they were smart. But they weren't smart. They were dumb. And I think they knew it, deep inside, on some level that they would never admit to being aware of. The quickest way to get yourself hurt in a place like the Hound's Tooth is to call one of those men on a bar stool stupid. They'll usually tolerate just about anything, but call one stupid and they'll cut you deep.

So Jackal had spoken of stars . . . pinpricks of light viewed from millions of miles away.

He had been there, physically present, when Mitch Krammer murdered Bernard Hilton . . . a man who employed a lot of the guys at the Hound's Tooth bar, including, one had to assume, Mitch Krammer himself.

Jackal was the key . . . the linchpin, and I didn't even know his real name. He was the link between Bernard Hilton, Mitch Krammer, R.L. Webster, and Frank Lyttle/Joe Pace. He was in prison with three of them; and he had been Joe Pace's lover . . . would have gone on being his lover, if Joe Pace would have had him. But things change after a guy gets out of the joint, by which Jackal meant, I have to believe, that guys who had been willing to sleep with men returned to women once they were again available. Webster and Pace stole something. Jackal knew them both . . . and he knew that Mitch Krammer had made a videotape of the murder of Bernard Hilton. The murder of his boss . . . the one time in his miserable life that the hulking, hairy, slope-browed motherfucker probably ever got close to the "star" that had, up until that point, probably controlled most of his world.

So where was Scene One?

Who had paid Captain Video's fee?

To whom was he contractually obligated?

I couldn't answer any of those questions . . . yet. But I could imagine something that might lead me to some answers, eventually. And what I could imagine was Jackal, hopped up on grass, or Jack Daniels, or whatever he used to blow his fuses. He's sitting at the bar, and Frank Lyttle is sitting next to him. Not R.L. Webster. Webster might have been there, but Jackal would be speaking to Lyttle. Jackal always spoke to Lyttle. He probably touched him when he talked, like a friend remembering intimacies not-long gone. He's drunk, and Lyttle's there, close enough to touch. Jackal wants him to stay, wants to keep him interested, wants the two of them to be, for a brief moment, as close as they were in prison . . . or at least as close as can be managed on the outside. He wants to have Little Frank's attention . . . to be the focus of his undivided attention for a little while. Just a little while . . . because things can never be the same.

"I knew they couldn't be, on the outside. I didn't even want them to be."

Liar.

Jackal's talking.

I can all but hear the words.

"We did a star, Joe," he says into his glass. "Me and the video man, we did him, clean and clear. Pumped him full of grain and pushed his car off a cliff to make it look like an accident. Big shot paid us too. A big shot with deep pockets and a line to the coroner's office. Not a chance of getting caught. Not a whisper of a chance."

Look at me, the Jackal is saying, in effect. Look at how important I am. How smart I am. How alive I am . . . here, in this cage, where the starlight barely reaches. Look at me. Love me. Listen to me because I'm worth your time.

And Little Frank does listen, and so does R.L. Webster . . . the two men who look so much alike, who could have been twins, and who shared a "big synergy." They listened all right, and they probably shared the same thought at the same moment.

"There's a tape of it! A record. An angle."

So they broke into . . .

Where?

Where did they break into to steal it? Who did they steal it from? Knowing that might tell me who ordered Bernard Hilton killed. It couldn't have been Captain Video's house that they had burgled, because he didn't have the kind of scratch that would make the risk worthwhile. For what reason could they want that tape other than blackmail? And they had wanted it, that much was obvious. I had it. I had found it where Frank Lyttle had hidden it after R.L. Webster was killed . . . tortured because whoever traced him from jail knew that he had taken it. They didn't know about Frank Lyttle—still called Joe Pace at the time—or else they would have picked him up by then; but they knew about Webster.

How?

Could Jackal have told?

Probably not, because Jackal wouldn't have known, for sure. But he might have guessed. He might have said, after the tape was stolen, "Hey, you know, I think we ought'a talk to Rob Webster 'cause I've got a hunch about him." He would never have admitted that it was he who had spilled the beans in the first place. But he might bring up the suspicion . . . without implicating Joe Pace, the love of his life.

But he would implicate Webster . . . might even deliberately implicate Webster. It might have been deliberate all along, to give Mitch Krammer a reason to kill Mr. Webster, who was still sharing something with Joe Pace that Jackal himself could never hope to share, and therefore coveted very much. It could have happened either way, and the result would be the same.

"Where is the tape?" Mitch Krammer would have asked Webster, tied, with his hands over his head in the warehouse bathtub. Burning him when he didn't reply. Probably videotaping it. "Where is the tape?"

"I don't know."

More fire.

More screams.

"I don't know; but Joe does. Joe Pace, he was in on it with me!"

Kill Webster to keep him quiet, have Dr. Wolf, who covered up Bernard Hilton's murder, so he's fucked forever, cover up this one too, and go on to find Joe, and get that tape back. But Joe Pace is smart. So he goes underground, changes his name, and hides the tape where nobody would ever think to look for it: right under Captain Video's nose, in his own back yard. Two years go by, and nobody hears a word about Joe Pace. For all anybody knows, he fell off the face of the planet. Gone. Joined the stars.

"But you couldn't leave it alone, could you?" I whispered to the darkness. "No, you were hooked. It was like a drug, wasn't it? Like booze to me. Once you took it, you knew you had it. You knew it was just sitting there, and you couldn't leave it alone. So you used it to get money when you needed it. And that's how they found you . . . because you were greedy, and you led them right to your door."

So Scene One was gone because Joe Pace had edited it out and sold it back to the people who wanted it. He'd been cutting that tape up and selling it back one piece at a time . . . that's where he got the money he used to get over the rough spots, and why he had said that he didn't want to "piss his stash away a nickel at a time."

So where was the glove compartment key?

Who had it?

Just then the door of the prep room opened, and the light from the hall went from a pencil-sharp line along its edge to a bright wedge on the floor and ceiling intersected by Nat's shadow. Silhouetted against the light, she stood in the doorway and spoke into the darkness.

"They're not coming," she said.

"Who's not coming?" I asked without turning my head, still lying on the embalming table, my hands folded over my stomach, my face aimed at the ceiling.

"Ellie Lyttle and her brother."

"Her brother?"

"That's who he said he was. He just called. Mrs. Lyttle's in the hospital. She's having her baby."

"Since when?"

"Since Jerry called her to come down here to talk. It looks like all the excitement helped her labor along."

"Wonderful."

"Bill?"

"Yes?"

"Are you all right?"

I swung my legs over the edge of the table as Nat flipped on the light. Jumping down, I looked at her, considered my words for a moment, and said, "Frank Lyttle was using the tape of Bernard Hilton's murder to squeeze money out of whoever paid for it. He was going to that junkyard on the nights he knew Mitch Krammer and his dog would be at the dog fights across town, and he was taking that tape somewhere, probably to the hotel across the street, and he was chopping pieces of it off and selling them, either to Captain Video himself, or, more likely, to the person who paid to have Hilton killed, with Captain Video acting as a go-between. That's why he was killed. Because, once he made contact for the blackmail money, it was only a matter of time before he was traced to where he lived. Then whoever he was putting the screws to used Congo to torture him, hoping that he'd reveal where the rest of the tape was hidden. Since the tape was still there when we went looking for it, I have to assume that he didn't talk. And I think Ellie Lyttle's known the whole story all along, and that she's been holding out on us."

"What makes you say that?" Nat asked, still in the doorway.

"Because she only gave me one key," I replied. "To get to the tape, you needed two: the car door key, and the one that fits the glove compartment. I had the one for the car door, but I had to break into the glove box. She was being clever . . . I'm just not sure what the point of it was. But baby or no baby, I'm going to find out what she thought she was doing. And I'm going to do it, even if it means that my brother ends up hating me for the rest of my life. Now come on."

I led Nat into the office and punched Rusty Simmons' number up on the speaker phone, glancing at the clock and seeing that it was nearly five in the afternoon. When Rusty answered I asked him to do me a favor. He agreed, warily, and when I explained what I needed, he said, "I should be at work by eleven, so I'll call you then. This all you need, a list of the names of all the folks done worked security down here for the past three years?"

I thought it over, and added, "I guess so . . . unless you could swing pictures too."

"What for?"

"Just a hunch," I said.

"You sure got a lot'a hunches all of a sudden. I'll see what I can do, but that'll probably cost a bottle. Edgar still likes his Absolut."

"Put it on my bill." I smiled, remembering Edgar Wilkins, the head of morgue security, and the left-hand drawer in his desk where he stored his "secret" vodka bottle that everybody knew he had.

When I turned the phone off, Nat asked, "What was that all about?"

"You'll see," I said. "Just listen."

Margaret Taylor had given me a phone number, and I ran upstairs and got it out of my wallet. Then I dialed it on the speaker phone, and when it was answered, I asked to speak with her.

"Name please."

I gave it.

"One moment. Go ahead."

When Margaret Taylor came on, I said, "Bill Hawley here. I think I might be onto something interesting, but I need some help."

Ms. Taylor waited.

"Can you produce the original dental X-rays that you removed from R.L. Webster's file, as well as a set from when he was a prisoner at the New Jersey State Penitentiary? Not the ones from when he was in in Ohio, but a certifiable copy of the New Jersey records?"

After a moment's thought, she said that she could.

"Good. I need those as soon as possible. And I'll also need fingerprint sets from the same sources. Understand?"

"Yes. Mr. Hawley, what are you doing?"

"Researching the possibility of orchestrating a tactical victory that looks like an accident."

"Is there anything else you need?"

"Yeah," I said. "And this is important. I also need the dental X-rays and fingerprint charts for a second New Jersey inmate who was in at the same time as Webster. The name is Joseph Pace. You got that? Joseph P-A-C-E. And I need this stuff a.s.a.p."

"I can probably have them FedExed in by tomorrow."

"Good. When you get them, bring them right to my funeral home. You've got the address. I'll be waiting, and, hopefully, I'll have something to tell you."

When I hung up, Nat said, "I don't get it."

"Get what?"

"Why fingerprints?"

"For identification."

"Of who?"

"The bodies."

"But you already know who the bodies are. The first was R.L. Webster, and the second was Joe Pace, a.k.a. Frank Lyttle. What can you achieve by proving it again?"

"We'll see," I said, rising and signaling for Nat to follow me up the stairs. "Come on. Let's get dressed. I've got to go gun shopping."

TEN

■ ■ ■ ■ ■ ■ ■ ■

I HAD A permit to carry a gun, and I decided that it was about time I started using it. I'd kept a gun in the night stand next to my bed from the time that Nat and I were married. My father had given it to me because, in his opinion, every home needs protection. It was a long-barrelled, nickel-plated Colt .357 Magnum revolver; and it was less a pistol than it was a cannon. I considered carrying the magnum, but finally decided against it because it would be nearly impossible to conceal. What I needed was a little .38 like the one Larry Fizner carried in a holster clipped to his belt at the base of his spine, where his sport coat would cover it. So, on the way to the hospital where Mrs. Lyttle was having her baby, we stopped at a gun shop to browse. Jerry was impatient, and wanted to get to the hospital as soon as possible. Larry Fizner was sitting in the back seat of the van monkeying with a tiny portable tape machine equipped with a set of headphones and, strangely, he refused to accompany me into the store. He mumbled something about it not being right that the state should hand out pistol permits like they were food stamps, or something to that effect, concluding with, "Just go ahead and make it snappy, Mr. Private Eye."

"I think he's pissed about you getting your license without having to take a test or anything," Nat said as we stepped into the shop.

"Tough," I replied. "He's the one who's always talking about the strings being pulled behind the scenes. Well, that's all that's happened here. What's good for the goose . . ."

I had never been in a gun store before, and the place made me nervous the moment I stepped inside. While I looked around, Nat looked at me. There were bars on the door and windows, and police patches lining the walls. Hundreds of police patches from cities all over the country. And guns. My God! I've never seen so many goddamn guns in my life.

"What the hell would anybody want with such a thing?" I asked, staring into a glass case containing a pump action, 12-gauge shotgun that was designed to look like an assault weapon. There had to be a thousand different kinds of pistols here, and bullets, and holsters and . . .

I swallowed, my tongue feeling strangely dry. I looked at Nat. "Well?" she asked. "Do you see anything you like?"

Just then a man emerged from the back room, stepped behind the counter, and spread his hands on the case. "Help you folks?" he said, with a grin that was moist and inviting.

The effect disturbed me.

He was a short, pudgy little man, with a floppy moustache and glasses. Not at all the sort I would expect to be "packing a rod." But from where I stood I could see his artillery, nestled under his armpit in a shoulder holster with leather straps that criss-crossed his chest. I glanced at the butt of the pistol, and then back up at the man's smiling eyes, trying to reconcile the two.

I guess what was bothering me was that if this man, with his myopic-looking stare and soft, blubbery belly were, say, a taxicab driver, I might not think anything of it. He looked as if he could probably operate a car all right, if he took it slow, and was careful. But if he were, say, the man who poked his head out of an operating theater, scalpel in hand, eyes squinting as his greasy hair hung into them over his cheap white dress shirt with the spaghetti-sauce stains on it from his dinner, I don't think I'd be all that thrilled about his working on me. Know what I mean? He was just a guy; an ordinary Joe. Nothing special. No special skills apparent; no extraordinary features. And yet there he stood with a weapon at his side, fully capable of killing me if he so chose.

Killing me.

Or anybody else.

He could simply withdraw his pistol, point it, and, BOOM! Clean and simple. End a life without taking a step. It chilled me to the bone, and made me shudder. And . . .

"No," I said reflexively. "You can't help us. We're in the wrong place. Please pardon the interruption."

Grabbing Nat's elbow, I hustled her out of the store, the bell jangling merrily overhead. When we hit the sidewalk I was breathing hard and my skin was moist. My wife looked at me, and I looked back.

"No gun?" she asked.

"No gun," I mumbled.

She smiled softly, and leaned forward, kissing me on the cheek. "Good," she said. "You had me worried there for a second."

I was trying to think of something to say in response, when the side door of the van slid open, and Larry Fizner stuck his head out, shouting, "Bill, get over here! I think I got something!"

When we got up closer, Larry produced an audio cassette tape from the little hand-held recorder he'd been playing with for the past hour, saying, "Listen to this."

Nat and I climbed into the front seats, and I started the van and put the cassette into the player in the dash. Jerry, who'd been grumbling steadily about hurrying to the hospital, didn't complain, but just sat there, in his wheelchair, his head ducked down a little because of the low ceiling, listening to the garbled sound of an indistinct voice.

"What is it?" I asked, turning in my seat to face the back, where Larry Fizner was hunched forward, lifting his hand to indicate that I should be quiet and listen.

I did.

After a moment, the voice, which was heavily reverbed, and sounded as if it had been recorded underwater, resolved itself into words. It was not so much that the sound quality of the tape improved; it was just that my ear adjusted, and started picking out meanings.

"That's Mitch Krammer," Larry explained briefly. "Remember, I bugged his house."

"When was this recorded?" I asked.

"Earlier today. I've got my van parked about six blocks from the junkyard, and on the way back to the funeral home I stopped to pick up this tape, and to load a fresh one in the machine. The transmission range on my equipment's not that great, so I had to leave the van on the street. The microphones are transmitting to a voice-activated tape recorder. Only runs when someone's speaking . . . even distinguishes TV and radio noises. Only records human speech. Fancy Japanese shit. I was going over what I got on the way here, and that's when I heard this. Now listen . . ."

He raised one finger as if to say, "Here it is," and everybody in the van strained to hear.

From the garble, Mitch Krammer's words seemed to fall in on me, as if from a great height, starting out as fuzz, and sliding into sense:

" . . . ssssslllllllbbbbggllll . . . lllll . . . I think it's about time we maybe pay up," he said, referring to God knew what.

"What the hell?" I said, and Larry Fizner shushed me angrily.

"Listen, goddamn it!" he growled.

Nat put her hand on mine to steady me.

Krammer was apparently talking on the telephone, because his sentences started and stopped abruptly, with no reply that I could hear. Okay. I had that much.

He continued:

"I know it's a lot of money," he said, his voice much more intelligible now . . . easier to understand now that I had the concept. "But jail's no place for a lady; believe me, you wouldn't like it. And I don't want to go back either. No, I can't find the fucking tape. I tried everything I know how. Yeah, I know it's a shame he died, but it happens. He wouldn't talk . . . I tried for an hour. But we can get him when he comes for the cash. Yeah, I know it's another murder, but what can we do? We cough up the scratch, and what's to say he don't come back in another two years with a copy? We thought he was gone the last time, remember? How long you willing to go on like this? Yeah, I know it was dumb to make that tape, but you wanted proof. Hey . . . don't gim'me that! You're the one who came up with it, remember? It was your house they got it from.

"Okay. Sorry. So what's the plan?

"Yeah, that's what I think. So I should go along with it? Uh-huh. Okay, I'll set it up."

The tape suddenly went silent for an instant, during which Larry Fizner said, "Now listen to this!"

Tape hiss.

Then:

"Yeah, this is Mitch. Okay, the lady said it's a deal. Where and when? Wait a second, let me get a pencil. Okay, shoot."

Silence.

"Come on!" I whispered, imagining Mitch Krammer sitting in his pink shack in the middle of the junkyard, writing out his instructions. "Repeat it!"

And he did:

"Slip fourteen, dock C; eleven-thirty at the pier. Yeah, I got it. You just make sure you're there on time. There better be no fuckin' around or you're gon'na wish you really were dead. Get it? Yeah."

The tape went quiet again . . . and this time, it stayed that way.

"Is that it?" Nat asked.

Larry nodded.

"But who was he talking to? And what's it mean?"

"Bill?" Larry said.

I frowned. "It means that whoever ordered Bernard Hilton's death is going to pay up. It's a woman, from what Krammer said. And she's going to cut the deal with whoever's been selling her pieces of that videotape, at eleven-thirty, on a pier."

"Eleven-thirty when?" Nat asked. "And what pier?"

I glanced at Larry Fizner, who shrugged.

Then I said, "Yeah, what pier?" with a sigh, as Jerry, from the back of the van, piped up, "Are we going to the hospital today sometime, or we gon'na sit in this parking lot till Ellie's kid's in high school?"

Oh yeah, I thought. I almost forgot about that. But then I said, "Just a second," rewinding the tape of Mitch Krammer's voice and playing it again. There was something he said . . . something that stuck in my mind. . . .

There it was!

" . . . what's to say he don't come back in another two years with a copy? We thought he was gone the last time, remember?"

"There," I said. "Did you hear that?"

I played it again.

" . . . gone the last time, remember?"

And again:

" . . . gone the last time . . ."

I looked at Nat, but her eyes were dull with confusion. Then I looked at Larry, finding, to my distinct disappointment, pretty much the same condition.

"You really don't get it, do you?" I said, feeling a tingle in my fingertips that frightened me a little. "You really don't see? It's been right there all along! Right in front of us, and we missed it!"

Then, with a sudden rush of positive joy, I slapped the steering wheel with the heels of my hands and shouted, "I'VE GOT IT! GODDAMN IF I DON'T!"

"What?" Nat asked. "What have you got?"

But instead of answering, I turned and looked at Jerry, saying, "You still want to go to the hospital, or you want to come with us?"

He blinked, and said, "I want to go to the hospital. Why, where are you going?"

"Okay," I said, throwing the van into reverse and backing out of the parking spot. "The hospital it is. We'll drop you off."

"Where are we going?" Nat asked.

And I, still alive with excitement, said, "We're going to visit a star."

ELEVEN

■ ■ ■ ■ ■ ■ ■ ■ ■ ■

THE HOTEL ACROSS the street from Captain Video's junkyard was a shabby building, ten stories high, with a glass-enclosed lobby that I could imagine filled with hookers resting their tired feet later in the evening. I wanted to leave Nat in the van while Larry and I did what we had to do inside, but in this neighborhood I decided that even four locked doors wouldn't keep her from being molested for long. So we all went in.

It was going on eight o'clock in the evening, and since it was April, the sky had gone a dusky grey, with darker grey streaks of cloud finger-painted over a hint of pink on the tip of the horizon. Our breath made steam that shimmered yellow beneath the single light burning on a pole. And our steps were loud on the asphalt. The hotel was an ugly, brick block of a building, with broken windows covered with cardboard, paper and trash strewn over the parking lot. The front door hung limply on one hinge.

"I hope the elevator works," Larry said, looking up.

"I wouldn't count on it," I replied.

Stepping up to the counter, I rang the call bell, which was answered by an older man in a white shirt, no tie. He looked bored and uninterested, and when I asked if he had a man living on the premises who had a swastika tattooed on his neck, he leaned on the counter with both elbows and shrugged. "Who knows? I don't pay no mind to who comes and goes round here. Ain't my business. What's it to ya anyway?"

I glanced at Larry Fizner, who sighed, and, quite politely, placed the barrel of his pistol in the man's right ear.

Leaning forward, I said, with my face deliberately close to my subject's, "Once more from the top, and this time, with feeling. How about a room number for a guy named Jackal."

For an instant, the man looked as if he were going to laugh in my face, or simply take the gun out of Larry Fizner's hand. But when he moved his eyes Larry's way, I think he must have seen something of what I saw in the old detective's expression . . . which was a cold, flat, unemotional detachment that advertised, quite clearly, that the man holding the gun had nothing left to lose. The desk clerk couldn't know the reason for Larry's lack of fear . . . couldn't know that he was dying and therefore unafraid . . . but he could see as plainly as I that Larry would indeed pull the trigger—there was simply no doubt about it—and I think he picked up the vibe on the spot, because the smile that was just starting to flicker at the corner of his mouth died when he lifted his eyes.

"He asked you a question," Larry said, drawing the hammer on his .38 back with his thumb.

The clerk seemed to think things over for a moment, and then he answered with a sixth-floor number.

Larry Fizner very politely said, "Thank you," replaced his pistol in its holster, and indicated with a wave of his hand that he would follow Nat and me to the elevator.

I was wrong about the elevator not working. It worked just fine, though it smelled like piss inside. Nat wrinkled her nose, and I examined the buttons, looking for the right number under a fuzzy line of black spray paint that had been run over the entire inside of the car. The sixth floor hallway smelled like a locker room. The room doors were made of steel. Number 603 was closed, but not all the way. A band of amber light seeped out into the gloomy hall, and Larry Fizner, glancing over his shoulder at where I stood at his back, with Nat behind me, withdrew his pistol before reaching out to knock. He rapped three times, waited, and then rapped twice more, calling out, "Hello? Jack?"

No reply.

He looked at me, and I stepped back, moving Nat and myself out of the line of fire as Larry licked his lips, settled his shoulders, and pushed the door open.

The amber light was coming from a single lamp, lying on its side on the floor, still bolted to an end table that also had been upended. Larry led the way, crouched, gun held before him with two hands, and Nat and I following behind. There was a smell of smoke from where the lamp lay with its shade cocked and smoldering against the bulb, and with the light coming from so close to the ground, our shadows stretched out behind us, squirming up the cracked-plaster wall.

A woman was lying on her stomach on the floor near the couch, legs flat and wide apart, red high heels splayed, tight skirt torn, one arm at her side, pointing down, bright pink fingernails shining, the other arm up, crooked at the elbow. Her face was aimed away, but her long black hair was heaped in a pile of curls so deep that at first I couldn't tell which way she was facing. Her stockings were sheer pink, with tiny red hearts stitched into them. Cushions that had been pulled off the couch lay around her in disarray.

The whole room was a mess, the furniture—what there was of it—scattered, overturned, and busted. All the lights were out, except for the lamp jutting out of the overturned table, which I bent and lifted, immediately altering the shadows in the room, sending them dancing as if to right themselves as I set the end table back on its legs.

Nat pushed past me and knelt at the woman's side while Larry inspected the bathroom before finally announcing, "There's nobody else here."

"My God!" Nat whispered, putting her hand to her mouth. I stood beside her, and she looked up at me, saying, "It's a man."

I nodded.

It was Jackal, dressed up for a night out . . . a special evening, judging by the care he had taken with his makeup, which was mostly all smeared now, but thick and colorful. But not nearly as colorful as his skin, which was puffed, bruised, split, and bleeding.

"Help me," I said, sliding one hand under his arm and beginning to lift him. Nat and I got him up on the couch, flat on his back, arms lolling. But he was breathing, and, after Nat had wiped his face with a wet towel she got from the bathroom, his eyes rolled, and he licked his swollen lips. He didn't speak, at first, but simply groaned and moved his head. Nat sat next to him on the couch, looking concerned, not because she knew him, but simply because he needed help. I loved her for that. It touched me, and reminded me of the alternative—the other side of the coin—one of the reasons, I think, that I do the things I do.

Jackal's hand moved jerkily over his stomach, touched Nat's hand, went on, and found mine where it was hanging close to my side. With surprising strength, he grabbed it and squeezed, pulling me down close enough to smell his perfume, and the alcohol on his breath as he exhaled. His eyes nearly crossed as he rolled his head around, trying to focus on my face. His lipstick was smeared whorishly over his mouth, and his wig had slipped back on his head, revealing his high forehead and shaved scalp.

"He's so . . . mean," he whispered, at last, a tear escaping the corner of one eye to roll down into his ear. "He said that he loved me . . . but he never . . ."

His lip quivered. Then he squeezed his eyes shut, sobbing.

I knelt next to him, seeing in my peripheral vision Nat leaning in close next to me, with Larry Fizner behind her, searching through something on the bed.

"Why?" I asked. "Why did he hurt you?"

Jackal wiped his eyes, recognition registering plainly on his face for the first time.

"Cowboy!" He half smiled, laying his head back down and sighing with a very effeminate emphasis. "You're about the last person I expected."

"Why'd he hurt you?" I repeated.

He looked at me, and asked, "You know?"

"It's Webster," I returned, and heard Nat inhale sharply. "He was the security guard on duty at that warehouse on the night the body was burned, wasn't he? And you were what, the 'homeless' man who reported it to the police?"

Jackal nodded.

"Listen," he said. "There's a bottle of champagne in the fridge. I bought it for tonight. Could I have a drink, please?"

He was trying to sit up, but he couldn't make it. His head dropped back and he collapsed with one hand over his forehead.

Nat handed the champagne to me. I popped the cork, glanced around for a glass, found none, and gave the bottle to Jackal, who took it and swallowed gratefully. With a belch, he rested his head back, saying, "Somebody took the tape. When Ron went to get it this afternoon, somebody had broken in and taken it. He blamed me. Me! He said I told somebody where it was. He said I let him down. The son of a bitch!"

Jackal was sulking, drinking, closing his eyes.

Larry said, "Bill, look at this."

I stepped around the couch to where he was standing over a VCR built to accommodate two tapes at a time. There was also an editing machine with a tiny screen, next to a stack of blank cassettes.

"This is where they spliced the original," I said, looking up at the window, which overlooked the junkyard, affording a splendid view of Captain Video's pink shack. "They watched him come and go from here. So it's Webster who's got the second key. Webster and Pace were partners to the end. I should have guessed."

"I'm calling an ambulance," Nat said. I turned to find her fishing the phone out from under the bed by its cord as Jackal was trying to get to his feet, swaying, and collapsing back down on the couch.

"No!" he insisted. "I'm fine."

"You're not fine, you're badly beaten," Nat said, jiggling the button on the top of the phone and trying to get a dial tone.

I was staring at Jackal. He caught my eye and returned my gaze. Suddenly, it was as if the two of us were alone in the room . . . we were locked together by a shared knowledge that until that very second, I hadn't even realized I was privy to.

"He told you to say what you said on the roof of the warehouse, didn't he?" I asked. "He told you to act like you were interested in helping me so that I'd think it was Joe Pace you loved. Right?"

He nodded.

"He wanted me to think that it was your love for Joe that gave you a reason to want to see my investigation succeed. But all the while it was just a way to throw me off the track. Like what you said about Ellie Lyttle actually being Joe's daughter. It was all a smoke screen. All bullshit. While I was out there looking for Joe Pace's life story, you and Webster were taking care of business here, with Webster being a dead man, as far as I, or practically anybody else in the world, knew."

Jackal didn't move. Nor did he look away.

"How did Webster know that I was even involved?" I asked.

Jackal put his hand to his forehead as he said, "Eddie told him."

"Who's Eddie?"

"You know Eddie. You met him on the stairs."

"The one who pushed me?"

I got a brief flash of an image right then: two men, Jackal and Eddie, with their backs to me, descending the stairs, hand-in-hand.

Jackal nodded, champagne bottle tipped as he drank. Then, with a choking sound he was stumbling into the bathroom, where he vomited into the toilet, retching violently.

"That's it," Nat said. "I'm calling the fire department. He needs a doctor."

I placed my hand over hers to stop her from dialing. "So Eddie works at the morgue, huh, Jack?" I said as I stepped toward the bathroom, where I found Jackal on his knees, wig on the floor, face aimed down as he hugged the toilet.

"Go to hell, cowboy," he muttered without lifting his head. "Just go to hell."

"Tonight's the night, isn't it, Jack?" I pressed, leaning on the door frame as casually as I could. "When he found the tape missing, he panicked and put the screws to the video man but good. Said it was his last chance to come up with the money, or he was going to bring down the house. Right? It's tonight! That's why he wailed on you like he did . . . because he was convinced that it was you who fucked it all up . . . he was teaching you a lesson."

"Get screwed," Jackal said, sitting down on the bathroom floor between the toilet and the tub.

"He said he was coming back for you, didn't he?" I asked. "This was just a whipping to teach you a lesson, but he's still coming back for you when it's over. Isn't that the plan?"

Jackal was looking at me with a superior expression, despite his obvious pain.

"You pathetic little queen," I muttered, shaking my head. "He's not coming back for you, Jack. He's never coming back. You want to know why? One, because he doesn't need you anymore. You served your purpose. You're finished, as far as he's concerned. And two, because he's going to fall. I'm going to see to it. He's going to fall, and you're going down with him."

Jackal's swollen eyes sparked with anger as he started climbing to his feet, holding onto the toilet, his torn skirt hanging in tatters around his legs. But before he could stand fully upright, Larry Fizner aimed his gun from where he was standing at my back, drawing the hammer back with a loud click that froze Jackal in a crouch.

"We're leaving now, Jack," I said. "Once we're gone, what I suggest you do is puke a couple more times to make sure you're feeling better, take a shower, put on some fresh clothes, and go down to the nearest police station . . . the one on East One Hundredth Street would be good. When you get there, tell the nice officers that you want to turn yourself in, and that you'd like them to take care of you. Because when this evening's over, there's nothing in the world anyone's going to be able to say to convince Mr. Webster that you didn't rat on him. No matter what I say, he's going to think that it was you . . . and he'll get you for it.

"Understand?

"I know things that I have no right knowing, as far as Webster's concerned. So he's going to think I learned them from you . . . no matter what you or anybody else says to the contrary. All he's got to do is get the word out to the guys at the Tooth that you snitched, and somebody down there's going to take it as his civic duty to straighten you out. No matter what rotten shit Ron Webster was up to, ratting on him's a mortal sin to those guys, and you know it. As long as you're on the street, your ass is going to be on somebody's list. So go to the cops, have them put you up for the night, and maybe tomorrow, when it's all over, I can help you cut a deal with the D.A. It's your only hope, Jack. That's my advice to you."

"Screw you, cowboy." Jackal grimaced, lowering himself back onto the floor. "Just screw you and the old fuck too. Get out'ta here! Leave me alone!"

He was crying again, his shoulders rising and falling rhythmically, his hands over his smeared face. Larry, Nat, and I left, leaving him there. In the hall Nat said, "But what if he runs away?" Making me shrug as I replied, "Where's he going to go? What I said was true about somebody in his circle of friends cutting his throat once the word gets out that he snitched on his partner."

"But he didn't snitch," Nat said sharply.

"Sure he did," I said. "How else would we know to do what we're going to do next?"

"What are we going to do?"

"Visit Dr. Wolf."

"To convince him to give up, too?"

"No," I said, holding the elevator door so that Nat and Larry could step in before me. "To pull his ass out of the fire."

It was nearly nine-thirty at night before we got to the morgue, where Dr. Gordon Wolf received us less than graciously.

"I was just heading home," he said when he opened his office door. "It's been a long day. And, considering your reputation, I doubt very much if you and I have anything to discuss, Mr. Hawley."

Dr. Wolf made no secret of the contempt he felt for private investigators in general, and me in particular. To a degree, I actually share his prejudice. Private eyes are notorious for screwing up the cases developed by the legitimate criminal investigative agencies of a city. While the cops go about their methodical business of accumulating evidence, it's not unusual for a private eye to come along and say the wrong thing to the wrong person, or to step into situations where vital information ends up being compromised. With my being a licensed funeral director, a profession at least a few inches closer to Dr. Wolf's own than when I wore my investigator's hat, the times I had stepped into the role of P.I. were tantamount to a betrayal of everything the good doctor stood for as a professional. I had heard rumors about his opinions of me through Rusty Simmons and others, but I had never felt it necessary to confront him on that score. Until now. Now, we were going to have it out, whether he liked it or not.

He was trying to push his way past where I was standing in his office door, blocking his way into the hall, when I reached out and, quite firmly but with as much decorum as I could manage, shoved him back inside.

"That was a serious error," he said, his face coloring as he pulled his frame up to its full six foot something height.

"Whatever," I said, stepping into his office with Nat and Larry Fizner following. Nat was carrying an overflowing file folder, and the video cassette I'd gotten out of the glove box of the Cutlass in the junkyard. Larry had the two binders full of materials Margaret Taylor had faxed to me during the course of the past few days. We'd stopped for the stuff at the funeral home on our way to the morgue, and, having found Ansel howling in the garage, had brought him along too. He was now waiting in the van, smearing dog snot all over my windows.

"I suggest you sit down, Doctor," I said as Larry slapped the binders down on his desk. "Because we've got a lot of information to process, and not a hell of a lot of time to do it. May I use your phone?"

Without waiting for him to reply, I lifted the receiver, hit the intercom, and said, "Rusty? Good, I was hoping you'd be here early. Do me a favor, okay? When you've got that stuff I asked for together, would you bring it up to Dr. Wolf's office? Yeah, that's right. Dr. Wolf's office. We'll be waiting."

I hung up and turned to the doctor, who was standing in front of a blackboard covered with anatomical drawings done in three colors of chalk, and next to a human skeleton hanging on a metal tree from a screw implanted in the top of its skull. "Does the name Ronald Lancing Webster mean anything to you, Dr. Wolf?"

Some of the angry color drained from the doctor's face. His eyes narrowed.

"How about Frank Lyttle?"

I could see by his tense expression that I had his attention.

"Aha!" I smiled, indicating the chair behind the doctor's desk as the place he should occupy. As he stepped past me, his eyes never leaving my face, I continued, "You thought that since Margaret Taylor agreed to cover up the misidentification of those two bodies that no one would ever ask you any questions about them. You probably even thought that you were the luckiest guy in the world, what with having an official representative of the governor's office agreeing to back you up in what could have been a very embarrassing situation. But what really happened, Dr. Wolf, is that you've been sold down the river. From every direction . . . up one side, and down the other. And that's where I come in. Believe it or not, I'm the best friend you've got right now. And I can prove it."

He licked his lips nervously and glanced at the binders on the desk before him.

Dr. Wolf was a wiry man, very thin, with, as I've mentioned before, hair that was so white that it virtually gleamed under strong light. His other outstanding feature was the color of his eyes . . . which was a very sharp amber, almost like a gemstone, shot through with slivers of gold. Those eyes sparkled as he rubbed one hand over his mouth and said, "What have you got to do with this, Mr. Hawley? What's your interest in this matter?"

"Originally, I didn't really have one," I replied. "But on Margaret Taylor's advice, you instructed Frank Lyttle's widow to call me to take care of her husband's funeral. Remember? Didn't you think that was a strange request for Ms. Taylor to make, considering that you folks wanted Mr. Lyttle buried with as little fuss as possible?"

"I assumed," he replied, "that given your reputation, you and she had come to some understanding, and that engaging you in the matter was tantamount to a guarantee of security."

"So you thought she'd bought me off," I said, shaking my head in mock abashment. "You really don't think much of me, do you? But if that's the case, then why'd you go along with it, Doctor? Even if you thought that I could be bribed, didn't you know that what you were doing was wrong? Didn't you think it was unethical for a man in your position to agree to covering up faulty pathologist reports made directly to the coroner herself?"

"Ms. Taylor explained it in such a way that I was forced to agree with her reasoning," he said. "I didn't like the idea, but I felt I was obligated to comply."

"Obligated?" Larry Fizner snorted, snapping the doctor's head his way. "What a crock! Your shoes are shitty, Doctor, and you're tracking it everywhere you go."

"What's he talking about?" Dr. Wolf asked, turning a very worried face my way.

"No idea, Doctor?" I asked in return. "You don't have anything to say about, oh, for example, the results of the autopsy you conducted on the remains of a gentleman named Bernard Hilton?"

"What's Bernard Hilton's autopsy got to do with anything?" he demanded, beginning to rise. Lifting my hand for him to remain seated, I removed a sheet of paper from the file folder and handed it to him with grave solemnity.

"This is a copy of an anonymous letter sent to the police department's Special Operations branch suggesting that you deliberately distorted the results of the autopsy on Bernard Hilton for some unexplained, possibly nefarious, reason," I explained.

Dr. Wolf's face went white as he read the letter.

"What's the meaning of this?" he asked, his lips pale and dry.

"No idea?" I said. "All news to you, I suppose. Well, how about this, then?" I handed over another sheet of paper, saying, "Pay special attention to the paragraph I've highlighted in yellow, Doctor. In it you will read that according to the official police report filed on the date R.L. Webster's burned body was discovered in a warehouse on East One Hundred Seventy-first Street, you and another individual are specifically recorded as having spent time examining the remains alone. You will also note that according to that same report, the condition of the body as originally discovered varied significantly from the body you subsequently described in your report. And, I might add, there are pictures to document the discrepancy."

"But this isn't true!" he insisted, fluttering the paper. "It's a lie!"

"Ah, then there's this little gem," I said, sliding the open binder toward him. On the pages displayed were the drawings of the body of Frank Lyttle he had made during his autopsy, compared to the Polaroid photographs I had taken in my prep room.

"They don't match very well," I said, shaking my head sadly. "Which makes me awfully suspicious as to the accuracy of your observations . . . in this case, or any other in which you're involved. It's a shame, really. When so many people think so highly of your qualifications. There's going to be a lot of disappointed city officials mouthing your name when they find out what a sloppy pathologist their golden doctor actually is."

"But I didn't make these drawings!" Dr. Wolf shouted. "Where did you get these? They're all wrong!"

He was on his feet now, trembling with indignation, facing me straight on.

"Dr. Wolf," I said, my hands on my hips, my eyes locked on his. "Please answer the following questions truthfully, and without hesitation. And make me believe you, because the only way I'm going to help you out of this mess is if you convince me that you're playing me straight.

"Now:

"Have you ever, at any time in your career, deliberately concealed or distorted autopsy results officially reported as representing the findings of the county coroner's department?"

"No," he insisted vehemently.

"Have you ever tampered with evidence in a criminal investigation by either removing said evidence from the scene of a crime, or by altering in any way said crime scene evidence in hopes of concealing pertinent facts from the police?"

"No! Never!"

"Are you presently engaged in a scheme to extort money from a citizen, or citizens, as yet unnamed?"

"No! What the hell are you talking about?"

"Did you realize that during the past two years you and your office were the subjects of at least two investigations conducted by the city, as well as by agents representing the governor?"

"What? No! I had no idea. Is that true?"

"Yes, Doctor, I'm afraid that it is. Please, sit down."

He did.

So did I, pulling up a seat in front of his desk and leaning forward, with my elbows on my knees.

"Dr. Wolf," I said, conscious of how closely Nat and Larry Fizner were listening to what was going on. "Here's the situation:

"A little over two years ago two men came into the possession of a videotape . . . this video tape—"

I lifted the tape for the doctor to see.

"—which records, in excruciating detail, the murder of one Bernard Hilton . . ."

"Murder!" the doctor exclaimed.

I nodded gravely.

"Yes, Doctor, murder most foul, and most carefully carried out."

Briefly, I ran over what was on the tape, keying it with the fact that the doctor, given the extent of Hilton's injuries resulting from the severity of his automobile accident, had neglected to note the existence of a single hypodermic puncture wound in the victim's right thigh.

"A perfectly understandable oversight on your part, Doctor," I said, "but one for which it was intended that you pay quite dearly. For, you see, what happened next was even more ingenious.

"Someone then wrote that anonymous letter claiming that you deliberately falsified Mr. Hilton's autopsy results, and sent it to the Cleveland Police Department's Special Operations Division, knowing that that particular city agency was already interested in Mr. Hilton's activities. Coming as it did in the middle of their existing investigation, it made your position look very suspicious. But, lacking any solid evidence, since the letter didn't say specifically what it was that you supposedly overlooked, the police simply

opened a file with your name on it, and held on to the letter
while keeping an eye on your activities."

"My God," Dr. Wolf groaned. "This is so, so, Kaf-
kaesque."

"That was the first event," I continued, "designed to cast
a shadow on your reputation. Step two served to deepen
that shadow, and it happened the day R.L. Webster was
killed. Because, in fact, Mr. Webster was not killed that
day; he did the killing, of an innocent homeless man, who
he burned to death after outfitting him with a set of parole
papers identifying the corpse as himself.

"A confederate, posing as a local street person who had
just stumbled over the body while looking for a place
to sleep, then called the police, who responded, taking
pictures of the crime scene when they arrived. But while
they were waiting for you to show up, they were called
away by the sounds of gunshots down the street . . . a fact
that's documented in their original incident report forms, as
well as in records of their radio transmissions. Together, the
two officers went to investigate, and, while they were gone,
Mr. Webster used the time to burn the body again . . . this
time, quite severely. When you arrived on the scene to
conduct your initial investigation, taking the photographs
that appeared in the final, official report of the case, the
condition of the body appeared to have been significantly
changed from the way the investigating officers had found
it, by *you*.

"But the only witness to what you actually did to the
body while you were alone with it was the man you had
with you taking pictures, who, it was suspected, was your
confederate, and would never contradict your story. So, for
the second time, information documenting the suspicious
activity of the county's head pathologist and chief medical
examiner enters the secret file being kept at City Hall.
Further evidence to serve as yet another brick in the wall
of your cell.

"Then, two years later, comes the death of Frank Lyttle,
whose dental X-rays, it is found upon examination, just
happen to match those of your second suspicious case,

as documented in the police department's file. How is this amazing development discovered? Why, by the even more remarkable discovery of a driver's license bearing another man's name in Frank Lyttle's shoe! Eureka! Isn't it amazing?

"You were being set up, Dr. Wolf. Can you see that now? Somebody was going to great lengths to establish a pattern of misconduct on your part that, if exposed, could lead to your utter humiliation by implying that you were in the pocket of someone committing murder. Interpreted as they stand, things look very much as if you were conned into agreeing to cover up Bernard Hilton's murder, and, because you dirtied yourself once, you had no choice but to go along with the others, for fear of exposure. Can you see it? Do you understand how the pieces all fit together to form that particular pattern?"

"But why, Mr. Hawley?" Dr. Wolf asked, his face ashen, all resistance gone from his demeanor. "Why would someone do this to me?"

"Money, Dr. Wolf," I replied. "Plain and simple. Money."

"But I've received no demands for money," he protested. "No one's contacted me at all!"

"It wasn't you they were interested in blackmailing," I replied. "Think back to the origin of all these problems: It was Bernard Hilton's murder. Bernard Hilton, who was already being investigated by the police. He's the source of your worries, Dr. Wolf. Somebody paid to have him killed. Oh, yes. Paid. Someone produced money to insure that Mr. Hilton died in a particular way, and that person demanded proof of the act in the form of a videotape of the actual event. It was that videotape which, when stolen, became the key to this entire affair. And that videotape was stolen from your house, Dr. Wolf. From your house. Now do you understand? Any light in the dark yet?"

"*My* house?" he demanded.

I nodded, and said, "Think about it."

I could see him doing just that. When the answer finally hit, he said, "You can't mean . . ."

And, when I nodded my agreement, he fell back in his seat with a gasp, his ability to choose words apparently escaping him for the moment.

During the interlude, I asked, "Does the location slip 14, dock C, at the pier, mean anything to you, Doctor?"

Numbly, he nodded, looking down at his hands, which he had folded atop the desk, saying, so softly that I could just make out the words, "Yes. It's where I keep my boat."

I felt a tingle overrun the skin on my face.

Then Rusty Simmons knocked on the door, bearing the photographs I had asked him to collect. I quickly searched the faces of all the people who had been taken on as morgue security guards during the past three years, found the one I wanted, and departed, leaving Dr. Wolf and Rusty looking at each other, with Nat and Larry following on my heels.

TWELVE

■ ■ ■ ■ ■ ■ ■ ■ ■ ■ ■

"*DR. WOLF'S WIFE?!*" Nat exclaimed once we were in the van, heading home.

I nodded.

"Obviously. Who else could it have been?"

"I don't understand," she complained.

So I laid it out:

"Bernard Hilton was a crook, okay? We know that, from the fact that the cops were investigating him, and even from the goddamn newspapers. Everybody knew it, including, presumably, his wife. Not only was he a crook, but he was a cheat, running around with any woman who would have him, which included quite a few, since he had so much money.

"But think about it: What did his wife do after her husband 'accidentally' died? She took over his businesses herself. She's a tough lady. A fighter. You think a woman like that is just going to stand by and let her husband make a fool of her, in public, in the newspapers, having his picture taken in his limousine jaunting from one bar to another with any young cutie he could grab? No way. She went along with it for just so long before she hooked up with one of the shady characters her husband employed, who she paid to do him in. But to make sure there were no mistakes, she insisted that the killer tape the event, so she could see for herself what went down.

"Okay?"

"Okay." Nat nodded. "But it gives me the willies."

"Me too," I agreed, heading the van onto the freeway. "But it's the one scenario that fits all the facts.

"Now:

"Captain Video wastes his boss. Mrs. Hilton, who's got a boyfriend of her own, namely, Dr. Gordon Wolf, guarantees that the cause of death will be ruled accidental. I personally don't think that Dr. Wolf was a party to the crime. It just isn't his style; it's too much for me to believe. Instead, I think that he was set up to take the rap . . . or at least to look as if he were in a position to take the fall. But what I couldn't see before today was why somebody would want to do it that way . . . I just couldn't find an angle. And that's where that tape of Bernard Hilton's killing came in. As soon as I saw it, it hit me:

" 'Who would dare to record a murder?' I asked myself.

"And the answer came: 'Somebody who had no fear that the murder would ever be discovered.'

" 'But who could be so sure that the murder would remain hidden?'

"Answer: 'Somebody with an in at the coroner's office. Somebody who could guarantee the cooperation of the pathologist doing the autopsy.'

"See?"

Nat nodded. "But how can you be so sure that Dr. Wolf's not consciously involved?" she asked.

"Because I know how smart he is," I answered, squeezing the steering wheel and pushing the van up to seventy. In the back I could see Larry Fizner holding onto Ansel, who was swaying where he sat in response to the rocking of the van, ears pricked forward, tongue lolling to one side of his grinning mouth.

"If Dr. Wolf was going to cover up a murder, he'd do it in such a way that nobody would ever suspect. And I do mean nobody. If Bernard Hilton's death were the only suspicious case we could link him to, then I'd say, 'Okay, he might have done it.' But three goofy killings, and every one with a paper trail? Funny photos and driver's licenses inexplicably popping up to link this body with the one that he's already examined? No way. It just didn't wash. It was too much to swallow.

"As far back as when Margaret Taylor was laying out the evidence for me in that warehouse, I knew something was wrong. I just couldn't tell what it was. But everything just seemed so clumsy, and stupid. You could follow the trail back to the doctor so easily that I knew an intelligent man like him would never have left such a glaring mess behind. If the Dr. Wolf I knew was really going to put his ass on the line, I knew that he'd do it in such a way as to fool even the brightest cop."

"So Dr. Wolf didn't misidentify Webster and Lyttle deliberately?" Nat asked.

I shook my head. "No way. He did as good a job as he could, given the evidence he had to work with. But that evidence was altered, in some cases even before he had a chance to see it, and it happened right there in the morgue."

"How?"

"Simple:

"Remember when Jackal told me that it was a guy named Eddie who worked at the morgue? That was the key. Here—" I handed over the photograph I'd taken from the stack Rusty Simmons had brought up to Dr. Wolf's office just before we left. "I had Rusty pull the files on everybody who's worked security at the coroner's office during the past three years. I was willing to bet dollars to doughnuts that Eddie's picture was going to turn up in that list. And it did. This is it. That's Eddie. I first met him on the roof of the warehouse the night Jackal sang me his song about looking to the stars. He's been a security guard at the morgue for over two years now. Security guards have passkeys. And a passkey is all he needed.

"Now follow this:

"Elizabeth Hilton pays Captain Video to kill her husband, stipulating that she wants a tape of the event as proof that it was done exactly in the way she prescribed. Captain Video does the job, with Jackal—with whom he was acquainted from prison and from the Hound's Tooth bar and the dog fights—as his cameraman, slash, accomplice. Okay?"

Nat nodded.

"Now," I continued, "Jackal, who fell in love with R.L. Webster when they were in prison together in New Jersey—I thought it was Joe Pace he was in love with, which is why it took me so long to figure this thing out—is indiscreet, and ends up telling Webster, the love of his life, about what he and Captain Video did. Webster, who's partnered up with Joe Pace on burglary jobs in the past, decides to scarf the tape of the killing and sell it back to the money lady at a profit.

"But something goes wrong . . . and once they have the tape, the two burglars get cold feet. Maybe the lady's tougher than they anticipated. Or maybe Captain Video is. But for whatever reason, they end up sitting on the tape for a while . . . during which R.L. Webster spends a little time in jail for a parole violation. When he comes out he rigs it, with Jackal's help, so that it looks as if he was killed in that warehouse. Remember, Bernard Hilton had a reputation for employing guys with criminal records, so it wasn't hard for Webster to land a job as a night watchman for one of Hilton's properties. Once it looks like Webster bit the big one for the final time, Joe Pace, his partner in crime, changes his name to Frank Lyttle, and the pair of them go underground . . . so to speak . . .

"For a while.

"They hide the videotape in that junkyard, and just to keep each other honest, they each keep one key: Joe Pace had the one that unlocked the car's door, and R.L. Webster had the one for the glove compartment. That way neither one of them could monkey with the tape without the other one knowing. Either that, or it was symbolic. I don't know. But they each had one key, that's the point. Okay?"

Nat nodded again.

"Okay," I said. "Time goes by. Money gets tight. Both Webster and Pace know that the tape's just sitting there, waiting to be used. There's no statute of limitations on murder, so whenever they feel like it, they can use the evidence they have to squeeze money out of Elizabeth Hilton—now Mrs. Elizabeth *Wolf*, after her marriage to the pathologist. And remember, not only has the lady just married a hot-shot doctor with a rising reputation, she's also taken over her late husband's business interests and is, without a doubt, one of the richest and most influential ladies in town. To Webster and Pace, contacting Mrs. Hilton would be like making a trip to the bank. Or at least that's how they'd see it.

"But she was tough once, and there's no reason to believe that she's any less tough now. So instead of squeezing her directly, Webster and Pace decide to go after her at an angle. Instead of setting her up personally as the target, they use her new husband's reputation and career as their point of attack. They already know that, as far as anyone on the outside is concerned, it can easily be made to look as if Dr. Wolf was in on the killing of Bernard Hilton, since he didn't discover the hypodermic mark during the autopsy of a murdered man whose widow he would soon go on to marry. He was also duped by the burning death of R.L. Webster . . . another costly mistake. With a little finessing, it wouldn't take much to create the impression of a connection between the two events, thereby making a case for the doctor's being crooked. Which is exactly what they did:

" 'Either pay up, or we ruin the Wolfman professionally for life.'

"Elizabeth Hilton, now Mrs. Wolf, might be a tough lady willing to go toe to toe for herself. But now she's got her new husband's life on the line. Dr. Wolf's professional reputation is everything to him, and it always has been. So she makes her fatal error: She agrees to pay. But instead of the whole tape, she gets a piece, a couple of minutes. If she wants more, she has to pay more. And it goes on that way. But all the while, Captain Video's zeroing in . . . sniffing the ground like a bloodhound, trailing his master's tormentor.

"Eventually he figures out where Joe Pace works . . . remember? The foreman on the construction job told me that a 'Hell's Angel-looking guy' had been visiting Little Frank for about two weeks before his death. I think they gave him a chance to make good and come up with the rest of the tape. When he didn't, Captain Video chased him down and tried to force him to tell where it was hidden by turning Congo loose on him. But Pace didn't talk. And Webster, who was dead as far as anybody else knew, used his partner's death as yet one more link in his chain of blackmail.

"This Eddie, the security guard at the morgue, was the guy who insured that the bum who was burned would be identified as R.L. Webster. The scam was easy enough. While they were waiting for the dental X-rays to come from the Lucasville prison, he took the authentic X-rays of the burned body out of the file and replaced them with a pre-arranged set taken of Webster specifically for the purpose. Then, when the charts from Lucasville arrived, they couldn't help but match, and since the body was so badly burned that fingerprint comparisons were impossible, Webster was officially entered into the book as deceased, and the case was closed.

"Then, when the time came to confuse the issue with Frank Lyttle's body, Eddie removed Frank Lyttle's X-rays from his file and replaced them with yet another copy of R.L. Webster's. Then, when the two-year-old Webster file was pulled, lo and behold, the charts matched again . . . and Dr. Wolf looked like a schnook twice over. The whole thing entailed nothing more complicated than the opening of a drawer and the exchange of a couple of films. And since Eddie, the security guard, had a passkey, opening a drawer was simple."

"But how can you be so sure that Dr. Wolf really didn't agree to cover up Bernard Hilton's killing?" Nat asked, frowning in concentration as she tried to follow my reasoning.

"I'm not sure," I admitted. "At least not absolutely. But it just doesn't sound right to think he did. To me, it sounds a hell of a lot more likely that he inadvertently gave his girlfriend the idea for the murder after she pumped him for information. You know, like pillow talk: 'Oh, Gordie-poo, you're so smart. If you were going to kill somebody, how would you do it?' Or maybe not. Who knows? But whether he knew about the murder in advance or not, Dr. Wolf very considerately went along with the plan by ruling Bernard Hilton's death accidental. When he did that, he set the stage for this whole, goddamn mess."

"So what do we do now, go to the police?"

I shook my head.

"We can't. We haven't got enough evidence."

"Not enough evidence? How much do you need?"

"What we've got's circumstantial, at best. And open to interpretation at worst," I said. "Which is exactly why Margaret Taylor got me involved in the first place. I haven't dug up all that much that's new. I've just worked out what's underneath it in a way she couldn't. Plus I got the tape. We can't use it to make a case against Webster, or even Mrs. Wolf, because the only people on it are good old Mitch Krammer and Jackal. But it's enough to satisfy Margaret Taylor's needs. Now she can call the dogs off Dr. Wolf, and send them yapping in a different direction. Dr. Wolf's in the clear, and, as far as I'm concerned, this job is finished."

"Really?" Nat asked.

I nodded, and glanced up at the rearview mirror, saying, "That sound about right to you, Mr. Fizner? Don't you think that it's about time for us to retire from the field?"

He didn't answer. But his serious eyes held mine in the mirror.

I looked back at the road. The silence in the van grew, got heavy, and then became positively oppressive. I glanced into the rearview mirror, then at Nat, then at the road, and then back at Larry Fizner in the mirror.

"Jesus Christ!" I cursed, pulling the van over onto the shoulder and slamming it into Park so hard that it lurched on the gravel. "Okay, what do you guys want from me? Huh? What am I supposed to do?"

Neither of them said a word, but their unexpressed dissatisfaction was so plain that they didn't need to.

"Gim'me a cigarette," I demanded of Larry Fizner, who complied, holding his lighter up for me and briefly illuminating the van's interior. Over the flame I looked at Nat, expecting her to protest that I shouldn't be smoking. But she wasn't going to make it that easy.

I leaned back in my seat, staring at the cones of light thrown by the van's headlights and feeling the swoosh and bounce of passing cars. It was dark . . . nearly ten-thirty at night. A light drizzle was falling—more like hanging— glittering like tiny bugs in the glare. I inhaled and blew smoke out my window.

Finally, still staring straight ahead, I said, "Okay, so Krammer's probably going to waste Webster when he shows up for the money tonight. Or at least that's what it sounds like the plan is from the tape. We could call the cops, I suppose; explain it all and let them handle it."

I fidgeted with my cigarette.

"Although, even if we called right this second, they'd have less than an hour to organize and get there, so they'd either be late, or, if they did show up in time, end up scaring everybody off. So Krammer and Webster would just make another arrangement for another meeting some other time, and we'd probably never see them again. But so what?"

I inhaled . . . blew smoke.

"Fucking Krammer is a sadistic son of a bitch. There's no telling how many people he's done in. And Elizabeth Hilton! Now there's a piece of work. But . . ."

I looked at Nat's eyes, twinkling in the dashboard lights.

"But what can we do?" I asked earnestly.

"I don't know," she returned. "But we ought to do something. We can't just leave it."

"Mr. Fizner," I said. "Any suggestions?"

Silence from the back.

"Ansel? How about you?"

Ansel yapped when I said his name, which didn't help me much at all.

"Dammit!" I hissed, pitching my cigarette out the window and picking up the car phone. Calling information, I got the number I wanted, dialed, and listened as the line rang. When I got through I asked my questions, got my answers, left my phone number and hung up, sighing and setting my hands on the steering wheel as I said, "Jackal's real name is Jackson Tucker. He went to the police station, just like I told him to. When he got there, he said exactly what I told him to say. Margaret Taylor's on her way down there right now. When Jackal mentioned her name, the cops at the station house had sense enough to call the number I'd given him. When she shows up, they're going to have her call me."

"So?" Nat asked.

"So, we've got a witness against Mitch Krammer, and R.L. Webster too," I said. "Jackal knows plenty. He can burn them both, which changes things." Glancing at her one last time, I asked, "But you're sure about this now? You really think we've got to see it through?"

She looked at me for a long moment before finally saying, "Yes. I'm sure. Let's do it."

When I hit the gas, Larry Fizner whooped in the back.

The pier wasn't far from where we were, maybe twenty minutes away, which meant that we pulled up a good half hour before Mitch Krammer had scheduled his meeting with R.L. Webster. Being April, and Cleveland—where it's been known to snow in May—there weren't very many boats outfitted for use yet, and the pier, which was part of an exclusive yacht club, had a spooky, ghost-town feel to it, lying there next to the dark lake, with boats wrapped in canvas, and limp rigging lines swaying like dead vines in the chilled night breeze.

Personally, I don't know shit about boats. But Nat does. She was raised on the water, and had sailed Interlakes all during her childhood and right through high school. If you don't know what an Interlake is, don't feel bad. She's explained it to me three times, and I still couldn't pick one out; though I understand they take three people to crew.

The setup looked like this:

The pier was not a beach. It was a rocky strip of shoreline that had been heavily developed and built upon, with a section of tended lawn leading up to a spot where the ground just dipped, falling sharply thirty or forty feet to a perfectly flat area that ran to the water. Atop the drop was a high cyclone fence, and along the decline, railroad ties had been set into the hillside like steps. Where the flat area started at the bottom, the ground had been paved into a private street which ran along the shore, accessible only from a tended entry gate a mile and a half or so east of where we were sitting. The boat slips were lined tightly along the water's edge, demarcated by flag poles upon which yellow triangles were posted, marked with black numbers and lit by light bulbs at the top. Nearly every slip had a boat docked in it. And nearly every boat was wrapped up for the winter. The slip closest to where we were parked—at the top of the hill, headlights out, looking down on the long stretch of docks below—was number 128. We were looking for number 14. Apparently, it was a ways down the line, which diminished the chances that someone might have noticed our arrival.

I turned the engine off and leaned back in my seat, heart pounding. We had arrived . . . we were there: flying. That's how I think of it, as flying, when I get that sensation: queasy stomach, tingling digits, cotton mouth, head rush. I had it back at the Coffee Grinder when Rusty Simmons first told me of the inexplicable details concerning R.L. Webster's death, and then, in a slightly more pronounced fashion, at the construction site when I first started asking the questions that had led us here, and again, in varying degrees of intensity, all the way through to the present. This was the culmination . . . the rush . . . the payoff. This was what it was all about, though I hated to admit it. I'd given up the booze, and taken up risk instead. I was hooked.

"Well?" Nat asked, making me blink as I turned her way. "What's the plan?"

I blinked again.

"Ah, Mr. Fizner. What do you think?"

"I think that this Krammer guy's the brass ring," he replied, coming up to the front and sticking his head between the seats. "If Jackal's playin' us square at the police station about really being ready to cut a deal, then he can finger Krammer as the button man on the Hilton job. Then Krammer can turn around and try to save his own ass by fingering the dead guy's wife as the one who hired him to do her husband's killing."

"But what about Webster?" Nat asked.

Larry kind of shrugged, saying, "That's iffy. Jackal can testify against him, since he was there the night they cooked the hobo, but who knows if he will or not? He went to the cops 'cause he was scared. It's anybody's guess how long he's gon'na stay that way. Besides, not only would it be Jackal's word against Webster's that the hobo was murdered in the first place, but admitting that the murder ever happened at all would essentially mean that he'd be confessing to being an accessory to a second major crime. There's not a shred of physical evidence left to verify his story, and the body's been long since cremated. No jury's going to convict in a capital offense on the word of a guy who's already admitted to being an accessory in another killing, and how much plea bargaining is a judge going to do for a guy like Jackal, anyway?"

"So we should do what?" I asked.

"Well," Larry mused, "I guess we should try to keep Krammer and Webster from killing each other. 'Cause that's what I imagine they're gon'na try to do."

"You mean Webster's going to get away with it?" Nat asked, still dwelling on Larry's previous point. "Are you saying that there's nothing anyone can do to him for burning a man alive?"

Larry nodded.

"Yup."

"Jesus," Nat whispered.

My car phone rang.

Margaret Taylor was at the police station, her voice sounding tight with restrained enthusiasm. I could see her in my mind, probably sitting behind some off-duty detective's desk—"Use that phone, lady. Such and such won't mind"—with four or five curious cops standing around, listening to her conversation and wondering what the hell was going on. She would be conscious of their prying eyes and ears, and therefore wouldn't dare show what she was feeling. Keep it cool . . . keep it simple. Keep it on a par with the way the boys would play it, because that's what she always did . . . She always knew that the game was rigged against her because she was a woman, and therefore she had to be just that much tougher, win that many more times, and score that many more points along the way. And with that foot of hers . . . God, it was no wonder that she was such an overachiever.

"It's a very positive development," she said, referring to Jackal's surrender. Then she explained that she and Jackal had spoken briefly, and that he had expressed his willingness to cooperate in exchange for certain considerations. He had mentioned my name. And, without specifically revealing the extent of his knowledge, for fear of diminishing its value in a trade, he had brought up certain names and dates which had sent Ms. Taylor's professional head spinning.

"He says you've got physical proof to back up his claims," she concluded. "Is that true?"

I told her that it was, mentioning the videotape for the first time.

"My God," she breathed. "Okay. Where are you, Mr. Hawley?"

I was thinking about the wisdom of telling her, weighing it against the notion that we would be better off without the cops rushing in. But finally my sense of self-preservation overruled my flair for the dramatic, and I told her, explaining the situation, and saying that care had to be taken in the capture of our suspects.

"It should go pretty easy," I said. "We'll go down and watch, while you guys cordon off the exit. Then you can just pick them up as they're trying to leave. If we keep it low-key, there shouldn't be any trouble."

"That's exactly what I don't want," Ms. Taylor agreed. "Trouble. I don't want any hostages, and I definitely don't want any shooting. Can you promise me that, Mr. Hawley? I'm not going to even bother telling you to stay out of the way, because I know you won't listen. But can you promise me that you won't do anything foolish before we arrive?"

"Now would I do that?" I asked, and clicked off the phone.

"Well?" Nat said.

"She's sending the cavalry," I replied, opening my door. "So all we've got to do is sit tight and wait."

Right.

I had a set of tools in the drawer under the passenger's seat of the van. As I used a pair of wire cutters to snip a hole in the cyclone fence through which we could pass to the hill and the tarmac below, I was thinking that maybe what I was doing wasn't such a hot idea. Let them kill each other, a voice in my head was saying. Who cares? Having seen Congo, my money was on Mitch Krammer anyway. As far as I could tell, he was the one who was going to walk out of this thing in one piece, and he was the one we wanted anyway. So why should we risk our butts playing referee until the cops arrived? As Larry had already said, we didn't have much of a case against Webster anyway. If Congo ate him, it would be no more than what he deserved. Actually, as the last snip set the section of fence upon which I'd been working curling into a loop that went rolling down the hill before I could grab it, I had just about decided that a scenario in which Mitch Krammer killed R.L. Webster, and the cops caught him red-handed at it, would be the best for everybody concerned.

But then I thought, What if it doesn't work out that way? What if Webster's too smart, and it's him who ends up walking away with the money, leaving Mitch Krammer lying on the dock with a bullet in his head?

That would be fine too, I decided. Even better, maybe. Then the cops would nab Webster for Krammer's murder, and justice would be done the long way around.

So why were we doing it—Larry, Nat, and I? Why were we crouching down and stepping through the hole I had cut in the fence?—Nat with Ansel on his leash, flowing blackly like a panther in the dark down the hillside, the rest of us picking our way by the feeble light of a moon filtered through clouds so dark that the sky looked heavy. Then I thought, They've both got it as bad as I do! They're hooked, and they need to know.

When we got to the paved road at the bottom of the hill, Ansel's toenails clicked on the concrete, his dog tags jingling as he trotted along at Nat's side. We were so close to the docks, we could now hear the water lapping below, and smell the lake rot rising from the debris that had accumulated around the hulls of the boats during the winter: dead fish, floating junk, gunk, slime, and dirty bubbles. I didn't see it, but then again I didn't need to. I'd seen it before, and the smell was enough, even in the April chill. Larry already had his gun out. I was almost regretting that I hadn't bought one earlier in the evening. Then I thought, So if you had one, what would you do with it? Shoot somebody?

No . . . I knew I wouldn't shoot anybody . . . but the gun might have been nice as a kind of display . . . something to wave around so that the bad guys could see how formidable I was.

I checked my watch, finding that it was nearly eleven-thirty, which was zero hour.

I was looking for the motorcycle with the sidecar . . . or some kind of vehicle that R.L. Webster would have used . . . or a limousine. Yeah, I was looking for a limousine, because the wealthy, former Mrs. Hilton was involved, and in my mind I could see the hand-over going down as a kind of set piece from a movie, with the black six-door Cadillac sitting on the dock, its tinted, mirrored windows rolled up, and Webster standing at its side with a briefcase. A window rolls down, a woman's hand in a white, elbow-length glove passes a bundle of money wrapped in brown paper to Webster, who takes it with one hand, passing the briefcase over with the other. The window silently slides back up, and the limo pulls away, leaving Webster to chuckle and skip back into the darkness. But in reality I didn't see anything. Not a single vehicle was anywhere around.

When we got to slip 40, Larry whispered, "This'll do it," and Nat reared back on Ansel's leash. From where we were standing we could see that there were lights on at slip 14, and that the boat that was docked there, a long, low, gorgeously expensive-looking thing that had to be a good sixty feet long, was not outfitted for storage like its slip mates, but set and ready to sail. The lights came both from the docking lamps set along the hull of the ship, and from the portholes in the cabin, which glowed yellow with light from within.

"You know," Nat whispered, "I just thought of something. Since we've got the tape, what the hell is Mr. Webster planning to sell?"

"A copy," I answered. "That video machine in the hotel was equipped to duplicate. I'm sure he made more than one copy, just to be safe."

"Then how can Mrs. Wolf be sure he'll ever leave her alone? What's to stop him from coming back with another copy in a couple of weeks and demanding to be paid again?"

"Nothing," I said. "Which is why Krammer's going to kill him. A guy like Webster's too greedy to back off. He'll be nothing but trouble as long as he's alive."

Larry Fizner, standing a couple of steps to my left, lifted a hand to indicate that Nat and I should be quiet. Then he said, very softly, "You know, the one thing that's bothering me about this is that I can't spot a baby sitter."

"A what?" Nat asked.

"A baby sitter," Larry repeated. "Somebody to act as a lookout. On something as important as this, I'd think that both of 'em would bring somebody to watch their backs, just to be safe."

I hadn't thought of that before, and the notion ran through me like a shudder. Immediately I was tingling, reaching out to grab Nat's hand, and looking over the dock with renewed suspicion. I had been concentrating all my attention on the boat lights, forgetting entirely that there might be other eyes watching from the dark.

It was at that instant—and I do mean at that very, god-damn instant—that we heard the sound of running feet. Not a man's feet, but an animal's—a big animal—running right at us over concrete.

Congo looked like a demon in the dark. His shape was vaguely defined in its most elemental dimensions, creating the fluid impression in my mind of a flowing lick of dark-ness moving toward us from the lake. He had apparently been sitting at the land end of the gangplank, up between the boats, and had watched our approach in silence. He had obviously been waiting for us to get even closer, but since we'd halted, he'd given us a few minutes to decide if we were going to close the distance between ourselves and him any further, given up the notion, and decided to charge. Now he was bearing down in a rush, running silently, save for the heavy patter of his feet on the cement and a kind of rumbling purr that came at us as a hard-edged series of grunts and growls.

There were maybe thirty yards between us, and the big dog was closing it fast . . . covering the distance much more quickly than it's taken me to describe him doing it. We had an instant to act, and we wasted it because all three of us simply froze, the image of the dog bearing down doing something to us that shut down the human part of our brains for a second, and left the animal part of our makeup to tremble nakedly in sickly fascination at the predator that had chosen us as its prey.

Congo finally barked when he was no more than thirty feet away, and the sound made something in us snap, sending us scattering like birds. I went for Nat; Larry went the other way, fumbling with his gun. But before he could squeeze off even one shot, the Tosa was there, snarling with an explosion of pure rage.

But it wasn't us that Congo wanted. It was Ansel, who, inhibited by the leash Nat still held, yapped once, and then—

Congo was on him.

They came together with a horrible crash, rolling immediately into a ball of thrashing fur as the leash was torn from Nat's hand, and she screamed. Then, even more quickly than it had taken to happen, Ansel was up and running, with Congo on his heels in pursuit.

I turned, finding that Larry Fizner, gun still in hand, was giving orders.

"Let them go!" he said, waving his free hand at the water. "You and Nat get over there, on one of those boats. I'll see what's going on with the meeting. All this noise is going to fuck up everything!"

For a second I was stunned by Larry's single-minded focus on our original task, and angry, just for an instant, that he seemed to have written Ansel off as a loss. But then I saw the sense in what he said, and, pulling on Nat's arm, I practically dragged her toward the water. She fought me at first, straining the other way and insisting that we had to do something to help the poor German shepherd. But it didn't take long for her to realize that there was nothing we could do, and that we needed to be ready when Congo came back . . . because he would come back.

He would.

Kicking off his shoes as he ran, Larry was in a crouch that took him around and out of the line of sight of the big yacht's forward-most cabin. The door on that cabin was opening in response to Congo's barking, throwing light out in a yellow arc onto the gleaming teakwood deck. Nat and I were moving the other way, down the dock between the boats, toward the aft portion of the yacht, where there was a second boat, done up for storage, docked close enough for us to jump aboard. For some reason I wanted to climb. Go figure. But literally all I could think of at that instant was that, when Congo finished off Ansel and came back for me, I wanted to be sitting on top of one of the docked boat's masts . . . like a raccoon treed by a hound. Which brings me to a very uncomfortable admission:

During that initial instant when Congo first showed himself, something had happened to me that doesn't make me very proud: With the first realization of what was happening, a rolling wave of panic absolutely paralyzed my mind. All I could see was the dog that had mauled me when I was a boy, and a sheer insensibility nearly blinded me with an unutterable desire to run . . . to hide . . . to do absolutely anything that would remove me from the path of the oncoming dog. I didn't think of Nat. I didn't think of Larry. I didn't think of anyone or anything but myself. It was pure self-concern, self-interest, self self SELF, that was in my eyes, in my mind, in my bones. It didn't last long. But it would have if I hadn't consciously forced it away. And even after I had, I'm not so sure it was completely satisfied. I was so scared, I was dizzy with it. If it hadn't been Nat, my wife, my life's center, who was with me, I don't think that there's another human being on the planet whose presence could have cut through my totally irrational absorption with myself.

But it was Nat . . . Nat's hand was in mine, her flesh was touching my flesh, we were together, and, in a way, my self-concern extended to her as well, for I didn't think of her as separate at that moment. I saw, I think, the pair of us as a single entity . . . and all my heart wanted nothing more than to protect that entity from Congo's teeth and jaws.

So as I threw Nat—literally threw her by grabbing her around her waist and heaving her aboard the docked yacht next to the one with the burning lights—I wasn't paying nearly enough attention to what was going on around me as I should have been. It took me a few minutes to re-orient myself—and by the time I did, things were moving way too fast.

THIRTEEN

■■■■■■■■■■■■■

THE YACHT ONTO which I'd heaved my wife had a canvas tarp stretched over it so tight that it was like the surface of a drum. The tarp started at a peak over what I assumed was the cabin's roof, and proceeded down at an angle to the edge of the deck—pardon me if I don't have the nautical lingo right—where it was secured by a series of deadeyes with nylon rope, like the cover for a back-yard swimming pool. Near the cabin, a white pole jutted straight up, which was the mainmast of the boat, and that pole had little foot rails running up it, leading to a crow's-nest thingamajig at the top. That's the spot from which I wanted Nat and me to see the rest of what was going to happen . . . that crow's nest. And I said so, loudly, almost shouting.

When I threw Nat, she landed on the canvas as if she had hit a trampoline, and for a nauseating moment I thought she was going to bounce right off and back onto the dock. But, as I've already said, she's been on boats for most of her life, and with an incredible dexterity she slid along the tarp, hands and feet splayed like a cat on ice, until she'd gained a purchase and was able to kind of bounce along toward the mast. I was still on the dock when she reached it, turned back, and looked at me.

"Go on!" I shouted. "Climb it!"

"What about you?" she asked.

I turned, wondering what I should do.

When I turned, this is what I saw:

A series of lights set into the ground had flashed on, probably controlled by a switch inside Dr. Wolf's yacht, though the logistics of connecting a free-floating boat to an electric line escaped me for the moment. As the lights blazed, I caught sight first of Larry Fizner disappearing around the doctor's boat, and the two dogs on the tarmac.

"Come on, Bill!" Nat urged.

But with a deep breath and a terrible flexing of the muscles in my chest and shoulders, I replied, "Get safe; I've got to help Larry!"

"No!" she was calling behind me, but I didn't reply. Moving instead along the doctor's yacht, approaching the cabin from behind, I saw the silhouetted shape of a man's head rise as he exited the door that had been opened, and I heard a muffled shout from inside the boat, saying, "What the hell's going on!"

"Looks like Congo snagged a stray," Mitch Krammer replied, the back of his head still all I could see as it peeped over the top of the cabin.

"Keep 'em up!" R.L. Webster ordered from inside, and Krammer raised his hands, one on either side, creating the classic portrait of a man held at gun-point. But instead of both his hands being empty, one gripped a rectangular black object, which immediately told me that he and Webster had already concluded their exchange. Krammer had the videocassette of the murder, which meant that Webster would have whatever money he'd been able to squeeze out of Mrs. Wolf, there, on the boat, in his possession.

That's when I thought of the bullet at the end of the key chain Mrs. Lyttle had given me, and the box of bullets I'd found in Frank Lyttle's dresser. I had wondered where the gun for the bullets was, and it looked like I had just found out.

I'd also wondered about all those CD's a much younger man than Frank Lyttle would own, realizing at that instant that they belonged not to Little Frank, but to his wife's brother, who had been following me in his dark green Nova earlier in the day.

Wonderful, I thought.

Then . . .

That was some plan, Captain Video. How the hell had he intended to finish Webster off if he had gone and allowed the other man to get the drop on him like that? Obviously, since it was Dr. Wolf's boat, and Krammer worked for the doctor's wife, it was Krammer who had been waiting aboard for R.L. Webster to arrive for their meeting. Hadn't he made preparations? Hadn't he known that Webster would come armed? Or had he made other arrangements that I had yet to discover?

A sound from shore caught my ear, drawing my attention back to what was transpiring between Congo and Ansel. Apparently, Krammer and Webster were also watching the confrontation. And by all appearances nothing was going to happen until it was over. Then Congo would come back, I knew, so I decided that I had best be ready.

But still, I couldn't help but watch. Despite all my intentions, I couldn't help it.

From where I was crouched next to the yacht, hidden in the darkest shadows between the boats, with the lights from the cabin and on the shore to illuminate the area in front of me, hiding me even more completely, I had a clear view of Ansel and Congo as they faced one another on the street. Seen this way, the remarkable difference in size between the two dogs was immediately apparent. Congo was easily twice as long as Ansel, and twice as heavy. As he moved, the musculature straining beneath his short tan fur was so defined as to make him look strangely developed . . . as if he, a dog, had been lifting weights. Ansel, on the other hand, looked almost scraggly in comparison. His brown and black fur was longer and less tight than the Tosa's, his posture less aggressive, more settled for defense, as if he knew that he didn't have a chance and was simply looking to stave off the inevitable for as long as he could.

"Congo's gon'na rip the shit out of him," Captain Video boasted happily, hands still upraised, one on either side of his head. His tone of voice was remarkably relaxed, and I wondered if his compliant attitude before Webster's gun hadn't been a part of their arrangement after all. He certainly didn't sound like a man who feared for his life, or who had been taken by surprise. And Webster, for his part, seemed at ease as well. There was no urging for Captain Video to either return to the boat's interior or to let Webster pass. The two men seemed content to just stand there and watch the dogs fight . . . as if they had all the time in the world . . . which, I realized, as far as they knew, they did.

When were Margaret Taylor and the cops going to show up? I wondered suddenly. Why wasn't I hearing any sirens?

Congo's style of attack was instantly obvious from the way he moved. Ansel, after that initial charge in which he had been bowled over by the Tosa—I quickly searched him over with my eyes, finding nothing that looked as if he'd been hurt yet—had deliberately led Congo away from where the three of us had been standing. He had run toward the center of the street, and stopped at a point that was virtually parallel to where Dr. Wolf's yacht was docked. Overhead, a street lamp glowed, a drifting haze of drizzle undulating in the glare. Below, dead center in the circular pool of light cast onto the concrete, Ansel had turned to face his opponent.

Congo apparently appreciated the situation, because he had settled into what I can only describe as a boxer's stance. He planted his back feet, more or less keeping them in one place as his front feet skittered on the ground, constantly making the tiniest adjustments to the angle of his head to his target. The muscles in his haunches were coiled and ready. He barked almost constantly, showing his awesome teeth, saliva flying, his eyes alight with fury. Several times he made as if to charge, pulling his great weight up as if he meant to lead not with his jaws but with his chest in an attempt to tackle the shepherd. But each time he must have seen something in Ansel's attitude that prevented him from making his move.

Ansel, for his part, couldn't have appeared less like the Tosa. Where Congo clearly fancied himself as the aggressor, Ansel seemed focused on his own, inner thoughts. He neither growled nor barked. His fur didn't bristle, and his teeth never showed. His tongue lolled as he breathed, very fast, making steam. But he didn't prance or jitter. He stood firm, eyes locked on Congo's every move. To the Tosa, this was the pit, a repeat performance of an experience he had obviously engaged in hundreds of times before, and one in which he had met with nothing but success. To Ansel, this was serious business, and he seemed to be approaching it more as a puzzle than a fight.

Congo froze for a micro-second, and then lunged. But instead of trying to avoid the burst, Ansel simply dipped his head, going in low and showing his teeth for the first time.

I don't think Congo had ever seen an opponent do anything but cringe before his roaring onslaught, because I swear the bigger dog looked downright surprised as he overshot his target and snapped at the air. Ansel, front legs bent so that his chest hugged the ground, came up under Congo, snapping twice, which sent the Tosa's back legs to pumping as he snarled, rolled, and, faster than I thought anything in the world could move, recovered and altered his angle of attack to bring his jaws in tight against Ansel's neck. Ansel pulled in on himself and folded up, looking as if he had simply collapsed, pulling himself out of the way of Congo's bite. But Congo, so fast as to appear to be a blur, still got a mouth full of fur, and at least a little skin, because, even from where I was standing, I could see a spurt of blood erupt behind Ansel's ear, and hear his yip of pain as he was up and biting back, grabbing hold of Congo's front leg and shaking hard before letting go and dancing back, ready for another assault.

"Jesus!" I heard Webster say. "He's good."

" 'Stray' my ass," Captain Video responded. "But still, Congo's gon'na turn him to hamburger."

"Wan'na bet?"

"How much?"

"A thousand?"

"Done."

"If I win, you can send my check to the Bahamas," Webster said, making me wonder what he was talking about.

As I glanced over at the two men, I caught sight of something moving on the yacht to my left, silently moving on stockinged feet to come up from behind where Webster and Krammer were standing, crouched low, gun silhouetted in one hand. Larry Fizner had climbed aboard, and was apparently getting himself in position. For what, exactly, I didn't know, but I didn't have time to worry about it. For, during the split second I had taken my eyes off the dogs, the Tosa had altered the tide of the exchange, and Ansel was in trouble.

I looked back just in time to see Congo charge, abruptly leaping forward and landing on his back legs as his front feet came down and collapsed, lowering his chest and neck so that his head came up and under, butting Ansel, who, not as fast as his opponent, had only been able to complete half an evasive move to the side before the Tosa got in his lick. Congo hit Ansel square on the chest with his snout, jerking his head up and to the right so hard that it lifted Ansel off his feet, hurling him back and sending him squirming, desperately trying to swing his own head back around so that the Tosa would at least remain in his line of vision. But Congo was just too damned fast, and by the time Ansel came down, landing on his side and rolling, all four legs pumping, teeth bared, the Tosa had anticipated his trajectory, and was planted close enough in to land a vicious series of bites in Ansel's flank. Ansel yelped and snapped ineffectually back. But by the time he got to his feet, Congo had placed two or three yards between them, and was settling himself for another charge.

There was blood on Ansel's side and neck now. True, there was a little blood on the Tosa's front leg too, but it was scant by comparison, and seemed to affect the bigger dog's mobility not a bit.

Now, it's important to visualize the physical lay of the
land around the dogs in order for what happened next to be
absolutely clear. The stretch of concrete was like a ribbon
laid along the very edge of the shoreline, ending in a curb
and a short fence made of iron posts set about four feet
apart and strung with three lengths of light, stainless-steel
chain. Every twenty feet or so the fence was interrupted
by a projection that jutted straight into the lake; and it was
between these projections, which were made of treated-
wood planks, that the boats were docked. From straight
overhead, the effect would have been to create a kind of
gapped-tooth pattern consisting of a dock, a rectangle of
water with a boat aimed nose to the shore, another dock,
another boat, etcetera.

Got it?

Okay.

Now, the reason it's so important that you see that particular physical arrangement clearly is because Ansel sure
did, and he used it in the only way he could, considering how badly he was doing in a straight-out match,
one-to-one.

Ansel tried an attack of his own, and the Tosa countered
it, snapping hard. Ansel tried to make an evasive move, and
Congo anticipated it, and landed a bite. Everything Ansel
did seemed useless, and he was slowing down. Even I could
see that. The brutality and force of the Tosa was sapping
his strength. And, given the disadvantage with which Ansel
had originally gone into the fight, his fatigue was sure to
give that final, fatal edge to his opponent. Ansel was going
to die, I was sure. He was going to die because he had
deliberately sacrificed himself by drawing the Tosa away
from the rest of us in order to give us time to escape. It was
a noble, and remarkable, action, and I truly, in that moment,
understood and appreciated the bond that Mr. Schimmel
felt for his dogs, this one in particular.

But Ansel wasn't finished yet.

Not by a long shot.

Congo's muzzle was flecked with the German shepherd's blood, and there was a madness in the bigger dog's

eyes that seemed to indicate that he sensed the end of
the match was at hand, and that the part that he enjoyed
the most, the killing—the final, snarling assault—was just
around the corner. He seemed so engrossed in what he was
doing that even the appearance of strategy left him, and he
abandoned himself to simply lunging and biting, falling
back, and lunging and biting again.

Just as he must have done to Frank Lyttle, I thought
sickly. That was the motion he performed, like a machine.
In, bite, and out. In, bite, and out. With Mitch Krammer
standing back with his leash wrapped around his huge fist,
inserting questions in between. For the first time the impact
of the scene struck me, and I knew that there was no way I
would ever let Krammer get away with what he had done.

No way.

From where the fight had begun on the street under
the lamp, the two dogs had more or less worked their
way toward the shore, their exertions taking them ever
closer to the water. Now they were directly in front of
Dr. Wolf's yacht, standing face-to-face not ten feet from
the big boat's nose, panting, dripping, each locked on the
other. Their attitudes since that initial, searching motion of
the battle had altered absolutely: Where Congo had been
the more active, and Ansel the steady, studying strategist,
now it was Congo who had settled into a quiet, deadly
calm, measuring the shepherd with his eyes, judging the
distance, preparing for the end. And, as if to keep the
Tosa's attention one hundred percent on himself, Ansel
had taken to barking and jittering, dancing around in his
place with his tongue virtually dragging on the ground,
saliva flying, blood seeping over his fur. At first I thought
it was desperation that was making him so overwrought,
but then I noticed a pattern.

The Tosa made as if to lunge twice, but Ansel's maneu-
vers prevented him. From standing face-to-face, Ansel to
my right, Congo to my left, the angle of the two dogs to
the lake had undergone a subtle change, and now Congo stood with his tail pointed directly at the nose of Dr.
Wolf's yacht—named *Sawbones*, I noticed for the first

time. Ansel was facing me, so that I could see his expression, and, I swear, as I watched—with the muscles in Congo's haunches flexing before my eyes so that I knew that the big dog was preparing for his final attack—I saw a look of absolute determination and abandon come into the German shepherd's eyes. Then he did something that he must have planned out carefully in his mind. He had been maneuvering Congo into place with his display of panic, feigning fatigue, and getting ready. Now he was giving himself over to one last, calculated move.

Ansel, to my utter astonishment, leaped to the attack. His body simply burst forward, his teeth a twin line of grinning, vicious white, his growl a rapid-fire staccato punctuating the air with its anger and strength. But instead of aiming himself at the Tosa, Ansel overshot his mark, and his momentum took him up, and over the bigger dog, who simply lifted his head, and elevated himself from the ground, aiming his teeth up at Ansel's exposed underside, intending, I'm sure, to eviscerate his victim with one horrendous bite.

"Ansel!" Nat screamed from behind me, lifting every hair on my body straight up.

Congo's roar was clear over the water, deep, and satisfied.

Ansel was airborne for a very long time.

Congo's teeth were perfectly aimed.

But—

Ansel had not overshot his mark, he'd hit it dead on. Where I had thought he had made a fatal error in judgment based on his excitement and terror, he had instead lulled both me and, much more importantly, the Tosa, into believing himself an easy kill. As he flew over Congo's head, Congo followed, snapping viciously and following Ansel's trajectory with his jaws, the rest of his massive body lifting and turning in the air as he did. Ansel cleared the Tosa, and for an instant I thought he'd end up in the lake, but then I saw the object of his leap, and my heart sang in my chest.

Ansel had used the lay of the dock to his advantage. He had jittered himself around until he had placed Congo with his back to the water, and he had made a jump over the bigger dog that took him from the concrete shore, cutting the corner of the slip where the *Sawbones* was docked, and down, onto the wood plank projection that jutted between the *Sawbones* and the boat in the next slip. Congo, trying to follow the shepherd's flight, had lifted himself into the air, but where Ansel cleared that corner of water that lay right behind the Tosa, Congo, in his blood-lust and excitement for the kill, snapped, turned, and brought his front legs down on empty air, plunging off the edge of the pier and down, five feet or so into the water.

He landed with a tremendous splash as Ansel, graceful, fluid, even dignified, alighted on the dock, turned, and looked back to see the result of his jump.

"Son of a bitch!" Mitch Krammer was shouting, apparently having missed, in his concentration on the fight, Nat's outburst of a moment before.

R.L. Webster was laughing as he pushed Krammer from behind, saying, "I'm out'ta here." Congo was splashing and snarling in the water, moving toward the dock and churning with black foam. And suddenly, from my extreme left, an engine started, bursting into life with a roar that startled me into motion.

I'm looking back at it now, so I might be adding things to my thoughts that weren't really there at the time. Or, more likely, I've been able to sort through the impressions racing through my mind and define them a little more neatly than they existed at the moment. But there were two separate notions screaming in my skull as I raced along the dock as the *Sawbones*' engine started, laying out a blanket of diesel fumes over the water and rumbling the air as Congo reached the pier. They were:

The yacht was part of the deal! Mrs. Wolf had given Webster whatever money he wanted, and she'd given him the boat as well! When he said that Krammer could send him a check in the Bahamas, he'd meant it. The fucker was slipping through our fingers, right before my eyes! He was slipping through our fingers, and there was nothing I could do about it!

And . . .

Congo was going to get out of the water, and when he did, he was going to kill us all!

Those were the two thoughts that were driving me forward, and the second only goes to show how little I really know about dogs, because, as Nat explained to me later, once he's in the drink, a dog can't pull himself back up. He doesn't have the right muscles in his chest and shoulders to go from his position in the water up to the dock, like a swimmer pulling himself up on the edge of a pool. Congo would have floundered there all evening, presenting absolutely no danger to anyone, and I could have concentrated on what I needed to do without fear. But my terror of dogs had overwhelmed me, and, irrationally, I had decided that it was Congo who I had to worry about. Not Mitch Krammer. Not R.L. Webster and his gun. But Congo. And that's where I was going . . . to get that dog.

There was a rowboat wrapped in canvas set on two pegs just a few feet down the dock. Atop it were a pair of oars. I could hear Mitch Krammer shouting, "What the fuck!" as soon as I showed myself, but I didn't care. I was concentrating on the oars, and as soon as I had one in my hand, I turned and lifted it over my head.

A loud THUD echoed on the dock behind me as Krammer landed, jumping from the *Sawbones*, shouting Congo's name. The oar in my hand was about five feet long, and made of wood that was slick with moisture and worn smooth in gentle contours. The yacht's engine raced noisily, washing out whatever Krammer was shouting and replacing it with a white-noise kind of sensation that made my ears ring. Congo, his wet fur pasted back on his face defining the contours of his predator's skull in a way that made his eyes bulge in their sockets and his teeth stand out even more prominently in a demonic, snapping grin of angry exertion, looked up at me, and then at the oar I had raised over my head. In that instant something inside me snapped, and all the hatred—no, not even that—all the fear, all the secret terror I had been harboring for so long, all the dog faces I had seen snapping at me through nightmare swirls as I churned the sheets on my bed with my legs and sweat poured from me in cold rivulets as I clawed my way back to consciousness from my own, private visions of fear, played out from childhood to the present, ripped to the surface and overcame me, making me tremble as I prepared to bring the oar crashing down on what I would later learn was actually a defenseless animal.

Then I felt hands on my back, and with a scream I pitched forward as Mitch Krammer pushed me from behind, sending me into the lake atop Congo, the oar flying from my hands, the world tipping wildly as my legs kicked up and over my head.

The water hit me with an icy blast that was like a solid punch to the gut. It drove the breath out of me as everything went black and my hands clawed through nothing. When my face broke the surface of the water again, my mouth open and gasping, my chest a simple spasm of muscle gulping air with a jerking arrhythmia that didn't really do much to fill my lungs, I saw a dark shape lift itself from the dock and bowl Mitch Krammer over as Ansel attacked.

I also saw something that made me think I'd been hit on the head: lights, flashing everywhere, like stars.

Red and blue.

The cops had finally arrived.

FOURTEEN

■ ■ ■ ■ ■ ■ ■ ■ ■ ■ ■ ■ ■

WHEN CONGO'S HEAD came blasting up from beneath the water, directly in front of me, no more than a foot away, I screamed and beat at it in a panic. All I could see was the big dog's jaws working on me in the dirty foam, churning it with my blood until my own head disappeared beneath the surface in a roar of bubbles. But Congo didn't bite at me. Instead he pumped his front legs and dog-paddled my way as I tried to swim back, keeping a distance between the two of us that he easily closed in less than thirty seconds. Then he was on me, like a drowning man, his steaming breath hot on my face, his eyes rolling with fear, his big front legs pawing at me so that his long nails gouged at my skin and his weight pressed me down.

"Bill!" someone shouted, as I fought to keep my head above water. "Grab on!"

My hand found the end of the oar Nat dipped toward me, gripped it, and held on as she pulled me toward the shore. Congo whined as I lifted myself up on the dock, pumping his legs desperately and snapping at the air. Mitch Krammer was on the ground, his back against a post on the pier, one hand lifted up as if to protect his face from

Ansel, who, molded in an attitude of defense, was keeping him prisoner where he lay. I quickly went over to the shepherd and disengaged the length of leash that still dangled from his collar, then returned to the dock, where I knelt and reached for Congo, who paddled instantly toward me. Grabbing his collar, I snapped the leash onto it and pulled him up, wrapping the leash around a docking post so that the big dog wouldn't drown, but not daring to pull him out of the lake for fear that his panic would fade and the old, aggressive monster he had been trained to be would re-emerge.

Then I turned, in time to see Larry Fizner running absurdly in place along the side of the *Sawbones* as it backed out of the slip. As the boat moved, Larry's feet pumped on the deck, and had the boat been stationary, he would have covered a lot of ground really fast. As it was, he remained parallel to one spot on the dock as from the aft portion of the cabin a flash erupted, and he threw himself forward, off the boat, to roll on the dock's planks, producing an echoing THUD!

The flash from the back of the boat was R.L. Webster's gun—an automatic from the sound of it—which cracked through the air with a quick BANG BANG BANG that sounded like firecrackers at a distance. At the end of his roll, Larry lifted himself immediately to one knee, his right arm held straight out, steadied by his left hand on his elbow as he leveled his .38 to return fire. But at that moment the *Sawbones* turned, pulling the stern of the ship across his line of sight, and hiding the aft portion of the cabin where Webster crouched, spinning the big steering wheel with both hands and throwing the accelerator full-throttle to blast up a roar of sound and throw bubbles and spray beneath a rolling cloud of exhaust that poured, it seemed, from all along the hull of the boat.

"Call him off!" someone demanded, and I turned to find a uniformed police officer, gun drawn, speaking to Nat from the end of the dock. Ansel had turned to face the cop, and was growling, his lip curled back, his long, curved front teeth exposed.

Nat went and knelt at Ansel's side, calling his name and putting her arms around the big dog's neck. Ansel relaxed then, nuzzling her, licking, closing his eyes. The cop immediately moved down the dock and drew Mitch Krammer to his feet by one arm, hustling him off the dock and removing the videotape from his hand. Larry Fizner, returning his gun to its holster at the base of his spine, stepped all the way down the dock, standing at its very end and watching as the *Sawbones* roared into the center of the bay and began its long, lazy turn to place its stern to the west, where R.L. Webster would take her out into the dark.

From the place that I stood, near where Congo still paddled in the water, I saw Margaret Taylor limping down the embankment from an unmarked police car, its red and blue lights flashing in the rear window, its headlights ablaze to silhouette her through a mist of exhaust pouring from its idling engine. They hadn't used the siren at all, keeping it off in order to arrive unannounced, I realized. They'd only turned the lights on at the last moment, to declare their presence. There was a second cop pulling himself from behind the steering wheel as the first hustled Mitch Krammer off the dock. And, when I had judged Margaret Taylor to be within earshot, I shouted, "He's getting away!" pointing out at the *Sawbones* as its running lights snapped on out on the water, outlining the big yacht against the solid black regularity of the breakwater lying low against the horizon to protect the bay about two hundred yards out.

It was at that instant that the arrangements I'd suspected Mitch Krammer had made to deal with R.L. Webster, but had failed to figure out, finally erased, once and for all, any hope I might have harbored that Webster would ever be apprehended.

As I watched, the *Sawbones'* engine sputtered, the long boat's shape gliding gracefully back and turning to place the yacht across my line of sight. The sky was overcast, and very dark, though the rain had stopped falling. There was therefore no moon, and the only light came from aboard the boat, three yellow circles along the cabin that reflected tiny licks of gold on the water's rippling surface. Near the back of the boat, Webster's dark shape was working the wheel, and, as the engine started into life again from the relative quiet of his shifting gears, he lifted one hand over his head as if to wave goodbye, a split second before the entire rear third of the boat was engulfed in the brightest light I have ever seen in my life.

The shock wave of the explosion hit me an instant later, knocking me back on my ass as my teeth came together with a CRACK! and my glasses, which had miraculously stayed on my nose all through my dip in the drink, landed in my lap. My ears were ringing and my hands trembling as I struggled to put them back on my face, then lifted my eyes in time to see flames erupt over the *Sawbones* as its stern came up out of the water and pieces of black debris spiraled slowly down all around, landing in the water, which was suddenly alive with golden fire. Flames danced and junk splashed and the yacht creaked and rolled over on its side, sliding under so quickly that it was hard for me to follow.

There was silence around me.

No one spoke.

Nat, I thought, climbing woozily to my feet and feeling the dock sway beneath me, either from the shock of the cold lake water or from the residual pounding of concussion in my ears. Before I could set myself to search for her, Nat had her hands on my arms, helping me to stand. I looked at her and pulled her close. She was crying, and I wasn't really all that surprised to discover that I was too. I don't know how long we stood like that, but when we finally broke our embrace, Larry Fizner was there, standing nearby, pointing toward the police car and saying something that I couldn't quite make out.

He repeated it, and the second time the words came through, though their sense escaped me.

"They shot him down," he said, for the third time, and I finally let Nat go and turned my eyes to follow his pointing finger.

Up on the street, lying like a pile of rags on the pavement before the idling car, vivid in the headlights, Mitch Krammer's body was motionless at the feet of a cop with a gun. There was smoke still swirling in the glare. The figure of Margaret Taylor stood off to one side, her back to the scene, facing the water where the *Sawbones* burned. The noise of the explosion had apparently drowned out the sound of the gunshot that had dropped Krammer where he lay.

I was running, I guess, before I even knew that I was doing it. Junk was still sailing down from the explosion, pattering on the pavement. The ringing in my ears had faded to a dull buzz.

"What happened?" I puffed, coming to a stop very close to the woman in the suit.

She turned to me, her eyes glittering with the reflection of the distant blaze, and said, "It was a bomb. He put a bomb on board and killed Webster."

"No!" I shouted. "There! What happened there?"

I was pointing behind me, in the general direction of Mitch Krammer's body, from where I could hear the crackle of static as one of the cops called for backup on his car radio.

"He tried to get away," Margaret Taylor said dully.

It was at that moment that I noticed the videocassette in her hand.

"I believe you said you also had a cassette," she said, extending her free hand as if expecting me to turn it over on the spot.

But I didn't make a move. Instead I said, my voice trembling, "He wasn't armed. You had them shoot down an unarmed man!"

"The cassette, Mr. Hawley," Margaret Taylor said, moving the fingers on her extended hand impatiently.

It was then, with the wreckage of Dr. Wolf's yacht burning to my left, and the body of Mitch Krammer lying on the street to my right, that the whole thing suddenly made sense. The truth was stunning, and lousy, and it made me curl my lip in rage as I shouted, "You didn't ever care about identifying those bodies! This is what you intended all along! It's her you've been protecting—HER! How much money does it take to buy a politician, Ms. Taylor?

Did she do it with cash, or were there fancy transfers of assets involved?"

Margaret Taylor's eyes narrowed, and the reflected fire dancing in them seemed to fade as another, hotter flame rose up from inside her head.

"I told you where my priorities were when we spoke at the warehouse, Mr. Hawley," she said, her voice hard and unequivocal. "I hardly think I need repeat myself. Now hand over the tape of Bernard Hilton's murder before I ask one of those policemen to relieve you of it!"

"But what about Jackal?" I asked. "He knows all about it. He was there!"

"Mr. Tucker and I have already come to an understanding," she replied. "His testimony will only serve to verify the obvious. Now, the tape if you please, Mr. Hawley. Now."

"Give it to her," a voice said at my back, and I turned to find Larry Fizner standing nearby, with Nat behind, Ansel at her side.

"No," I said.

"Give it to her, Bill," he repeated. "Then we'll go home."

"But it's not right," I cried, clenching my fists and setting my shoulders.

"He was trying to escape," Ms. Taylor repeated.

I turned to her, really mad.

"No!" I said.

I think she must have seen something in my face that made her decide to try another tack.

"You've got your licenses, Mr. Hawley," she said, apparently in an attempt to be reasonable. "And your funeral home's safe. The O.O.F.P. will be informed that you're a hero, and you'll be free to do as you please from this day forth. What else do you want, for God's sake?"

"The truth," I demanded.

An expression of quiet sadness came over the woman's face, as if she were trying to explain something obvious to a child.

"Mr. Hawley," she said. "Don't you see, there are so many things going on beneath the surface that you simply have no idea. And believe me, you don't want to know."

"I want the truth," I reiterated, pulling the videocassette from my pocket and holding it up. "Last trade, or no dice."

"Or else what?"

"I walk."

"I doubt it."

"Are you going to have your thugs shoot us all?" I asked. "Is that how far we've gone?"

There was a siren in the background, and the corner of Ms. Taylor's eyes crinkled in reaction to the sound. Time was running out. It was do or die.

"It's better this way," she said, nodding toward where the body of Mitch Krammer lay. "He was trying to escape after having been taken into custody. He killed Webster over a disagreement that's totally unrelated to either Dr. Wolf or his wife. They may even have been trying to steal the doctor's yacht. We haven't figured that part out yet. Given the unfortunate conclusion to their dispute, we may never know all the details. But that happens in these cases. The police often have to piece things together from what's left behind. There are usually gaps. The public realizes that, and expects it."

"But Dr. Wolf's wife paid to have her first husband murdered!" I cut in.

"Prove it," Ms. Taylor countered.

I froze.

"See, Mr. Hawley?" she added. "With Mr. Krammer and Mr. Webster both gone, there's not a shred of evidence left to say that anything happened here tonight other than a dispute between criminals. Even Mr. Tucker, Jackal, knows that."

"But the tape . . ." I began, looking down at it and realizing that she was right.

"Believe me," she said, still holding out her hand. "It's better this way. Mrs. Wolf is a very influential lady. Her financial holdings stretch from one end of the state to the other. The potential for positive results because of her good will far outweighs the urge for revenge I'm sure you're feeling. . . ."

"Revenge!" I shouted, lifting my head and looking her directly in the eye. "It's not revenge—it's justice I'm concerned with."

"Oh, really?" She smiled knowingly . . . a smile I didn't like at all.

"What are you talking about?" I asked.

"I suppose you'd like to include Mrs. Lyttle in your sweeping cut of justice, eh, Mr. Hawley?" she said. "Since it's fairly obvious that she must have known what her husband was doing, if this whole story should come out."

"But she's innocent," I countered, startling myself because I suddenly realized that I actually believed that to be true.

"Really?" Ms. Taylor replied. "That's going to be pretty hard to prove. And, while we're on the subject, how about you, Mr. Hawley? Would you like to explain your motivations to a jury, considering the events of the past few hours? Would you like to explain what you were doing here tonight, with that tape?"

"I was . . ." I began.

"Yes?"

I swallowed, seeing my position clearly.

I was fucked, plain and simple.

Screwed, and done with.

With a frown, I extended my hand and passed the cassette tape to Margaret Taylor. She took it with a grim expression and a single nod of her head, saying, "That's more like it."

"I don't want anyone to know that I had anything to do with this," I said.

Margaret Taylor cocked her head, asking, "No glory? I'm a P.R. specialist, Mr. Hawley; I could make you look very good."

"Nothing," I said, feeling cold inside, my wet clothes sticking to my skin, goose flesh breaking out all over me. "I don't want my name in it at all."

Margaret Taylor shrugged, lifting the cassette I'd just given her and squeezing it. Looking me in the eye, she said, "Have it your own way."

She was just turning, as if to go, when I asked, "How do I know it's over?"

She looked back my way, one eyebrow upraised.

"How do I know you won't try to hang me up anyway?" I asked, as a clarification.

"Why should I?" she replied.

I thought it over, nodded, took Nat's hand, and turned my back on the whole thing. It was over. I was tired, and beat, and bruised. I was sick of it, and I was giving up. My brother, Jerry, was still at the hospital with Ellie Lyttle. With Nat at my side, and Larry Fizner—limping, I noticed for the first time—bringing up the rear, I headed back the way we had come, back toward where I'd left my van, while the fire on the lake burned, and the sound of an ambulance bouncing down the street toward us, siren blaring, cut through the dark and washed away any hope of speech. Which was fine. I didn't have anything to say anyway. I just squeezed my wife's hand, and walked, as quickly as I could, feeling cold.

Really cold . . .

As it started raining again.

And the sirens behind me faded to silence in the mist.

EPILOGUE
■ ■ ■ ■ ■ ■ ■ ■ ■ ■ ■ ■ ■ ■

ON THE TELEVISION screen suspended in the corner of Ellie Lyttle's hospital room there was live local coverage of the explosion and fire down at the lakefront pier, complete with an earnest-looking news lady speaking into an oversized microphone, promising exclusive details as they developed. How she expected her details to be exclusive, since even as she spoke news trucks from the other local stations could be seen behind her, she didn't explain. But she went right on chattering, pointing out fire trucks and other interesting things while men in uniforms purposefully milled around in the periphery of the shot. Using the remote control, I turned the sound down to zero. I'd heard enough. I got the gist.

About fifteen minutes before, Margaret Taylor, official spokesperson for the investigating authorities, had made her statement, which though sketchy had included the mention of my name at least five times. Apparently, nothing I had said about keeping me out of it had made any impression on her at all. She had her agenda laid out, and she was sticking to it. At first I thought she was just being inflexible. But then it dawned on me that what she was actually doing was insuring my future cooperation. If I was officially known to have been involved with whatever it was that she finally settled on as her story of what had happened down at the pier, then there was little if anything I could ever do to contradict the details for fear of digging myself into a mess.

So be it.

What was done, was done.

Ellie Lyttle had delivered a five-pound, four-and-three-quarters-ounce baby boy at 1:29 A.M. The child had been jaundiced, and anemic, and had been rushed straight from the delivery room to an incubator, where he was sleeping fitfully, crying softly every so often, and jerking his little arms and legs as if he were swimming in his dreams. One of the doctors attributed the child's sickliness to emotional stress experienced by his mother during her pregnancy, a diagnosis that, as far as I could tell, sounded as if it were right on the mark.

It was now nearly three in the morning, and Nat, Jerry, and I were all sitting around Ellie Lyttle's bed. She was awake, but pale, holding Jerry's hand from where he had parked his wheelchair up close, and drifting in and out of a sedative-induced stupor. The delivery had been rough, and had wrung her out. But she had smiled just moments before when a nurse stuck her head into the room to inform us all that Gerald William Lyttle—or Jerry, Bill, one for my brother and one for me—was doing fine.

I don't know how much of what I described about what had been going on with her husband and his burglary partner Mrs. Lyttle had actually absorbed. But nothing I said seemed to have much of an impact. There was an indifference in her reaction that could have been brought on by the drugs in her system, or by the many years she had spent dreading the consequences of her husband's activities. She had been through a lot, and I think she had gotten to the point where her nerves were callused; with Ellie Lyttle, I believe you'd need to go a long way to shock her anymore. Years on the edge can do that to a person . . . something I was beginning to understand myself.

Mrs. Lyttle's brother, Stanley Marcus, he of the frizzy clown hair who had followed me earlier in the day in his dark green Chevy Nova, stepped into the room bearing a bunch of flowers he'd bought after convincing the lady at the gift shop to open up the refrigerated case, even though it was off hours. When he saw that his sister's eyes were closed, he laid the flowers gently at her side on the bed, and took a seat in one corner without saying a word. He was a quiet, morose young man, who had done all he could for her, and who now appeared glad that everything was apparently over. I didn't look at him as I spoke to my own brother, but I was perfectly aware that he was listening to every word I said.

"You should have seen Mr. Schimmel's face when I dropped Ansel off at his place on the way here," I offered, continuing what I had been describing before the news story about the pier had come on. "I thought he was going to punch me right in the nose. I had promised to take care of his dog. Then I brought him back looking like he'd been hit by a car. Hildie went right to work on him. And Ansel didn't fuss at all. He just stood there while she cleaned his fur and examined his wounds and pronounced that he looked a lot worse than he actually was. Mr. Schimmel watched for a while before demanding that I go over the story in detail. When I told him that Ansel had beaten a Tosa in a fair fight, I swear he got six inches taller.

" 'I have said already,' he said with that cartoon German accent of his, 'that Ansel is the best I have ever trained.' He was stroking Ansel's head when he said it, and there was blood on his fingers, but neither he nor the dog seemed to notice. 'The best,' he said, a couple more times. And, I swear, he looked like he was going to cry. Gunther Schimmel! He didn't . . . but for a while there, I think it was pretty close."

Jerry looked at me, his face drawn with fatigue. He had sat through the story of what had happened to R.L. Webster, and Captain Video, Mitch Krammer, in dignified silence. His only comment was that I looked pretty beat.

Which I was. Other than that, he didn't seem to have an opinion.

After leaving the dock, the three of us had dropped Ansel off at the Schimmel Kennels; then we'd gone back to the funeral home, where I quickly showered the lake muck off myself and changed into fresh clothes. Larry Fizner, looking drawn and sleepy, had declined our invitation to go to the hospital, preferring to go right to bed. I don't know if he's been undergoing any kind of therapy—chemo or radiation—for the cancer he so recently told us about, but his stamina certainly isn't what it used to be. The Larry Fizner I knew just a few months ago could run circles around me, and the thirty years difference in our ages be damned. Now he looked old, the lines in his face cut deep, the circles under his eyes dark and pronounced. It saddened me profoundly to see him like that, and I held onto his hand for a lingering moment as we shook hands before he left, saying, as sincerely as I could manage, "Thank you, Mr. Fizner. For everything. I can't think of anybody I'd rather have watching my back than you."

His reaction had been a simple shrug of the shoulders, and a question:

"So, is Hawley and Fizner Investigative Services official, or what?"

Without hesitation, I had said that it absolutely was official. I was even willing to take an ad out in the Yellow Pages to prove it.

I think that my initial motivation for saying it was to appease him . . . as kind of a reward because I knew that it was what he wanted to hear. But upon reflection, and not much reflection at that, I knew in my gut that it was what I really wanted as well. I hated the funeral business. Not that I wasn't going to continue with it, but there had to be more to my life than what my daily routine there could offer. What that something more was, I knew, centered upon who and what I was as an investigator. What had happened with Margaret Taylor, and the awful miscarriage of justice that she had overseen, did nothing to dissuade me from my belief that what was right was simply right, and that what was wrong was repugnant in the extreme. If anything, it had strengthened that view, and if there was anything I could do to prevent such things from happening again, I'd do it. Period.

When Jerry looked at me from beside Ellie Lyttle's bed, I said, "If I asked you to serve your apprenticeship for a funeral director's license, what would you say?"

He blinked, and frowned.

"What?" he mumbled. "So that I can feel useful? Is this supposed to make me feel like a man?"

"No," I returned. "It's supposed to make you worth your pay check. If I'm not around—and I have a feeling that I'm not going to be, sometimes—then we're going to need somebody on the premises qualified to take a death call, and deal with a family. If you don't do it, then I'm going to have to hire somebody that will. The job's open; I just thought you'd like first shot."

"You're serious?" he asked.

"Dead serious," I replied. "No pun intended."

"I'll think about it," he said, though I knew he'd agree.

"Bill," Nat said, and I looked at her. She was nodding toward the television, saying, "Isn't that Dr. Wolf?"

I looked up at the screen, and rolled the volume control on the remote. Dr. Gordon Wolf had arrived at the pier in a dark brown Buick four-door something or another, resplendent in a white smock, carrying a little black bag: the county's chief medical examiner, on the job. The reporter lady was busy singing his praises, throwing in for color his recent marriage to the former Elizabeth Hilton, noted socialite. Weren't we all lucky to have a man like him representing the interests of the community? Dr. Wolf was a recognized authority on forensic . . . blah blah blah.

I turned the TV off, realizing at that moment that I had never so much as laid eyes on Elizabeth Wolf, widow of Bernard Hilton. After all was said and done, I hadn't even met her . . . which was just fine with me. With any luck at all, it'll stay that way, I thought, rising from my chair.

Nat was staring at me.

"Come on," I said, indicating that she should accompany me out of the room. "Let's go look at the baby."

Gerald William Lyttle was sleeping in his incubator, which was equipped with a series of glass and rubber tubes. He had a little bit of white tape holding something on his tiny arm, and his fingers, so small, with their almost imperceptible yet perfectly formed fingernails, moved slowly, opening and closing . . . ever so slowly . . . as if to touch and hold. His eyes were a little puffy, squeezed tightly shut. His lips were pressed into a thin, firm line. On his head there was just the hint of blond fuzz, nearly white . . . hair like his mother's, making me wonder how much of her he had inherited, and how much of his dad . . . his dad, who he would never know.

Silently, with Nat's hand in mine, we stood before the nursery window, looking down at him as he slept. To myself, I wished him luck. He'd need it. And, while I was at it, I wished a little luck on myself . . . though, thinking about it, I've got to say that, all things considered, I seem to be a pretty lucky guy. How long that luck would hold was anybody's guess. And that was true for everyone. How long would Larry Fizner's luck hold in his fight against the rebelling cells in his own body, or Jerry's luck, in the budding romance between him and a young widow with a child, or Margaret Taylor's luck in concealing the incredible tangle of lies she would surely weave around what had happened on that dark and dangerous pier? All I could do was hope, and pray for the best.

Turning, I was about to say some of this to Nat. I don't know what part exactly, but some of it, anyway. But she was sticking her tongue out and wiggling her fingers at a tiny little girl in a bassinet close to the window. Even though I knew that the baby was too young to actually see her, for the moment I let myself believe that I wasn't projecting my own wishes on the scene. What I saw was a baby girl swaddled in the pink trappings of a newborn, grinning, kicking with her arms and legs, drooling, laughing, and, though I couldn't hear it, squealing inside the nursery as if Nat's funny faces brought her no end of pleasure.

To hell with it, I thought.

Who needs luck?

I've got Nat.